# THE
# BRIGHT
# &
# THE
# PALE

## JESSICA RUBINKOWSKI

Quill Tree Books
*An Imprint of HarperCollinsPublishers*

*To my parents, Jason and Rebecca, who fostered the dream, and to Mark, who*
*helped me achieve it*

Quill Tree Books is an imprint of HarperCollins Publishers.

Library of Congress Cataloging-in-Publication Data

Names: Rubinkowski, Jessica, author.

Title: The bright & the pale / Jessica Rubinkowski.

Other titles: Bright and the pale

Description: First edition. | New York : Quill Tree Books, an imprint of
HarperCollins Publishers, [2021] | Audience: Ages 14 up. | Audience:
Grades 10-12. | Summary: "Seventeen-year-old Valeria has been on
the run ever since she escaped the curse of Knnot, a magical happening
that encased her entire mining town in unbreakable ice"— Provided by
publisher.

Identifiers: LCCN 2020039164 | ISBN 9780062871503 (hardcover)

Subjects: CYAC: Blessing and cursing—Fiction. | Magic—Fiction. |
Fantasy.

Classification: LCC PZ7.1.R82758 Br 2021 | DDC [Fic]—dc23

LC record available at https://lccn.loc.gov/2020039164

ISBN: 978 0 06 287150 3
Typography by David DeWitt
21  22  23  24  25   CPI   10  9  8  7  6  5  4  3  2  1

First Edition

# ONE

THE KNOCK AT MY DOOR can mean only one of two things. I've finally been discovered and should prepare for my immediate shipment to a tyur'ma, a prison in the middle of a freezing wasteland. Or I've got another mission.

Neither sounds appealing.

I roll from the warm cocoon of my quilt and wince as my feet hit the floor. The bite of the cold boards rolls through me and reminds me why I wasn't able to sleep in the first place. It's the type of night that makes me remember. My dreams would be haunted by crawling frost and frozen bodies. My mother, swallowed by ice; my father, trapped forever, laughing at a joke I never heard. I squeeze my eyes shut against the thought, willing the dull sheen of ice covering my mother's face to fade from memory.

The knock comes again, more insistent this time. I swear to the Bright God above, this had better be urgent. I rip open the door midknock. Blistering wind forces its way into my home, wicking away the heat of my anger. A person in a dark cloak stands on the stoop with their face hidden in shadow, a bag slung over their arm. Not the bright-gold-and-black uniform of a Storm Hound, then. The tight ball in my chest loosens slightly. Another night of freedom.

I step silently to the side, already knowing who lies deep within the hood. The street outside sits empty, as always. Everyone knows what this building is and likes to pretend it doesn't exist. It is under the Czar's protection, after all, and who were they to question the might of the Czar?

The stout form slips inside. Crystalline snowflakes cling to the midnight fabric of the cloak, stark and vibrant in the dull glow from the hearth on the other side of the room. I close the door slowly, shivering as the last whispers of cold wind curl around my ankles. My chest grows tighter as the memory of icy fingers closing around my leg races through my mind. The absolute hunger of the frost, clawing at my family, my home, Ludminka. I swallow hard as I lock the door tight, as if that will keep the memories from consuming me.

"Couldn't use the front door?" I point at the wooden door on the opposite side of the room as I walk to the fireplace and toss on another log. That door leads to the Thieves Guild headquarters, and if I'm doing guild business, I prefer it to come from there.

The fire roars to life, and warmth begins to leak out toward the small two-person table in the center of the room. I sit down while my guest perches primly in the chair opposite me, hood thrown back and chestnut hair gleaming in a waterfall down her back. I can't help the smile that tugs at my mouth.

"You know I can't risk having the others see." Luiza, master of the Thieves Guild, returns my smile. "I can't be playing favorites, now can I?"

I let a chuckle escape my lips and the iron vise in my chest loosens a little.

"They already know you love me best. I don't know why you try to pretend otherwise," I say.

"To maintain my mysterious and aloof cover, of course."

I laugh again. Luiza has been master of the guild since before I came to her, cold and very alone. She didn't have to take me into her network of thieves and assassins. She could've turned me over to the Czar or tortured information about the Freeze of Ludminka from me. She didn't, instead using me and the other orphaned children she found to gather all the information the Czar could ever need to keep control over the population of Strana.

"What brings you to my room tonight?"

Luiza's eyes drift from my face to the small window above my bed. Bright moonlight spills across the worn, buttery-yellow quilt, and my heart gives another painful squeeze. I'd helped my matta make that quilt, the year before the freeze. It was the only thing I still had of my family.

"I knew you shouldn't be alone with your thoughts tonight." Her eyes venture back to my face. "You look like you haven't slept in days."

Her hands, calloused and lined with the beginnings of wrinkles, circle mine. She rubs a thumb over my knuckles and I try to contain the swell growing inside. She's right. I haven't slept. No more than a handful of hours the past couple of days. The season turned to winter, bringing with it blistering winds and the slow curl of frost across windowpanes.

I used to think the panic that came every time I saw a snowflake or heard the crunch of frozen grass beneath my feet would dissipate.

But as the years passed, my fear had only grown. Thinking *this* winter would be the one when the frost finally claimed me like it had my entire town. That *this* time would be when my luck finally ran out and whatever curse had sickened everyone from Zladonia would finally find me.

My hands tremble and Luiza squeezes them tighter.

"Valeria, take a deep breath," she says. I obey and try to release the tension through my nose. "Another."

I follow orders and my racing heart calms. She captures my gaze and takes a deep breath, which I mimic.

"You've been with me for ten years now, since you were just a girl of seven. You know I will keep you safe. This is your home, and I will never let anything happen to you again. What happened in Ludminka—"

4

My face tightens at the name of my village. She gives me an apologetic half smile before continuing.

"It has never happened again. You are safe."

"I think it's getting worse," I say, hating the way my voice sounds small and fragile.

"It's been worse since Alik," she says.

My heart constricts so hard and quick, I'm almost left breathless. Luiza squeezes my hand again. A year ago, I lost Alik—my best friend and only other Zladonian I'd known since my parents' deaths—to the Czar's cruel militia, the Storm Hounds. Specifically created to hunt down Zladonians and round them up into prisons strung across Strana.

The Czar said it was to protect the people from the plague. To contain the strange sickness that seemed to crawl through us. Yet aside from the few scouts who'd ventured into the Zladonian region at Strana's northernmost point, no one had gotten sick. It was clear the plague lay in the North, not inside the Zladonians. But the Czar still refused to free them.

"I want to talk about something else. Anything else," I say.

Luiza gives my hands a final squeeze before releasing them. She studies my face and I know what she's going to say before she opens her mouth.

"Let's check your hair."

I sigh and swivel to face the fire, trying to relax as Luiza slowly undoes the plait down my back. She lets out a disgruntled hum as the tangles at the top free themselves. I don't need a mirror to know exactly what she sees. The ends of my hair are a dull chestnut, almost identical to Luiza's, but the roots are bone white.

"You should've told me as soon as it started to show," she says.

"It's winter. I'm always in caps anyway. I didn't figure it mattered."

"It always matters," she mutters.

She pulls a forest green pot from the bag on the floor beside us and I make a face.

Every Zladonian bears the same marks: colorless hair and nearly translucent skin. Years spent mining Strana's prime resource, lovite, had turned all of us. The ore lies deep within the mountains strewn throughout the North, and Zladonians dutifully harvested it for the Czar.

No one complained when the dust from the pale ore infiltrated their lungs and dyed their children the same color in the womb. Not when there were riches to be had. Everyone had profited from the wealth lovite brought into the country. When melted down and paired with iron, the alloy became unbreakable. Walls across the world had been built with lovite, ensuring a city's safety and a building's resistance to flame. Weapons forged with it gleamed on battlefields, their edges never dulling.

And Strana controlled the only deposits of lovite the world over.

The freeze stole it all. Now Strana is nothing but a shadow of its former self, scraping by on exports of fish and lumber.

Luiza sighs and slides the lid from the pot in her hand. A pungent chemical stench circles me. I almost don't notice anymore. Luiza's been dyeing my hair ever since she found me. My hair is the only thing that marks me as a *malozla*, a "little evil." A sick twist of the Zladonia region's name.

She takes a bit of the claylike substance from the pot and moves to stand before me, beginning the process of pressing it into my roots. She hums as she does it, a favorite from when I was little.

"You're quiet," Luiza says.

"You know I don't like doing this."

Luiza's mouth pulls at the corners, and she lets the comb drop to her side. Her dark brown eyes meet mine.

"I know," she says. "I just want to keep you as safe as I can. You don't know the things I hear. . . ."

Luiza has always done her best to hide what happens at the *tyur'mas* from me. She seems to forget I often receive the same unfiltered information she does. I work for the best Thieves Guild in the world. The information we get is nearly always right.

All the countries at our borders have attempted to mimic the success of Luiza's guild, establishing spies and thieves of their own in order to combat Strana's chokehold on the world. The country may have gained power due to lovite, but it kept

7

it because of Luiza and the secrets she gathered. The Czar maintains control and, in turn, Luiza is granted freedom to run the guild outside the law.

Luiza finishes combing the dye through my hair and adds a swipe of it to each eyebrow. I stare at the dark smudges in the mirror, hating Czar Ladislaw for making this a necessity. Hating the Storm Hounds for being more than willing to round us up. Hating the entirety of Strana for turning anyone like me over to the hands of the Czar like it might cure their poverty.

Luiza presses a hand to my face and my eyes flick to her. Her brows knit together, almost as if she could feel the anger radiating off me.

"What?" I ask.

"I have something that may settle your mind. It affects the Czar. *Specifically.*"

"Why target your employer?" I ask, wanting more than anything for Luiza to be telling the truth.

I'd worked for Luiza and the guild to survive, thinking the Czar would never look for a Zladonian right under his nose, and trusting Luiza to keep me safe with her dyes and careful disguises. But if there was even the smallest chance that I could take down Czar Ladislaw for good, I would do it. He took everything from me. Fellow Zladonians, Alik.

Now it's my turn to take.

She gives a grim smile. "There is no easy way for me to put

this. The Czar still retains a stash of lovite, and I need you to get it for me."

"Oh." I haven't seen lovite since I was chased from my village all those years ago. The stores in Rurik, the capital of Strana, and the shipping towns along the Iron Sea to the east were depleted in a matter of months. The Czar has claimed for years there was no lovite left.

"What does this have to do with the Czar?" I ask.

"I've got a contact who has agreed to pay a mighty sum for any lovite he receives. He's building an army to raise against the Czar and needs it for weapons to fight the Storm Hounds."

I scoff. "No one in Strana is willing to raise a hand against their czar. They've let him rule this country for twenty years. We can't stop him. Why help this army instead of turning the rebellion in to the Czar? I'm sure he'd reward you for it."

Luiza kneels, so our eyes our level. She puts her hand on mine and her face flickers in the flames beside us.

"I'm not loyal to the Czar, Valeria. I'm loyal to myself. The tides turn in this country. The people are angry, the Zladonians suffer, our country dies. It won't be long until our enemies try to invade. I won't let it happen. I go where the tide goes, to keep us alive."

I brush the all too familiar scar on my left wrist, following the lines of it as I think. Red from rubbing, the scar looks emblazoned there by the hands of a god. Luiza grabs my hand

and stills its path. She's told me hundreds of times it's too obvious a tell.

"What makes you think this army will be successful?" I ask at last.

"One of Ladislaw's own Storm Hounds leads the charge."

"So?" I ask.

"He's the champion of the Bright God. I'm certain of it."

I can't help but laugh.

"There is no way," I say.

The Vestry teaches about champions of the Brother Gods, the Bright and the Pale. The gods despise each other, constantly at odds. The Bright God seeks to bring light and warmth to the world, while the Pale God consumes pain and brings suffering to fatten himself more. Since before Strana was called Strana, they have been battling each other. When their godly bodies returned to the heavens and the hells below, they extended their hands and chose a mortal champion to continue their war.

When a Bright God's champion rose, the world was in turmoil and he sought to right it. When a Pale God's champion arrived, he destroyed all in his path, taking no prisoners and showing no mercy. Their battles were always bloody, destroying thousands of lives. There hasn't been one in a hundred years. Why would the gods suddenly awaken? Years of pain had passed without the Brothers so much as lifting a finger.

Luiza levels a stare. She hasn't looked at me like this since I ruined a mission by falling into a vat of dye.

"You truly believe a champion has come to Strana to rid us of a czar? And that he's a *Storm Hound*."

"I met him. He proved it."

Luiza pulls the collar of her tunic to the side. On her right shoulder used to be a long, rigid scar she'd gotten as a child in a street fight. Now, it's gone.

"How?" I whisper. There'd been stories of champions blessed with the gifts of their patron god, but to see it . . . the proof is undeniable.

"A gift, he called it. To prove his usefulness," Luiza says. "So, what do you say?"

I smile. "Let's overthrow a czar."

# TWO

"THE PLAN IS COMPLICATED. BUT I know you can handle it," Luiza says as she combs the dry clay from my hair. It falls in crumbles to the ground, my hair now officially hidden once again. When she's certain nothing is left, she digs a long silver robe out of her bag.

I grimace as she lays it on my bed. There is only one group of people in all Strana who wears those: the Holy Sisters of the Brother Gods. The deep gray robes cover a beaded sarafan, a clear indicator Luiza intends for me to be a sister to the Pale God. What a cruel twist of the knife.

I stopped believing the Brother Gods meant anything decent for humanity the day Ludminka fell to the ice. If the gods truly loved us, as the priests claimed, they would've stopped it. They would've sent their champions or used their powers to aid humanity. Instead, they slumbered, turning a blind eye as we all suffered. Perhaps the Pale God wanted it that way, desiring to feast on the pain of the Zladonians who'd made him their patron when the rest of Strana prayed to the Bright God. If so, I wish to spit in his eye.

"Does it have to be a Holy Sister?"

"The lovite is inside the Royal Vestry. It's the only way you're getting in."

"You want me to sneak into the palace grounds? Breaking in isn't just complicated, it's impossible."

"Not impossible. You're the best. I trust no one else with this mission." Luiza crosses to me and takes my face in her hands. She smiles before kissing my forehead. "My little fox. You must be brave. We're changing the world. The champion has promised me he'll do right by the Zladonians and free them. You want that, don't you?"

"You know I do," I mutter.

"Then let me get you ready."

I sit back down before the fire. Luiza takes her time braiding my hair in a small circular crown before settling a thick veil on it, pinning it in place. The soft fabric flutters to a stop just above my nose. She lifts the shirt up next.

I slip into it, accustomed to the rough woolen fabric and embroidered bell sleeves. It falls to my thighs, and Luiza follows it with a silver sarafan, a beautiful long dress with sparkling embroidery up the center in a thick stripe, whorls of beading studding the collar and wide straps. Last comes a deep gray robe lined with velvet and fur. Luiza tosses me my utility belt from the post of my bed. It holds everything I could need: lockpicks, gloves, even small throwing knives. I slip it under the skirts of the sarafan, effectively hiding it from sight.

"You can barely see your face. You should be fine."

"So, what's the plan? Beg my way into the palace, hope no one stops me, and steal from the Vestry coffers?" I ask, flipping the fabric of the veil back.

"Essentially. There's a single guard who circles the gate this time of night. Lie your way in by telling him of the attack on the North Road Vestry. Say you need sanctuary."

"There's been an attack?"

"There's about to be," Luiza says. "After that, it's up to you to get to the Vestry and take your place with the other sisters. Once they retire for bed, you'll go to the priest's office. The lovite is hidden in a safe."

I nod. I'd had harder missions. Impossible hidden caches high in the mountains or trunks of manifests locked in a bog haunted by hungry *rusalka*. Aside from being in the Czar's palace, this didn't seem too difficult.

"You must be careful, Valeria. They can't trace this back to me. If they do, the entire guild will be compromised. Until now, he has granted us freedom because we helped him keep his throne. If he discovers our betrayal, his retribution will be swift."

Luiza takes my hands. "I'm giving this to you because I know you'll do right by me. I can trust you with anything. You're the closest thing to a daughter I'll ever have, and I'll be forever grateful."

My throat constricts at her words. She brings my wrist bearing the scar up to her lips and gives it a kiss, always aware of how much I hate it. I thought it ugly; she said it made me something special. She had since she caught me inside the guild storeroom desperately trying to stuff a tattered bag full of all the food I could.

I lean forward until my head rests against her shoulder and curl my arms around her waist. She pulls me into a tighter hug. I inhale her familiar smell, incense and the soft note of a rose, and let it calm me. She's all I've had for the past ten years.

She squeezes me tight before stepping back and leveling me with a weighted stare.

"We can't have you being followed. Take it to our drop location in the outskirts of Rurik, the one inside the burned house. Then slowly make your way back here in the most complicated way you can."

"Don't worry, Luiza. I can do this."

I *will* make her proud.

She smiles at me. "I know you can. I'll see you in the morning?"

I nod, expecting her to leave. Instead, she catches my hands. "I do love you. You know that, right? All I've ever tried to do is what is best for you."

"I know," I say with a raised eyebrow.

She doesn't respond to my obvious confusion. She just brushes my cheek with the back of her hand and makes her way to the door leading to the guild headquarters, giving me one final smile before she slips out, leaving me to prepare for an impossible mission.

Slipping out of the guild headquarters is easy enough. Not that it would've mattered if anyone had seen me. I just don't want to look at their pitying faces and questioning stares.

They've treated me like a crumbling leaf since I lost Alik a year ago, as if it isn't common to lose your partner in the guild. It was beyond rare to have him for the seven years we ran missions together. Normally, partners didn't last more than three, taken by foreign militia or killed in action. I shouldn't feel like I'd lost a part of my soul. We'd known it was the likely outcome.

But it never stopped me from hoping it wouldn't be us.

Luiza brought Alik into the guild around the same time as me. We clung to each other as Luiza ran us through grueling test after backbreaking practice. We were natural partners, but Luiza kept us together despite warning me that growing attached to guild members never ends well.

I suppose she was right.

I shove all memory of Alik aside and concentrate on the

job, wrapping the robe around me as I walk from the guild headquarters into the Pleasure Quarter, which is never at a loss for nighttime activity. Between the gambling halls, brothels, and opium dens, there's a little something for everyone. But no one looks to the shadows that cling beneath the eaves. Not when there are brighter, more desirable things to see.

The guild uses this area as a training ground for new initiates. Making sure they knew how to thieve petty coin before testing them on something much more valuable, like kingdom secrets. Luiza established the guild tucked behind two brothels, using the filthy alley between them as her personal choke point.

Alik and I had spent the better part of two years here. Choosing marks and concocting the best way to steal from them without being noticed. Every dark alley I pass as I pull deeper into the heart of the city seems stained by his memory.

I plod through the winding streets toward the shining peaks of the palace. Czar Ladislaw built it in the height of Strana's power, when wealth spilled into his coffers like a river of gold. The steep peaks jut high into the sky, hewn from pure lovite, the milky surface only marred by veins of cobalt blue. The palace sits against a bald rock cliff, the jagged granite dotted with watchtowers that burn bright even in the dead of winter. It's impossible to miss the building, even at this distance in the middle of the night. To visiting dignitaries from Adaman, Strana's northern neighbor, and Drangiana, its southern ally, it's a pillar of what Strana can do. It plainly displayed the one thing Strana had that they never would; and every country in the world wanted a little piece of lovite if just to say they owned some.

I amble through the streets, keeping my head down low enough to not be suspicious. I finally leave the district. The homes here share the same architecture, stolen straight from the streets of Drangiana. The buildings mostly square, with scrollwork along the trim near the roof. Drangiana, full of sun and heat, chose to flatten its roofs, while Strana severely slopes them to stop the snow from building up.

There isn't much Strana hasn't stolen from one of its neighbors. Architecture and foods from Drangiana, medicines and strategy from Adaman. Lovite was truly the only thing we ever gave the world. Once it stopped, so did the money and the trade.

People went hungry. Then they got angry. Rumors flew of revolt, of removing Czar Ladislaw for damning Strana to poverty, despite the story that the Czar's line was descended straight from a champion of the Bright God.

That is, until Ladislaw pinned all the blame on Zladonians. The country then finally had its villain. All cheered as Czar Ladislaw set up his prisons and turned on anyone seeking to escape the horrors of the North. It'd taken a year to round up nearly every Zladonian, but it didn't stop the people of Strana from being vigilant, reporting anyone who had a whisper of Zladonia about them.

I bite the inside of my cheek to calm my thoughts, and make my way to the edge of the palace grounds. Two long wings hug the interior courtyard; a massive lovite gate connects the wings and bars my entrance. There's no sense in trying to pick the lock. Storm Hounds would be on me before I could so much as move my arm. Instead, I sidle up next to the gate and bow my head, clasping my hands piously before me.

When my heart stills to a steady thump, I let out a soft sniffle. It's just pathetic enough to seem real, while being loud enough to be noticed. Luiza would be proud.

Soon enough, the heavy footsteps of a guard circle toward the gate. My heart climbs its way into my throat as the guard stares at me.

"A sister? Outside the gate at this hour?" he says, his voice deep and gravelly.

I chance a glance at him through my veil. His raven black uniform is cut to perfection and the gold epaulets lie across his shoulders like a mantle. Just the presence of the Storm Hound makes all my muscles coil, readying to run. Confronting them was always easier with Alik.

"Please," I whisper. "I was supposed to be aiding the North Road Vestry, but there was . . . there was an attack. They stole so many of our ceremonial treasures. I—I need to report it to Brother Gavriil."

"Very well," he says. "Do you have your palace papers?"

I nod once and grab the dull yellow parchment from my pocket and pass it to the Storm Hound through the gate. He studies it beneath the flickering light of the torch behind him on the wall. It's a brilliant forgery. The script curls in elegant lines across the middle of the page, ordaining me Sister Illma and granting me passage to the Royal Vestry whenever I wish. He takes a few more moments to study the stamps at the bottom of the parchment before nodding again and removing a key from his belt. He unlocks the gate, opening it just far enough for me to slip through before snapping it shut. "If you will follow me, please, Sister Illma."

"I know the way myself," I say, and the guard's eyes lock on me. I duck my head. "I do not wish to disrupt your rounds, sir. I know how valuable your time is."

He grunts and glances over his shoulder. I can almost see the wheels in his head moving. Allowing anyone to cross the palace grounds to the Vestry alone is frowned upon, but leaving his station open will get him punished.

I place my hand upon his arm. "Forgive my boldness, sir, but I have been graced with perception by the Pale God. I understand your hesitance to leave your post. I know the way well enough to the Vestry. I spent most of my girlhood there. I'll not tell a soul you let me slip through."

The Storm Hound relaxes beneath my touch, nods once, and turns on his heel. I slink into the shadows and don't breathe until I'm certain he is paces behind me.

The absolute stillness of the courtyard sets me on edge, and the crunch of the white gravel beneath my feet seems far too loud. It takes all my power to keep from looking over my shoulder for another Storm Hound. I swallow my fear and keep my eyes trained on the circled tops of the Vestry's towers.

I've been here only once before. The Czar had been afraid the priest was plotting against him, rallying the people to his side. Alik and I had been sent in as devout worshippers to gather any information we could. The priest had been nothing but a dullard with a bad habit of misspeaking in the most humorous ways. People had come to joke at his expense, not rally against the Czar. Alik and I had laughed ourselves silly at the Czar's paranoia, treating ourselves to warm taiga bread, a favored cinnamon treat from Northern Strana, for a mission well done.

Gods, it hurt to think of him.

I press two fingers firmly to the scar on my wrist, fixating on it until it's the only thought in my mind. It was the only thing that refocused me. Luiza always says emotions are the downfall of any good plan. I need every ounce of focus to fool Brother Gavriil. The man's shrewd enough to turn even the bitterest of sinners into a Brother to the Gods. Luiza has kept tabs on him for years now, just in case.

The Vestry's doors shimmer in the light cast from the giant braziers on either side of them. One golden, the other silver, just like the Brother Gods. Just like all those who serve them.

I let out a huff and push the door open. A vaulted entry soars overhead, taller than even the guild headquarters. The small chamber is perfumed with incense, and smoke rises from bronze bobbles hanging from two sturdy poles jutting out from the wall on either side of the door before me. My head goes dizzy at the smell, and I almost forget to waft it over my shoulders like a pious sister should.

"Sister Illma," a voice says from beside me.

I almost jump as Brother Gavriil steps from the small passageway beside the door, his broad hands clasped across the bright gold of his robes. A long auburn beard frames a wide jaw and his blue eyes hide behind bushy eyebrows. I swallow.

He shouldn't know who I am.

# THREE

"WE'VE BEEN WAITING FOR YOU to join us for midnight prayer compline. Please, if you will?" He gestures toward the chapel, and I duck my head as I follow him.

Our march leads us into the chapel. In the dim torchlight, the beams of the gold-painted roof above us remain hidden in shadow. We make our way down the aisle toward the other sisters, and my eyes drift to the painted ovals above each torch.

The icons display each champion of the Brother Gods. Some smile smugly out at us, their golden hair shimmering, while others give us stern, tight-lipped glares. Each champion had an important part to play in establishing Strana's power. Vasili the Bright fought back our neighbors with blasts of golden light, granted to him by the Bright God. Misha the Bold was said to be gifted with charm, allowing him to unite the roving bands of people into the solid nation of Strana. Their legends went on and on, each one granted something by his patron. Gifts of sunshine, healing, and communication from the Bright God. Ones of death, destruction, and cunning from the Pale God.

The aisle leads to a large stone altar situated between portraits of the Bright and Pale Gods. My eyes stray to the stern face of the Pale God and the familiar knot begins to form in the pit of my stomach. Seeing him reminds me of home, of our tiny altars tucked away in a corner and of praying with my father and brothers. The painting portrays a man not more than twenty, but his icy blue eyes seemed to hold an eternity. When I was younger, I'd been quite taken with him, thinking him far more handsome than any boy in Ludminka.

My gut squeezes in disgust at the thought. The gods did nothing to protect Ludminka, keeping their champions from us and leaving us to suffer at the hands of the Czar. They were nothing more than an idea to soothe a fearful country.

"Kneel." The stern voice of Brother Gavriil rings out across the cold flagstones.

We clasp our hands in front of us as we get on our knees. Some lift their heads toward the heavens; others stare at the large cup on the altar. My eyes only follow Brother Gavriil. He doesn't pay me any more attention than the other postulants.

Yet he knew I was Sister Illma.

Brother Gavriil goes to the altar and lifts the cup first to the

Pale God, then to the Bright God. He is his brother's opposite, with sun-warmed skin and hair the color of the sky at twilight. His eyes are deep brown and seem to accept any who stand before him. I find no more comfort in him than I do in his brother.

"Before the fall of our country, the people of Strana were strong. We were happy and fruitful. That is, until the *malozla* and their plague stole the lovite away."

I steady myself with a deep inhale as Brother Gavriil starts on a popular sermon topic, his rigid body burning with conviction.

"The Brother Gods do not wish for us to suffer. They have seen our country through many a dark time and will continue to do so only if we repent for the sins of the *malozla*. They were far too wild in their ways, shirking chastity, modesty, and their prayerful duties. Their taint soaked into the stone they walked on and turned the land against us, against the Czar. Now none can venture into the wilderness of Zladonia without falling victim to their plague. Come, sisters, we must pray for an end to this curse and for the mines of Zladonia to open once again. Call upon the mercy of the Brothers and beg them to rid us of the taint of *malozla*."

Silence follows his words, and blood thunders in my ears. It takes all of my power to remain quiet on the floor, the stone biting into my knees.

Brother Gavriil steps from the altar to the first novice in

line. He lifts the cup to her lips. She whispers something and sips. A prayer to the Bright God, then. He continues down the line and allows each girl to drink from the cup. Each one counts the blessings in their lives and the life of the country. At last, Brother Gavriil stops before me. I bow my head and sip from the cup. I hold the liquid in my mouth for a moment, allowing the bitter flavor to suck all the moisture from my cheeks. Then, I spit it onto the floor as one is to do when praying to the Pale God.

"I give to the Pale God all the hurt of this country," I say. "I give him all those who are in pain. All those cold and hungry. All those forgotten."

I stare into the eyes of the idol. The Brother Gods share the duties of aiding the world. The Bright God accepts the blessings and the praises of all things good, while the Pale God consumes the curses and evils of the world. The most devout worshippers of the Pale God claim he eats the world's evils to make room for the good. They take comfort in the Brothers, while ignoring the fact that the gods could have sent a champion to aid us if they wanted to. Brother Gavriil nods his head once and moves on to the sister at my side.

When Brother Gavriil is finished, he rings a small bell on the altar. All the sisters rise and turn toward a door on the right-hand side of the chapel.

"Sister Illma, if I could have a word?" Brother Gavriil asks.

I bow my head dutifully as the other sisters filter around

me. Once they leave, closing the heavy pine door behind them, Brother Gavriil steps forward, a strained smile painting his lips. I try to keep my breathing steady as unease spikes through me.

"I believe we have much to talk about." He gestures to the back of the chapel, and we walk in silence to the small wooden door that lies embedded in the stone wall.

As we enter, I see a plain wooden desk in the center with a sheaf of paper strewn haphazardly across it. Two bookcases stand on either side, laden with heavy tomes. A portrait of Czar Ladislaw sits between them, his gray brows drawn over a pointed nose, his chin just a little too large to be attractive. He looks every ounce the relation of the stern men on the champion wall outside.

"Please make yourself comfortable." Brother Gavriil points to an uncomfortable wooden chair before the desk, then settles in the plush one behind it. "Guards arrived at the Vestry a little before you. They say your Vestry was robbed?"

I nod, not sure I'm permitted to speak.

"I find it interesting you report this," Gavriil says flatly. He eyes me for a long moment, waiting for me to respond. When I don't, he sighs.

"I'll tell you why I find it interesting. We intercepted a correspondence to have your particular Vestry ransacked days ago. On parchment marked with the symbol of the Thieves Guild. I'm sure that, at least, is familiar to you."

He holds up the piece of paper. My mind reels as I take in the sharp line of the two crossed keys with ravens sitting upon them. I try to keep my face neutral as my mouth goes dry.

"Naturally, I killed the messenger and his compatriots and sent word the Vestry had been robbed myself, when it has been heavily guarded by our most esteemed Czar's Storm Hounds all night."

I say nothing, staring blankly at him. It's rare Luiza's plans go awry. She plots everything so tightly that she always knows when a piece doesn't fit. How could she have missed this? If the guild member responsible truly is dead, he may have met a luckier fate than any Luiza would've planned.

"It seems our guild leader has lost her touch," I say.

Brother Gavriil's eyes narrow and dart to the door behind me. He's expecting someone. Help, most likely. I need to end this before whatever aid he requested comes.

"What does Luiza want with the Vestry?" he hisses.

"What she usually wants. Information. Secrets. Things to ruin a kingdom." I refuse to betray Luiza. Her last words to me are haunting. *They can't trace this back to me.*

"Which kingdom?" His voice is a rasp in the back of his throat. He reaches slowly toward his desk.

"Yours."

I throw my gloves at him. He winces, and it's enough time for me to shove to my feet and crouch. I rip off my veil to see better as he brings a small dagger up to protect himself. Shock writes itself across his face.

"You're a . . . *malozla*," he says, and I curse my pallid skin.

I don't respond. His guard is down, and I need to use it to my advantage. I leap across the desk. He moves a second too late, slashing down with his blade in a clumsy stroke. It catches the skirt of my sarafan. I twirl the fabric around it and yank the dagger from his hand, the force of my movement sending papers sprawling. Brother Gavriil opens his mouth to call out as I press the dagger's tip to his neck.

"Speak and it will be the last thing you ever say."

His throat bobs as he swallows and closes his mouth.

"Where is your safe?" I whisper.

With shaking hands, he gestures to the picture on the wall behind him. A wry chuckle escapes his throat.

"You've come for our money, then? I'm afraid what we have won't do you much good."

"It will be good enough."

I raise the dagger. He closes his eyes tight.

*Coward.*

I turn my hand at the last minute, bringing the hilt hard against his temple. He drops like a sack of grain. I stare down at him, rage boiling inside me. I could kill him. It would be so easy now that he is unconscious. I envision shoving the dagger into his chest, all the way to the hilt. What is his life except one full of hate and anger at Zladonians?

I grit my teeth and turn away from his body.

I've never killed anyone. In all the jobs I've ever done, I've never had to. Or was too afraid to lift my blade and risk my own life.

Like the day I lost Alik.

Luiza always warned what killing would do to me, how it would change me from the inside. She wanted to spare me from it as long as she could. I won't kill one silly old man. No matter how loathsome.

I move quickly to the portrait. The hinges are visible now and the frame swings open with well-oiled ease.

The safe is different from the ones I've worked on before but not uncrackable. The tiny hole in the center is supposed to be for a special key. The idea being nothing could be made in the exact right shape to fit inside. But Luiza, of course, found a way around that. I remove the thin lockpick from my belt.

It's a slender rod made of lovite. It's the only form of it I have touched since leaving my village. How Luiza managed to get her hands on it, I'll never know.

I put the rod in the lock. Brother Gavriil expected someone to come help him. I have no doubt they'll be here soon. I need to get this done and get out.

I'm careful not to knock the minuscule rod against anything as I insert it. My mind goes blank as soon as I hear the familiar scrape that says the pick is in. My fingers sense every vibration, every slight bump or scrape. Slowly, as the rod explores the lock, a picture starts to form in my mind of the mechanisms inside. A row of tiny buttons sits at the very back of the lock, seven in total. Just a single press can send the safe open, or release a blinding spray of dye intended to mark the thief.

I carefully wiggle each one, looking for the loosest button. The movement will be slight, just enough to tell me the button has been used. I suppress the wave of warmth rushing through me. Seconds slip by as I wiggle each tiny piece again. Then, a third time.

They're all secure.

Sweat pours freely between my shoulder blades and dampens my lower back. I'm missing something.

A muffled thud sounds somewhere in the chapel. I'm running out of time.

I angle the rod a little lower. It hits nothing but air for one horrible moment until it brushes against one small button. My body sags when it moves. This has to be the right one. I suck in a breath and press.

A soft click whispers through the room. I squint my eyes, half expecting the dye to blow into my face and blind me. Instead, the safe shifts slightly and the door swings open.

My eyes widen. Atop a pile of paper money and golden coins sit six ingots of lovite, so white they almost look like vapor. If it weren't for the veins of cobalt tracking through them, I might think them nothing but air. In all my time thieving for the guild, I've never seen a hoard quite like this. I reach inside and pick up the ingots with trembling hands. The unnatural, smooth texture makes me shiver.

The ingots clang together and emit a pure, high note. I quickly cut a piece of my sarafan's skirt with Brother Gavriil's dagger and wrap the ore. It should dull the noise enough to reach the drop-off point. The tight knot in my chest constricts as the last glimmer of lovite slips behind the silver fabric and I shove the ingots into the small cloth bag I keep in my utility belt.

If I can just get the lovite to the drop point, the Bright God's champion can use it to supply his army. We can overthrow the Czar and start doing some actual good for this country. That is, if the Czar hasn't already moved against Luiza.

I have no idea if Brother Gavriil reported his findings to the Czar, but a sycophant like him would likely do anything for a single word of praise. I have to assume the worst. It's what Luiza would want me to do. Which means the guild is likely compromised.

Through the walls, I hear voices too quiet to make out. I press myself behind the study door and calm my breathing.

Slowly, the door swings open.

"What do you see?" a cold voice says from somewhere outside the room.

"He's here," says the man in the doorway.

"Anyone else?"

"No."

"Check the room instead of standing in the doorway like

an idiot," the cold voice says. His footsteps snap across the stone outside the door away from us.

The other man steps into the study and my heart starts to thud. He's easily a head taller than me, and much broader. His clothing is supposed to be nondescript, but I know a Storm Hound when I see one. His hair curls around his ears in dark swaths, cut close and clean. My face is still visible, my veil somewhere beside Brother Gavriil's fallen body. How had I been so stupid?

I press myself tighter against the wall and try to decide on my best course of action. I can't have him calling out. Who knows how many Storm Hounds are crawling around the Vestry? I need to move before he sees me. I close the door slightly to not seem suspicious, hoping his friend walked far enough away not to notice me. He stares down at Brother Gavriil's body as I dart out from my hiding place, dagger raised.

He whirls just as I reach him. His dark eyes widen in surprise. He's younger than I expected, likely just out of his first training season. He raises his hands, opening his mouth to shout, but I launch myself on the desk and swing myself onto his back, locking my arm around his throat. He stumbles toward the bookshelves. My spine slams into them and breath leaves me. I cling to his neck. If I let him go, he'll yell. I can't risk it. I wince against the pain and lack of air.

It takes longer than I would've liked for his arms to stop flailing. Ever so slowly, he loses his strength and falters. I finally release him, letting his heavy body thud to the floor. I quickly yank my veil from beneath him and throw it on. I tie the bag full of lovite to the belt beneath my sarafan and walk from the room as calmly as I can manage.

Storm Hounds indeed dot the hall. I keep my head down and make for the exit. With any luck, they'll think I'm just another sister going about her nightly duties. I can feel the cool air from the open door at the back of the hall. In ten steps, I'll be free.

"Sister, stop. None are allowed out at the moment," someone calls from behind me.

All thoughts of maintaining the false meekness of a sister of the gods leave me. I bolt. A roar sounds behind me, but I've got more of a lead than they can make up.

I race from the palace grounds. I can lose anyone I wish in the outskirts of Rurik. All I have to do is get there.

# FOUR

THE LIGHTS OF THE PALACE fade as I quickly slip between houses and press toward the outer rings of the city. Storm Hounds call out behind me, their heavy footsteps sounding far too close for comfort. More seem to pour from every alley.

They must have expected me, which means Brother Gavriil knew what the guild planned. They waited to see if Luiza would follow through with it before destroying the guild. I steal down street after street. The Czar's retribution will be swift, just as Luiza said. I can't return to the guild. Even if I wasn't concerned with saving myself, Luiza wouldn't want me to risk it.

I chance a glance over my shoulder. At least ten Storm Hounds give chase, their long strides almost double mine. My eyes dart from one building to the next until I finally find a tall lattice running up the side of a house to the steepled roof. I launch myself up it, scrambling far faster than I ever thought possible.

I throw myself onto the roof and look down. The Storm Hounds crowd beneath, their eyes pinned on me. A blond man pushes the rest aside and they part around him. If their respect didn't betray his status, the emblazoned patch above his right breast does: a knight astride a black stallion. He's a commander, decorated with the highest symbol of honor in Strana. He must've performed quite the service to the country to receive it. The sight of the emblem cools the blood in my veins. He starts up after me.

I flee.

The rubber-soled boots Luiza insists we all wear at last come in handy. They grip the roof's slick wooden surface and propel me upward. I fling myself from the highest peak onto the slope of the roof next door. The lovite clangs with each spring, despite the cloth I'd carefully wrapped it in.

I follow roof after roof, only looking down long enough to make sure the people chasing me on the ground have fallen back. The tall buildings nearest the palace start to fall away, replaced by the squat ones closer to the outskirts. Soon, I'll lose the ability to hide myself behind the peaks and falls of the roofs.

I glance back and find no one. The thundering in my ears starts to slow.

I throw myself to the lower house to my right, crawling up to the peak to study the darkened streets below. The shadows lie empty, the only sound a crying infant a few houses away. I slink toward the edge of the roof and try to catch my breath before lowering myself to the hard-packed dirt streets.

Silence follows. I wait for Storm Hounds to descend on me, but nothing happens.

I straighten and slip off the sarafan and veil, putting the robe back over the woolen shift. The silver fabric will be the first thing they look for. I shove it into the bag with the lovite, making sure to wrap it around the ingots to dull their sound.

The outskirts of Rurik circle the city like a ring of poverty and filth. Dirt streets filled with waste and trash wind their way between small houses filled with families. The Storm Hounds never come through here unless they have to, and I'm guessing they will tonight.

The palace stands behind me, still shimmering in the early morning darkness. Luiza's refuge lies to the west. The woolen dress I wear under the robe does nothing to stop the chill of the night from creeping into my bones. I curl my arms around myself, keeping my eyes trained on the lowest beams of the houses I pass. Luiza marks all her drops with the symbol of the guild—two ravens sitting on a key facing each other

I try not to think of what's happening to Luiza right now, but my mind runs away with all the possibilities. Word will have reached everyone by now that the guild tried to rob the

Czar. No doubt the Czar sent a battalion to capture the guild headquarters and take Luiza in. She might be on her way to some moldy dungeon by now.

Or already dead.

The thought makes me shiver more than the cold. I can't lose her, too. She is all I have left.

There has to be a way to save her. Maybe if I wait at the drop point, follow the person who comes to get the lovite, and beg the Bright God's champion for help, he'd do it. After all, Luiza is the reason he'll have lovite for his army. I'm not sure if it will work. I have no leverage. No way of returning any kindness he might extend to me. It's a feeble plan, but it's the only ray of hope I have right now.

I need that hope. I need to do something to save the only family I have left.

At last, my eyes catch the worn guild mark in the corner of a run-down home. The roof has long since collapsed on itself. I slip through the bowing door and make for the center of the building, peeling up a layer of the largest beam to reveal a carved-out cache inside. I place the lovite in as gently as I can before lowering the wood and smearing ash across the now visible lip.

It's as hidden as I can make it.

I'm considering the best place to hide when something suddenly slips over my head. I gasp and claw at the scratchy fabric. Luiza's training takes hold. I fling my fist back, low and as hard as I can and connect with something solid behind me. The person clinging to the fabric grunts and shifts their body farther away from me. The sack draws tighter over my face at their movement. Hot breath exits my mouth and gets trapped in the thick woven fabric. I can't breathe.

I fling my entire head backward and connect with something again. The person gives a cry and releases the bag. I scramble and manage to pull the sack away in time to see a dark form bringing the hilt of a sword straight down on my temple. And I feel myself falling. . . .

*Birds keen above me, taking off from their nests at the same time. A roar like a river around a boulder fills the air, and the hair on the back of my neck begins to rise. The birds take over the crystalline sky like a blanket of darkness and pull me from my daydream. My mother always said to beware a sea of birds, for it heralds death. I never believed her.*

*I should've.*

*I look down from my perch high above Ludminka and see miners trailing from Knnot Mountain like little ants, their task done for the day. My father and brothers would be among them, as would every other man in the village.*

*I grab the bundle of dried fir branches and my basket of pinecones, intent on trudging back to my mother's disapproval. The air stills, pressing down on me like a heavy blanket. Then the ground rolls. My stomach drops as my knees collapse into the frosty leaves beneath the trees. My head snaps up just in time to see Knnot shift.*

*My gut clenches tight. I know this nightmare, but I can't force myself awake.*

*My mother's cool voice finds its way into my mind, repeating the phrase she was so fond of telling me: "Fear the mountain, my dear. Fear the dark depths and the cold halls. Fear the call. For when the mountain sinks its teeth into you, it will never let you go."*

*Screaming starts from the village, then stops suddenly, as if blown out like a candle.*

*My heart thuds in my throat as my legs move of their own accord. I descend the small rise toward the village, a heavy rock growing in my stomach with each step. Gone are the excited shouts of children and the chatter of women hanging out their washing. I wrap my arms around myself as I near the first house.*

*Widow Cela lives there with her brood. I could never pass without at least one of her boys trying to tug my braid. But now not a single sound whispers from inside the closed shutters.*

*I approach a baby carriage set beside the front steps. She always let her youngest sleep outside, especially in early autumn. No coos gurgle from the blanketed form.*

*I don't want to look, but I do anyway. Perfect rosebud lips and a curl of white hair across his forehead greet me, but it's not what catches my attention. His skin is the color of new ice* with a sheen across the surface like he is nothing but a statue. My hands tremble as I reach out for him. Instead of feeling the smooth skin of a new baby, I feel the slick cold of ice.

I snatch my hand back. "Oh my gods."

I race through the streets, the sound of cracking ice following me as I go. Tears sting my eyes as face after frozen face rushes past me.

I have to reach my parents. They have to be safe. I'm certain that if I keep repeating it, that if I believe it, somehow it will be true.

At long last, our cabin comes into view, the roses my father carved for my mother proudly displayed on her windowsill. Smoke still curls from the chimney and merry lights flicker inside. The stone I've carried in my stomach since I saw the mountain shift disappears. Everything is okay. I hurry to the door and shove my way inside. "Matta?" I am determined to tell them all about the strange things I saw in the village.

Instead I come to a halt and crash to my knees.

My family is indeed still inside. My mother stands by the small iron stove, a spoon raised halfway to her lips. My father sits with his feet upon the table, smoke still twining from his pipe. My brothers sit by my father's side, caught in a mock argument, lips parted in laughter.

All of them frozen.

Even as I watch, frost creeps across the floor toward the warm hearth, undaunted by the fire inside. Long icicles drip down *before the open door that weren't there just moments before. I press my hands to my eyes and scream.*

*Hot tears flood onto my hands. I scrub my face, willing myself to stop. Crying won't solve anything. The frost on the floor curves around me, making an almost perfect circle on the wood.*

*Somehow, I've been spared.*

*Somehow, I'm still alive.*

*The frost, which had been at the door just minutes ago, now laces up the walls and wraps around the burning woodstove. The fire sizzles and then goes out, dousing me in semidarkness.*

My head pounds as I come to, my chest tight and my eyes wet. Guilt crashes onto my shoulders like it always does. I should've stayed. I should've done something to save them. In the end, I was a coward.

I attempt to move my arms, but they are caught in a tight knot behind me. Everything comes rushing back to me. The failed mission, the kidnapping.

I want to groan. I know I can't. Any sound will alert whoever did this to the fact that I'm awake, and I'll lose whatever small advantage I have. My thoughts instantly go to the Storm Hound commander who chased me, but I don't know if we are even in Rurik anymore.

"Wake her." A gruff voice sounds from somewhere above my head.

I brace myself for a blow. Instead, a shock of ice-cold water floods my face. I sputter and right myself, blowing the stinging fluid out of my nose. I blink a few times before lifting my head and glaring. I won't give the Storm Hounds anything.

But instead of a wall of black uniforms and cold glares, two bodies stand beside a low fire in the center of the room. A broad-shouldered male with a full salt-and-pepper beard and a slight girl no older than me with raven black hair, cheeks gleaming a golden brown in the firelight. She's clearly Adamanian, wearing a stiff, high-collared tunic and loose-fitting trousers. The man, however, looks Stranan, his stance wide and ready like he's spent years in the military.

What an odd pair.

Perhaps he was a Storm Hound and she a spy from Adaman sent to torture secrets from one of Luiza's guildlings?

"Who are you?" I growl.

Neither looks fazed by my tone. The man adds another log to the fire, and I try not to sigh as it warms my wet skin. The new fuel helps to illuminate every wall of the house. We must still be in the outskirts of Rurik. The rounded house has only one room with the firepit in the center. A low ceiling slopes upward in the middle, and the floor holds nothing but dirt and the rough blanket I'm sitting on.

"What do you want?" I try again.

"I have a proposal for you." The man steps forward and squats, his russet eyes studying my face.

"If you want guild secrets, I won't give them. Throw me in the *tyur'ma*, if that's what you're going to do."

The man chuckles and reaches for his shirt pocket, pulling out a thick piece of parchment. He taps it on his open palm.

"I want nothing to do with your guild. I was told you come from Ludminka. Is that true?"

I nod. There is no sense in lying, with my paper-white skin exposed to the world.

"I'm a man in need of a large amount of money. The Czar is a man in need of a large amount of lovite. I've heard tell there are still vaults full of it housed inside your mountain of Knnot that were never shipped. I need you to lead me through the mountain."

"Never." I spit at his feet. "I'll never go back there."

"What if I told you I could give you the one thing you miss the most in this world?"

"And what would that be?" My voice cuts cold and harsh.

"Alik Sokolov."

My hearts stops as I quickly realize this has nothing to do with the lovite I stole from the Vestry. These aren't people sent by the Czar. This is something else entirely. Somehow, the man before me knows Alik.

"Impossible," I whisper. My voice loses all venom. "Alik is dead. He has been for a year."

I saw Alik die. I watched his blood pour through the slats of that dirty pier in Oleg, a port city far to the east. I saw the Storm Hounds circle him and stab him as my boat floated out to sea. I never stopped seeing it. The scene haunts my nightmares.

I blamed his death on the Czar, the Thieves Guild, and Luiza. But most of all, I blamed myself. I left him to die without so much as lifting a dagger. This man can't be telling the truth, because if he is, I am an even bigger coward than I ever realized.

"It's true," the man says. "I'll prove it, if you promise not to run. If you do, we'll have to chase, and I'd rather not do that."

I nod, not trusting my voice. The girl, who stood behind the man near the fire, moves forward with a small dagger raised. She slices the bindings at my back before taking her post once more. I rub my wrists, my eyes never leaving the man before me. He lifts the small bit of parchment up, snared between two thick fingers.

"My proof." He places the paper in my hands.

I unfold it with trembling fingers. My entire body goes hot as I stare at the familiar neat handwriting. I can almost see the hand that wrote it, nicked with long scars, with one shaped exactly like a star beneath the ring finger. I swallow, my mouth suddenly bone-dry, and reread the note.

*Valeria,*
*I am alive.*
*—A*

# FIVE

MY BREATH CATCHES HARD AND fast. I want to believe it. My heart aches to let the hope of those words chase away the emptiness I felt for the past year. I search for a reason to deny the letter, but the left corner holds a sign only Alik and I ever used: a wide triangle with looped lines through the center, a combination of the first letters of our names.

"How?" I ask.

"I saved him," the man replies. "He nearly died but was strong enough to pull through. I've kept him with me this entire time."

"What, like a prisoner? And now you'll just hand him over if I lead you to Knnot?"

The man gives a shrug. "A boy for a mountain of money seems more than a fair trade."

"What makes you think you'll be able to retrieve any lovite? No one has returned from Ludminka since the freeze."

"I've got this," the man says, lifting a burning gem from around his neck. It almost looks like lovite, but gleaming orange veins lace through the stone, pulsing with power. I've never seen anything like it.

"What is that? What's it made of?"

"A charm given to me by a witch for saving her son. She promised it would let anyone pass through the frost and plague into the mountain. She said it was lovite touched by the hands of the Bright God's champion himself."

"You're a fool if you believe that," I say.

The man shrugs and tucks the stone back into his shirt. "You don't have to believe me. But your Alik is going whether you do or not. He has a debt to repay, and I won't let him go until I have it."

"He knows nothing of Ludminka. He wasn't raised there," I say. "He's useless to you."

"A skilled thief is never useless."

My entire world spins at his words. I knew better than anyone that something devoured everyone who stepped foot into Ludminka. I saw it.

Will I really refuse to save Alik when I've been handed a second chance?

I try to sift through the whirlwind of thoughts in my head. Of Alik and Luiza, the Czar and the Bright God's champion.

There is a plan there. I can practically feel it thrumming. It is too late to help Luiza now. She warned me as much before I left.

But the Bright God's champion needs lovite. It's what started this thing in the first place. If I can get my hands on enough lovite to outfit an entire army, he'll have to listen to me. It's the leverage I need. I'll get Alik and have what I need to save Luiza and the guild.

I'll have my home, my family, back together.

"We'll be rewarded?" I ask.

The man rolls back onto his heels and lets out a guffaw.

"I shouldn't have expected anything different from a thief. You'll get a cut. And Alik. I'll even swear it."

The man sticks out his hand. I stare at it. If I agree, I'll be going back to the one place I've tried to forget for ten years. The very place all my nightmares started.

But I'll get Alik back. I'll save Luiza and help the Bright God's champion right the world.

"Fine," I say. "You have a deal."

"Don't sound so happy about it," the man says, and stands, stretching his back as he goes.

"Who are you two?"

"I'm Ivan."

"Chinua," says the Adamanian girl.

"And you both just so happen to be lurking around a guild drop-off point—waiting for me?"

"Of course not. We received a tip," says Ivan. "Now, get changed. We can't have you freezing on the way to Oleg."

"Oleg?" I stop rubbing the raw spots on my wrist and snap my gaze to Ivan. "I thought we were going to Knnot."

"By way of Oleg, where I have a safe house. Where do you think I was keeping Alik all this time?" he says.

"You kept him in the same place he almost died?" I ask.

"He couldn't have gone any farther," Ivan says, his voice low and eyes downcast.

A pang lances through me at his words. I haven't stepped foot in the port city of Oleg since I watched Alik die. Or, I suppose, almost die. I've spent most of my days since then trying to forget the iron gray waters of the ocean and the sickening scent of dying kelp and salt.

Luiza had sent us on a mission to retrieve shipping manifests of Strana's most profitable trading partners. She'd wanted to make new agreements, or put pressure on the Czar's advisers to do so. If Strana wasn't making money, neither was Luiza or her guild.

We'd just escaped an abandoned warehouse when we were surrounded. Storm Hounds appeared out of the mist like they'd been waiting there for hours. Alik and I never saw them. To this day, I'm not sure how they knew we were there.

We ran toward the docks and a small boat. We'd almost made it when Alik suddenly screamed. I'd never heard him make a sound like it. I wheeled around to see a bolt from a crossbow protruding from his right thigh, straight in the back and out through the front. He collapsed to the dock. I raced to him, desperate to get him on his feet.

"Run," he whispered in my ear, his voice harsh and laced with pain.

"I can't leave you," I gasped.

"You can't stay here."

Heavy boots pounded on the dock. I could see the Storm Hounds over Alik's shoulder, their eyes fixed on us. I desperately tried to pull him up again, but Alik pushed me away.

"Run, Val. Run!"

I reached out for him one last time. If I could just get him to stand, I could get us somewhere safe.

I just needed him to stand.

He slapped my hand and his eyes met mine. They were wide with fear, but his brows pulled down over his long nose. I'd seen that look so many times, I knew what it meant without him saying anything. He was staying, no matter what I did. He'd made up his mind.

"Please, Alik, I can't." My voice broke.

"Go!" He put all his strength into kneeling and shoved me toward the boat as another bolt sailed over our heads. "Run!"

I threw one last look at him as the Storm Hounds descended onto the pier. Tears spilled down my cheeks as I turned my back and ran. I was ripping the ropes from the dock and jumping into the boat as the Storm Hounds reached him.

One raised his blade high.

I pushed away from the dock as the sword swung down. I put oars to water as Alik screamed again. The last thing I saw before I closed my eyes and rowed from the pier was Alik's dark red blood pooling beneath him and dripping into the lapping ocean below.

I grit my teeth against the memory. Now isn't the time for me to break down. I can't let these two strangers see the dark pit of weakness that resides inside me.

Chinua crosses the floor clutching a bundle. Her face betrays nothing as she places the clothing into my arms, but her hand lingers on my wrist. She opens her mouth like she might say something. Instead, she gives a curt nod and turns to repack the bag she took the clothes from.

Alik must've assured Ivan I would come because the clean, warm clothes, boots, and thick fur-lined coat I slip into fit perfectly. I sweat as I wrap a thick scarf about my face, drawing up the hood of my coat. The others gather up the scant things they used and shove them into packs. We aren't wasting time, then. We are going to Oleg *now*. I swallow down something hot and a buzz forms inside me, desperate to break the silence.

"You came all this way to get me?" I ask.

"You, and her." Ivan nods toward Chinua. "You're the last pieces of my puzzle."

I eye Chinua and wonder what she has to offer Ivan's expedition to Knnot. Do they even know of the plague and the freeze? I suppose they have to. Adaman lies closest to Zladonia out of all of Strana's neighbors. They raided the towns at our borders more than once for lovite.

Ivan stamps out the fire and covers it with dirt from the floor. He does it with such brisk efficiency, I know he's done it before. I narrow my eyes. He's hiding something, I'm sure of it.

We don't speak as we set out into the misty dawn. Rurik lies silent, as if I didn't run for my life just a few hours earlier. I expect Storm Hound patrols or checkpoints at the roads leading away from Rurik. We encounter nothing but a few bleary-eyed farmers with wagons full of pallid vegetables. Ivan's sturdy gelding leads the way, angling us down the long East Road toward the Iron Sea.

I cut a glance at Chinua on the horse beside me. Her posture betrays she's ridden before, her arms relaxed and back slouched. I have no such talent. Luiza taught me enough to keep steady for a mission to the farthest holding in Strana, where I'd had no choice but to ride.

"Did Ivan kidnap you, too? Or did he find a nicer way to ask you on his expedition?"

Ivan gives a chuckle from his mount five feet ahead of us.

"Chinua came voluntarily."

Chinua's cheeks redden slightly, but she gives me a smile.

"I've been in Strana for some time. This was far too much money to pass up, and Ivan was very convincing."

"Does he have one of your friends as a hostage, too?"

Again, Ivan laughs.

"Alik is far from my hostage. He simply knows he has debts he must pay."

"I don't see the difference," I mutter to myself.

"He's talked of little else but that boy since he found me at the border," Chinua whispers.

My forehead wrinkles. The way Ivan used Alik's life as a chip to barter with made it seem like Alik was nothing but a pawn to him.

"Did he say why he saved him?" I ask Chinua, but it's Ivan who answers.

"He was a dying boy alone in the cold. I couldn't leave him there."

The words cut deep. I *had* left him. A thought races through me hard and fast enough to make my stomach churn.

What if Alik hates me? He'd told me to leave, but I know he would've stayed with me if our positions were reversed. He would've made sure we left together or we didn't leave at all. Perhaps I should've done the same. Instead, all I thought about was saving my own skin.

He was alive this entire time and never once wrote. He must've told Ivan about me. He was the only person in all the guild aside from Luiza who knew I was from Ludminka. Since Ivan came to get me with that information in hand, it must have been Alik who'd given it to him. Ivan trusted Alik enough to stay behind while he ventured four days from Oleg to retrieve Chinua and me, so it wasn't Ivan stopping him from writing to me.

Yet he didn't once send a letter?

I never considered Alik might hate me for what I did. I left him to die, cold and alone, without a backward glance.

It should've been me who saved Alik, not a stranger. We were partners. We swore to always have each other's backs. The only free Zladonians in all the world, it seemed. But I'd run away from the only person who'd known me to my core and still accepted me.

Would he now, after all I had done?

We reach Oleg four days later. The road to the old port city hasn't been repaired since the lovite stopped flowing. Deep ruts and overgrown tangles of weeds make travel slow. Ivan had a small tent strapped behind his saddle that we slept in, and flint and steel to start a sputtering fire that we huddled around in silence almost every night.

Ivan finally draws to a stop at the top of a small rise and stares at the town below. Chinua and I pull up short behind him. The town, with its ramshackle cabins and winding streets, curls around a small inlet, long piers extending into an empty bay. The cold waters of the Iron Sea lap against the white outcropping of stones at the edge of the town.

I don't want to move. The thought of seeing Alik's smile carried me across half of Strana and pushed me through rain and bitter winds. Now, when he sits within a few minutes' walk, I'm frozen.

The horse beneath me shifts and noses her way forward. Ivan holds out a hand.

"What?" I say, pulling the mare to a stop. She gives an irritated swing of her head.

"Something's not right," he says. "It's never this quiet here."

"They've probably gone in to shelter from the storm," I say, nodding at the dark clouds gathering over the bay, promising snow. I tuck my nose into the fur lining of my coat as a sharp gust needles its way across my cheeks.

"No." Ivan shakes his head. "They're too poor to miss a day of work, no matter the weather."

I let the reality of his words settle on my shoulders. He's right. Even when Alik and I were here last time, in the middle of winter, people had bustled from house to house, hawking wares and bartering meager goods. In my desperation to both see and avoid Alik, I'd forgotten to really take in my surroundings. Luiza would chastise me for days if she knew.

My heart pangs at the thought of her.

"We should scout the city," I say.

"We can't separate. Things have changed in the year since you were here last. A Zladonian should not wander alone."

"What do you mean?"

Even as I ask, the eerie wail of a horn rises above the roofs of Oleg. Only one thing in all of Strana uses that sound.

A *tyur'ma.*

# SIX

A CHILL RIPPLES DOWN MY spine as the horn calls out again and another answers from somewhere near the heart of the city. In all my time away from Ludminka, I'd never once stepped anywhere close to a *tyur'ma*. The very sight of their dull black walls with spiked defenses tightened my chest. So many had been forced in, kept there under constant guard, and refused warm food and medicines.

"Why didn't you warn me?" I ask.

"I didn't think you'd have to know," Ivan says.

Chinua looks between the two of us, her brows raised.

"It's a *tyur'ma*," I hiss at her. "They've rounded up everyone from Zladonia and imprisoned us. They think we carry some sort of plague that will destroy all Strana."

"Do you?" Chinua asks, her voice small.

"No," I spit. "No one has had the sickness since they left."

"Why haven't I heard about these prisons?" she asks.

"The Czar keeps them quiet." Ivan's brown eyes sweep over the city in quadrants. "A whisper of this outside Strana and he knows all trade would halt. It's tenuous enough already without adding human suffering."

My eyes cut to Ivan. He is cunning and manipulative, but he lacks the venom with which most Stranans defend the Czar. Something about it strikes me as odd.

"You kept Alik *here*? Right next to it?"

"What better hiding place?" Ivan's voice is flat.

Three horn blasts sound. I'd gleaned enough information from Luiza's reports to know it means the *tyur'ma* is receiving a new shipment. It is likely getting ready to open its gates now.

Anger seethes in my chest, pressing against my breastbone. What if the person they are opening their gates for is Alik? What if Ivan is wrong? I can't just sit here and hope.

Not again.

I squeeze my horse, her warm sides pressing into my calves. She jumps into a lope and we careen down the hill into the town, chipped whitewashed walls rushing past in a blur of motion. I ignore the shouts of Ivan and Chinua behind me. I can't be this close to a *tyur'ma* and not help.

I slow the horse to a trot as we enter the city square. Leaning produce stands and food carts are scattered around the cobbled plaza, each one empty. A cold wind snaps through the tattered awnings, and I can't help but shudder.

I scan the streets, looking for some sort of clue as to where everyone is, though I already know. Stranans never miss a chance to scream hate at the people they believe ruined the country.

I pull the horse to a stop and listen. At first, I hear nothing but the soft roar of the waves a half mile away. A cold wind barrels through the streets to tug at my coat. At long last, I hear a shout. I spring from the horse, tying her loosely to a vendor's stand before darting down a side street, pulling my thick scarf over my nose and tugging down my cap until nothing but my eyes show.

The call of the crowd grows louder with each wide turn I make until I'm standing in what I can only assume is the warehouse district of Oleg.

Wide, squat buildings follow the slope of the land, leading into the long piers where large ships used to dock to take lovite around the world. A crowd gathers around a building close to the edge of the sea. One of the abandoned warehouses is circled by a high wall, thick spikes atop it. Storm Hounds stand at even intervals, their eyes sweeping the crowd as a horse-drawn carriage ambles toward the gates.

The people around me jeer, throwing slurs and curses like they were nothing more than crumbs. They're smart enough to stand far away from the Storm Hounds and allow a wide berth for the carriage as it makes its way to the gate. Through the heavy bars in the back, I can see them.

Two girls, no older than fifteen winters, sit pressed against the back of the carriage. Between them they clutch a small boy, no older than three. A man throws a bucket of water as they pass. They wince as the freezing liquid douses them. They clutch the small boy tighter, his cheeks red with tears and his nose covered in snot.

My heart shatters.

This is why Luiza worked so hard to hide my identity. This is what she's kept me from. I thought I knew. I read all the reports Luiza received on the *tyur'mas*, but reading and seeing are two very different things.

The crowd screams profanities and spits at them. They want this, our suffering. It's a mirror of their own.

My teeth grind so hard they squeak. I know better than anyone that the *tyur'mas* hold no means of escape. No way to break in. The Storm Hounds are given short shifts in order to stay alert. The inside is a maze and the walls are far too thick and protected to break through.

Yet every part of my body wants to free the children before me.

A solid hand clamps down on my shoulder. I spin and come face-to-face with Ivan. His cheeks are red from exertion. He shakes his head. I bare my teeth and try and rip away from him. His fingers dig into my flesh so hard I fight back a yelp. I can't just stand here and watch this. If I do, how am I any better than the jeering crowd around me?

Three horn blasts sound once more. I turn toward the prison as the gates open.

A large man steps out, draped in powder blue with a gold circlet resting on his graying black hair. I've seen his face in every home I've ever robbed, in the Vestry above the priest's desk, even in Luiza's office.

Czar Ladislaw of Strana.

Behind him, like a miniature shadow, is Crown Prince Yuri.

Yuri can't be more than ten but already holds every ounce of his father's self-importance. He's scrawny and pallid, nothing like his bull-broad father. His chin meets in the same point, but where Ladislaw seems proud and commanding, Yuri looks petulant. A snub nose only adds to his condescending features. His father's glossy black curls drape his head in lank sheets. On sight, I hate him as much as I hate his father. It seems fitting Ladislaw should spawn such a sour-looking child. As if all of the country's pain and sadness were trapped within Yuri's tiny body.

They step forward as one, marching to the stopped carriage. The crowd stares at Czar Ladislaw like he is the Bright God come to Strana. He raises his hands to quiet the crowd.

"Greetings, Oleg." Ladislaw's voice rings out. "I thank you for hosting my son and me on this wondrous day. We couldn't be more pleased with your city. When we first thought of raising a *tyur'ma* here, my advisers worried it was too close to the ocean to be defensible. I knew different. I knew the people of Oleg could keep the plague the *malozlas* bring behind lock and key."

The crowd roars as Czar Ladislaw beckons to the nearest Storm Hound. The guard grabs the rough rope connecting the children inside the carriage and yanks. They stumble, only barely managing to catch themselves before falling to the dirty snow at the Czar's feet.

The crowd cries for their death as the Storm Hound yanks them up. Ladislaw turns to them, the disgust on his face plain even to me from the back of the crowd. Yuri stands just behind his father, his face a cold mask.

"My Storm Hounds found these children just outside Oleg in a cave. Evidence shows they've been there for quite some time," Ladislaw says.

"No wonder we've had such terrible luck." An old man shakes his head beside me.

I shrink even farther into the shadows of my hood. I hate the fact that I continue to stand here, watching as the Czar throws yet another innocent set of people into a prison. Ivan's hand continues to hold me in place, his face a grim mask.

"I have granted Oleg another battalion of Storm Hounds for protection. They will make their rounds nightly, looking for any *malozla* in hiding. We will find them all." Czar Ladislaw's eyes sweep the crowd, and my heart stutters to a stop as they swing past me.

I'm a coward.

A spineless, useless coward.

Czar Ladislaw waves a hand, and the Storm Hound holding the rope tugs the children into the gate at the Czar's back. It takes only a couple of breaths for them to disappear. A sob catches at the back of my throat.

"I also want to show my thanks to Oleg for your selflessness in allowing our prison to be harbored in your town. I bring you gifts. You'll find the warehouses behind you stocked with all you could need for the winter. I've brought enough furs that every citizen should get a new set of warm clothes. There are food stores of grain, meat, even vegetables. I also am pleased to give you new windows, to keep the harsh winter winds from finding their way into your homes."

The crowd lets out a roar of joy. Czar Ladislaw smiles benevolently before flicking his hands. It's all the direction the crowd needs. They turn and descend on the warehouses like a horde of hungry insects.

My legs go numb as white-hot heat races through my entire body. It ignites a sick twist in my stomach. The Czar is standing not more than forty feet away. I might be able to kill him before the Storm Hounds stop me. Ivan's fingers dig into the fleshy part of my shoulder so hard I know I'll have bruises. He pulls me back from the warehouses and into the winding streets.

"Let me go," I grind out.

"Why? So you can throw yourself at the Czar and get yourself killed? Do you honestly think you'd be able to get more than ten feet before the Storm Hounds shot you full of arrows? It's what they're trained to do, Valeria. Dying won't help anyone," Ivan says.

"I should've done something." My voice breaks on the words, and I turn my face away from Ivan, trying to hide the tears starting to fall.

"We all should. We should've when the Czar branded you *malozla*. We all should've when he packaged you up and sent you into *tyur'mas*. But we didn't. No one in Strana did. This isn't your fault, Valeria. It's the Czar's. And all the people who failed to help before you." He gives me a sideways look and at last releases me.

I don't believe his words. He has the luxury of thinking the time for action has long since passed. He doesn't live in fear every day of the exact same fate we just witnessed in the town square.

He clears his throat. "I know what it is to feel helpless, to be trapped by your circumstances. I will never know how you are forced to suffer every day, and I'm sorry for the way this world treats you. There will be a time to act, but not today."

A war still rages beneath my skin. I want to scream. Instead, I nod and take deep breaths as I follow Ivan back to the city square. Logically, I know Ivan is right. I have no power, no way of helping anyone.

Luiza said the Bright God's champion would usurp the throne and destroy the *tyur'mas*. It's the entire reason I agreed to break into the Vestry. Only a champion of the gods has the power to destroy what the Czar built. If I could get to this champion, plead my case, and give him all the lovite an army could ask for, maybe he'd listen. It was better than another year under the Czar.

It's half-baked and relies on trusting someone I've never met, but it's better than no plan at all.

# SEVEN

IVAN LEADS ME BACK TO the still empty town square, the citizens of Oleg too caught up in pawing over the Czar's goods. My stomach continues to churn at the thought of the *tyur'ma*. Alik had been here the entire time. He'd been this close, heard the cries of the horns and seen the barricades. How had he been able to bear it?

I suppose he had no choice.

My mind circles with the logic of knowing I wouldn't have been able to save anyone, while also screaming that I should've tried. I clamber onto my horse. Chinua sits atop her own, her face an unreadable mask. Ivan makes a show of checking his girth straps as I stare dully at the saddle horn before me.

"You can't blame yourself." Chinua's soft voice comes from beside me.

"I saw the crowd Ivan dived into to stop you. There were too many eyes, too many waiting guards. You're a thief. Stealth is the best way to strike your enemy, no?"

I consider her words before a ghost of a smile touches my lips.

"Are you telling me to commit treason secretly?"

Chinua shrugs. "I don't know if anyone outside Strana would particularly care if your czar suddenly disappeared. Just do it in a way that looks like an accident."

"I'll have to keep that in mind when I plot the assassination."

Ivan swings up into his saddle and angles us northeast, toward the part of Oleg I know far too well. I swallow past the lump in my throat. It seems cruel I have to go there after what I just saw, but that's where Ivan's safe house must be.

"If they round you all up like that, why stay in Strana?" Chinua asks.

"I don't know," I say. "I guess I never thought about leaving. Luiza found me when I was a girl and raised me here. I have a job, a home, people I love."

"But you could be caught at any time. Doesn't that scare you?"

"Of course. I think about it every day. But if I leave Strana, I leave all the good parts of it behind, too." The thought of losing Luiza and the home she helped me make after losing my parents hurts. It may have already happened. I don't know what the Storm Hounds have done to the guild headquarters. It could be in ashes for all I know.

My heart already feels heavy when we turn on the street with an all too familiar quay. Docks jut out into a calmer part of the bay. Ragged boats still bob in the growing waves, undaunted by the coming storm. Icy wind rages across the seaside road and I shrug into my coat, wishing I could give the wind my anger and have it whisk it away.

I try to calm my roiling stomach, but it's impossible. I don't want to see Alik. Not now. Not like this, with anger and hate filling every part of me. I'm afraid I won't be able to hide it. It's always been the part of me he had the hardest time understanding.

My chest tightens as we draw level to the very pier I watched Alik fall to as I rowed away. I study the worn boards, looking for remnants of his blood, but the wood has long since been scrubbed clean. Ivan leads us past it without so much as glancing over. I train my eyes on his horse and continue to follow it down the narrow road that slowly curves along the bay. Sea spray splatters us in a fine sheen of salt and bitter water. At last, near what seems like the very edge of Oleg, Ivan turns onto a new road, which winds slightly toward a squat two-story cabin.

Ivan swings the horses around to the back of the house and into a small stable. It isn't much more than a lean-to, but it is enough to provide shelter. Two horses already stand within, their noses buried in a pile of hay at their feet. They nicker hello, and Ivan stops just before the opening.

"Remove the tack and brush down your horse with one of the currycombs hanging on the wall before going inside," he says. His eyes go from Chinua to me. "Take all the time you need."

He unsaddles his horse and hangs the tack on one of the thick timbers protruding from the wall. I mimic his motions with numb hands and a buzzing mind. Just inside the house behind me is Alik. Excitement and fear run rampant through my body. I go through the motions of caring for the horse without much concentration, brushing away the sweat staining its flanks, letting the smell of horse and fresh hay fill every inch of my nose.

I can do this. I'd done more impossible things for Luiza. Alik was . . . no, *is* my best friend. We've been through hundreds of missions together, heard Luiza's rough voice chastise our form and felt her slap our hands when we held lockpicks the wrong way. None of that disappeared.

It's just a bit more complicated now.

When I finally look up from my horse, I find the lean-to empty, Chinua's horse tethered next to Ivan's, glossy and happily munching hay. I sigh, and run a firm hand over my coat, attempting to center myself.

"Hello, Valeria."

My body goes slack at the voice I'd know anywhere.

I spin slowly to face Alik.

His familiar, beautiful face now bears a long scar, beginning in the hairline just above his right eyebrow and carving down over his right eye to end at his left cheek. It runs deep and whoever stitched him up did a shoddy job.

He's tried to train his hair over the scar and wears a thick eye patch over his right eye, but there is no hiding it. It surprises me, but it doesn't detract from the fact that I'm seeing Alik *alive*.

I take a step toward him. Then another, until we are a handspan apart. His eye follows me, his face set in stone. I reach out slowly and let my fingers brush against his warm cheek. A riot starts in my stomach. He's real, perfect. And he's Alik.

*My* Alik.

The edges of his mouth curve up into a smile. Heat rushes into my cheeks, and my eyes burn with unshed tears.

"You're really alive," I whisper.

I throw my arms around his neck and all the heartache and tears I shed over the past year seem to melt away. The dread of Alik rejecting me, of him screaming at me for leaving him, flies from my mind. How could I have ever believed he would be anything but happy to see me?

"I've missed you so much." My voice catches, and I don't spare the time to be embarrassed by the tears spilling onto my cheeks from behind my closed eyes.

Alik wraps his arms around me. His hug crushes the air

from my lungs, but I don't care.

"You have no idea how much I've missed you," he says into my hair.

I pull him closer. He smells different from how I remember, like sea salt and fresh snow, but it suits him. I almost say so but catch myself. I can't say those sorts of things. We are friends, nothing more.

"I was afraid you wouldn't come." His breath whispers along the shell of my ear.

I back out of our hug so I can stare at him. He doesn't stand as tall as he used to, his shoulders slightly rounded. I shake my head a little.

"How could I not? If there was even a chance you were alive, I had to see you for myself."

His forehead creases at my words, and I notice a small worry line now sits between his thick brows and a tiny nick lies just above his top lip. My fingers ache to brush across these new additions, to memorize them and relearn who he is. I clench my hand into a tight fist to stop myself. There are so many questions that I don't even know where to begin. I suppose there is really only one I want to know the answer to.

"How *are* you alive?"

He's quiet for a moment, glancing down to study my face. "You . . . you didn't get any of my letters?"

I step out of his arms completely, already missing his warmth as bitter air filters through my coat.

"Letters? What are you talking about?"

Alik's face goes slack.

"I wrote to you every week for the past three months. Each time, I explained everything and asked you to come to Oleg so you could see me for yourself. I knew you'd never believe it until you saw me."

I shake my head. "I never got them." I grab Alik's hands as a shadow passes over his face. "I swear to the Brother Gods I never saw your letters. Believe me, I would've come straight to you if I'd even heard a whisper you were alive. Life without you was . . . was horrible."

The words fall pathetically from my mouth, not doing justice to the black void of loneliness and longing I'd held in my heart since I left him.

Alik gives me a small smile. "I should've known you wouldn't leave me here alone."

"Never." I squeeze his hands tight, as if that will make him believe me. "I made you a promise when we became partners that I would never let you walk alone. I never meant to break it."

"I know, Val."

Silence hangs between us for a long moment. I notice my hands still wrapped around his and drop them, rubbing my palms down the sides of my legs to get the feeling of his warmth off them. He lets out a soft sigh before speaking.

"The first swing grazed my face. The next did—" He gestures toward his chest. "I thought I was dead for sure, but a man started picking off the Storm Hounds with a bow. He killed two before the rest turned toward him. He took care of them with his sword and picked me up. To be honest, I don't remember much after that. It was a while before my fever stopped making me delirious. Ivan saved me. I was all but dead. If it weren't for him, I wouldn't be standing here."

My first instinct is to make some joke about how I should thank Ivan for saving Alik, but I hug him instead. And I never want to let go again.

"I wanted so badly for you to be alive," I say. "And now here you are. I can't tell you how happy I am."

"I'm so glad you came. I spent a lot of days hoping you would."

My breath catches at his words. I want to look up into his face and see if he feels the same thing I do, but I keep my eyes firmly locked on our boots. It wasn't until after I lost him that I realized how much he really means to me. Losing him was like losing half of my heart. He means more to me than just a partner, despite Luiza's warnings, despite knowing better than anyone how much it hurts to watch people die.

Heat courses through me as I think of kissing him. Of him kissing me back. I stop the thoughts before they can charge forward. Alik doesn't know how I feel about him and he's never given me any indication he feels that way about me. I won't jeopardize what we have now.

"Do you want to walk with me? Just for a little bit?" he

asks. He gives a sheepish smile at my raised eyebrow. "I'd like to keep you to myself for just a little longer."

"Sure. Lead the way."

Alik heads back down the lane, drawing a thick hat out of his pocket and pulling it down low over his shock of white hair. A year without Luiza's concoctions has returned it to its natural color. I study Alik as we walk. A pronounced limp hinders his previously long strides. His face doesn't betray if it bothers him or not.

All too soon, we find our way back to the lane I'd just come down. Bile rises in my stomach as we walk down the street to the pier where I thought Alik died.

I can't stop looking at it. My steps falter as my knees buckle. Alik notices I'm not beside him and turns to me, confusion scrawled across his face.

"What's wrong, Val?"

I avoid his gaze, wondering if I should lie. Long ago we'd made a pact, after one of Luiza's half-truths had gotten us stuck in a waterlogged basement, that we would never lie to one another, not even to spare the other's feelings.

This is different.

How do you apologize for leaving someone to die? How do you explain that you've spent the past year tormented by your own cowardice? That you're terrified that when it matters most, you'll run again instead of staying to fight for what you love?

When I don't respond, he closes the distance between us. "Are you thinking about the last time we were here?"

I shudder as a wave crashes upon the quay and soaks my feet. I nod.

"Don't," Alik whispers, and cups my face, ensuring my eyes meet his before continuing. "I told you to leave. I begged the Brother Gods to help you escape. I *needed* you to live. I couldn't stand the thought of the gods being so cruel as to kill us both. You're just as I remember, and you don't understand how grateful I am for that."

I nod again and tears slip out, despite my desire to keep them back. The hollow feeling in my chest starts to close one small piece at a time. But a single question burns bright in my mind, threatening to consume me.

"Why didn't you write me sooner, Alik?" My voice breaks. "Even if I had gotten your letter three months ago, I still went nearly a year grieving you."

He smiles, a broken smile, a sad smile.

"Look at me." He lifts a hand to his face, tracing the long scar.

It shatters a small piece of my heart. I take his hand from his face. To me, he is as beautiful as ever. He is alive and whole and speaking to me. It's more than I ever dared hope for.

"Did you really think I would care?"

"How could you not?" He pulls away. Wind blows hard off the waves, sending them roaring through the space between us.

"I can't even walk properly anymore. I'm still training myself to use a sword again. I can forget working for the guild."

I reach out my hand and, after a moment's hesitation, grab his arm. His muscles are taut beneath my palm.

"That doesn't mean you aren't still the same person you were when I last saw you."

A rough laugh leaves Alik's mouth. He studies me so seriously that I'm almost certain he is reading my mind. Before I know it, he brings me in for a crushing hug. The waves crash against the dock again and spray us with chilling water.

He takes a step back with a sniff, the rims of his eyes a bit red. He grips my hand tight, his face sobering. "Valeria, you don't have to go to Knott. You can draw Ivan a map of the mines and go back to Rurik. To Luiza and the guild. That's why I wanted to get away from the house, to tell you without anyone overhearing. Ivan thinks having you with us will bring us luck. He talked of little else since I let slip you were from Ludminka. I'm sorry. I should've never told him."

I consider his words. Letting the idea of returning to Rurik without him settle in my mind. I can't do it.

"I'm never letting you out of my sight again."

"Are you certain you want to do this?"

With every part of my body and mind, I don't. But I won't let Alik walk into Knnot and never return. Not when I finally have him again.

I tighten my grip on his hand. "Absolutely."

# EIGHT

WE DON'T TALK AS WE make our way back to the house, too content being close to one another once again. Alik does a series of complicated knocks on the door, and muffled voices sound from inside before it opens a crack. A tall, blond woman maybe four or five years older than me looks down her thin nose at us.

"Took you long enough," she says, her voice almost husky.

We step into a small room, which could be in any other house in Strana. A warm fire already crackling sits in a hearth against the far wall, a staircase leading to the upper level just to my right. Comfortable chairs and a long settee circle the fireplace, Ivan and Chinua already slung across two of them.

The woman closes the woolen curtains before settling into the settee. Alik makes no move to join them, and I stay by his side, uncertain of what comes next. Ivan clears his throat and everyone in the room turns toward him.

"Now that we're all here, I suppose it's time to reveal my plan," he says.

"We've only been waiting three months," the blond woman says with a smile at Alik. My brows furrow, unsure what to make of it.

Alik finally moves, placing himself beside her. I take the remaining chair nearest the fire, both grateful for its warmth and intimidated by the way the woman and Alik seem so familiar with each other.

"You promised me riches, Ivan. Don't think I've forgotten," says the woman.

"I can't imagine you would, Serafima." Ivan retrieves a large piece of parchment from the mantel and spreads it before us.

The map is oddly detailed, with the points marking Rurik and Oleg mere smudges, while the two mountain ranges crossing the northern part of Strana are in vivid detail. Ivan looks up at Serafima.

"Have you found a path to Knnot that avoids the road?"

She squats, pointing a thick finger at Oleg. "This is the quickest route."

She traces a straight path from the city over the Biting Mountains, down onto a wide steppe, then up over the massive Ral Mountains that separate the Zladonia region from the rest of Strana. My legs ache just studying the terrain.

"It'll take us just east of Knnot, but we'll be far from the North Road and its villages. Most of the mountains will already have snow and I doubt the paths will be cleared. Few went this way when Knnot was profitable. I'd wager no one has used it since the mountain was closed."

I snort at her words. *Closed* isn't exactly what I'd call the freezing ice over Ludminka. Her sharp eyes cut to me, her mouth turning down.

"Have something to add?" she asks coldly.

"I'm no navigator."

"Well, I am. This is the best way to get there if we don't want you two getting caught." She nods at Alik.

I don't respond, and she looks back down at the map. She traces the path once more and nods, as if confirming it with herself.

"We'll be there weeks earlier than if we took the North Road."

"Even with the oncoming winter?" Alik asks.

"We'll take proper provisions, of course. But we should be able to make it before it's impassable. The autumn has been mild enough. The mountains shouldn't hold much snow yet, but I can't promise they won't close as we travel." She looks up at Ivan. "I can get us there. Are you going to tell us what we're planning to do once we've reached this mountain of yours?"

Something hot sparks in my chest. It isn't Ivan's mountain. If anyone in the room can claim it, it's me. I grew up there.

Survived the freeze that claimed my family.

It is mine.

I keep my mouth closed. I'm here for Alik. Once I have him, I'll take all the lovite I can carry and find the Bright God's champion and beg him for help in finding Luiza.

"Once there, Valeria will take us directly to the stores of harvested lovite still left inside. When we're at the vaults, Chinua will use her Adamanian powder to blow off the doors. We'll take all we can carry and become the richest people in all of Strana."

My lips thin. It was common knowledge Knnot held vaults of lovite where they readied shipments. I'd told Alik about following my father through the mountains when I'd been bored and looking for adventure, so Ivan probably assumed I knew the entire mine by heart. Even if I did, it didn't make it any less dangerous.

"You make it sound so simple," I say. "No one has made it back from Knnot since the freeze."

"We will," Ivan says.

"You're so sure? Because a lady gave you that charm around your neck and claimed it was magical enough to stop you from getting the plague?"

"Because Ivan saw a *vorozheia* and she predicted it," Alik says quietly.

"What?" I whisper, glancing at Ivan. He nods.

*Vorozheias* were rare in Strana now. The fortune-tellers rarely stayed in one place, too fearful of being caught. The

Czar had sought them out after the plague started assaulting the mines. When no one would tell him exactly how to stop it, he'd killed them and declared anyone who consorted with them a demon worshipper.

"She told me if I found people matching your descriptions, we would become the heroes who released Knnot," Ivan says.

"Did she say anything else?" I ask, my eyes narrowed. *Voro-zheias*'s visions often came with warnings or details that, if not followed exactly, would ruin the vision completely.

Ivan drums his fingers on his thigh before answering. "Nothing of note."

I consider pushing him. There's something he isn't telling us. Those gifted with the sight of the future are never wrong. If she truly saw us making it out, we would. I nod at last.

"Good. We'll leave in two days' time."

He rolls the map up and places it back on the mantel.

"We're safe here?" I ask as Ivan makes toward the stairs.

"As safe as you can be. If anyone knocks, we will protect you."

I wish his words comforted me as I watch him ascend the stairs. The Czar said a fresh battalion was to start searching throughout the city. Who was to say they wouldn't come knocking?

"Don't look so grim. We haven't had any issues so far," Alik says.

"You weren't with us today. The Czar is here."

Serafima drops the log she was about to place on the fire

with a solid thud. "He's here?"

"Yes." I make my voice as cold as I can. "I'm sure you're just dying to run to him and collect the reward money for Alik and me, aren't you?"

She stiffens, her pale cheeks coloring. "I could've turned Alik over at any point during the past three months. I have no interest in collecting money off you. The amount we'll get from Knnot is more than enough."

"So the only thing stopping you is the fact that we can get money from Knnot?"

The words slip out before I can stop them. I know I won't win anything antagonizing Serafima, but I don't trust her. I don't really trust anyone besides Alik.

"Valeria, stop," Alik says from behind me. "You have to be worn out from traveling. Why don't you take a bath and get changed into some new clothes."

"I don't think that will improve her manners," Serafima mutters. I don't get a chance to respond as Alik leads me away, the cool darkness of the hall stealing some of the heat of my anger. Tension hangs in the air between us for a brief moment before he huffs.

"We need her, Val. Don't prod her so much she leaves," Alik says in a hushed whisper.

"I don't trust her," I say.

"We don't exactly have the luxury of trust. Ivan won't release me until I follow through with this mission. I owe him a debt, and you said you were coming with me. Don't make us lose our navigator or we'll never reach Knnot in one piece."

I sigh at the collected calm of his voice. Alik hides his fear and anger better than even Luiza. It's a skill I've never been able to fully master, and he's never understood why. I swallow down the remains of my distrust.

Alik stops at a solid door and pushes it open. A tiny tub sits in the center of the room, a woodstove burning in the corner, a bucket of water already atop it. Steam seeps from heated rocks beside the fire, decorated with juniper berries and fir branches. We didn't have something this nice at the guild.

"This used to be Ivan's family home," Alik answers my silent question. "He made sure it was warm for his children."

"Where are they now?" I ask.

"I don't know. He refuses to speak about them."

I eye the bathroom, trying to stop myself from imagining a happy family laughing as they bathe their children. The image hurts my heart.

"Well, I don't think I'll ever leave."

"I was in here for a couple of hours the first time I used it." Alik chuckles. "I'll leave some wools outside the door for you. Ivan got several sets for the journey. Might as well be warm. It looks like it'll be a cold night."

"Thank you, Alik."

He smiles at me, and I close the door with a final glance back, still not really believing I am seeing him again.

# NINE

TWO DAYS LATER, WE LEAVE Oleg behind.

I spent the majority of the past two days in a small back bedroom, too afraid of the Storm Hounds to venture much farther than the sitting room. Alik didn't seem to share my hesitation. He busied himself with preparations for the trip to Knnot, happily going outside to care for the horses with nothing more than a loose hat on his head. We didn't get another chance to really be alone. The house was always full of bustling people determined to ready themselves for a trip they were sure would change their lives.

I had to acknowledge Ivan was more than prepared for the expedition. He'd secured all the right supplies—hats, balaclavas, several sets of thick trousers, and fur-lined boots. He even thought to bring sturdy winter tents and snowshoes for us all. I gleaned from a couple of jokes between Alik and Ivan that he'd been slowly amassing this small hoard since the fortune-teller confirmed the trip would be successful. Each of us ties saddle-bags to our horses, carrying all the gear we'll need for the trip.

Now gray skies mirror the waters of the Iron Sea, the waves lapping over the sides of the quay as if begging for just a nibble of my leg. We need to get out of Oleg as quickly as possible, and the predawn streets are quiet enough to let us slip past unnoticed. Ivan leads us on a winding path, going far out of our way to avoid passing anywhere near the *tyur'ma*.

My heart remains in my throat until the horses step off the roads and into the soft, new snow at the edge of the village. Serafima dismounts and connects a rough blanket to the back of her horse, taking the last position to cover our tracks as we walk. It won't hide our passing from a good tracker, but it should offer us enough protection to get far away before any-one notices. The Czar, besides throwing Alik and me in prison, would likely punish Ivan as well if we are caught. An unsanc-tioned trip to Knnot is illegal, the Czar fearing the plague and having no control over the mines if someone besides him managed to reopen them. We have to take every precaution.

The horses trudge toward the thick branches of a fir copse, keeping the ocean to our right. Alik and I ride side by side, and I glance over at him. A smile tugs the corner of his mouth as he takes a deep breath.

"This is going to be good." He nods at me. "I can feel it."

"You and your feelings," I say with a shake of my head.

"Have I ever been wrong?" he asks.

"Well, there was that one time you thought we'd slip into that merchant's house without waking his dogs. I have a scar on my leg to prove you were wrong."

Alik wrinkles his nose at me. "One out of one hundred isn't exactly bad odds."

I pretend to wince and rub my ankle where the faded scar lies. "It still hurts sometimes."

Alik rolls his eyes, but a smile pulls at his lips. "My gut is telling me this is going to be good for us. We are finally going to get what we want."

I cock my head at his words, suddenly very aware I have no idea what Alik dreams about anymore.

"What *do* you want?"

Color rises in his cheeks as he looks at me.

"What do *you* want?" he asks, avoiding an answer. "It has to be something big if you agreed to go back to Ludminka."

I narrow my eyes at his hurry to shift attention from himself, but it's not worth an argument. I purse my lips for a moment.

"I want . . . to have you and Luiza again. For things to go back to how they used to be," I say.

I expect him to smile and agree. Instead, he studies his hands, the grin gone from his lips. I burn to ask him what is on his mind. The press of Ivan and Chinua on either side of us stills my tongue. When we're alone, maybe I'll ask him.

Silence follows us as we make our way underneath the ice-laden branches of the forest. It sets me on edge. The trip would've been easier in the spring, but it seemed foolish even to me to wait that long. Besides, Storm Hounds will certainly be more active after the snow melts, and hungrier for blood after a winter of inactivity.

Oleg quickly fades to a dark smudge on a stormy sea, and I find myself almost missing it. I've always had the shadows of a city to hide in, the narrow alleys of Rurik like my personal shield against curious eyes. It feels too open now, too exposed. Like someone could pick me off with an arrow without me so much as suspecting it. I shift deeper into the thick fur of my hood and search for a distraction.

"Do you remember that game we used to play?" I ask Alik. "Fact or fake?"

He straightens a bit in his saddle and grins. "I'd forgotten all about that."

"What is it?" Chinua asks from beside us.

"Something Valeria and I made up when we'd be sent far from Rurik for a mission. One of us tells a story and you have to decide if it's a lie or not."

"Want to play?" I ask.

Chinua nods.

"I'll go first," I say. "Did you know there are creatures inside Knnot? They hide deep within the mines and draw unsuspecting people to them. My matta called them Those

Who Dwell Within. She said they tried to take me as a child. Swore up and down she saw one, that its long, pallid arms tried to drag me down into the belly of the mountain. Their eyes are as big as plates, to see better in the absolute darkness of the mine. They're smart enough to communicate, too, clicking rocks and building cairns to mark their passage."

"Fake," calls Alik.

Chinua considers for a moment. "Fact."

I smile at Alik and bare my wrist with the scar. "Where do you think this came from?"

"What? No way."

"Well," I say slowly, "I did get lost in Knnot. Once, when I was very small. I don't remember anything besides coming out of a passage and my papa crying and hugging me so tightly I couldn't breathe. He never did that. I must've been gone long enough they thought I was dead."

My throat constricts at the memory of Papa. It'd been a long time since I spoke of my family. It hurt too much. For years I wondered why I was spared when no one else in Ludminka made it out. I tried to bury the faces of my parents and brothers, preferring to lock them away rather than remember them over and over again. I grit my teeth as a chill both hot and cold rolls up my back, as it always does when I think of Ludminka.

Now I suppose it's inevitable. I'll have to see it again. There will be no more pretending.

"Why don't you tell us the fact of what happened the day the ice claimed Ludminka?" Serafima's cold voice cuts in behind us.

My shoulders tighten at her words. It's as if she knows exactly what I'm thinking and wants to needle me further.

"I don't think it's any of your business," I say just as harshly.

"Actually, I think it is. We are going straight to your village, after all," Serafima says.

I look around at the open, questioning faces of Alik, Chinua, and Ivan. No one in all of Strana knows exactly what happened that day. I'd never told a soul. Not even Luiza. It was a memory I revisited only in the worst of my nightmares. I chew the inside of my cheek, trying to tamp down the slow squeezing in my chest. They do need to know. I can't let them walk into the village unprepared, can I?

"I was young," I say, and suppress a shudder at the memory. "My mother sent me to gather fir branches to keep the smell of my father's and brother's boots out of our house. I'd gotten sidetracked."

The memory seems burned into my mind. I didn't want to go back home to be teased by my brothers and knead dough with Matta. The bright red winterberries had been too tempting to resist. I sat in a small bramble, gobbling down as many as I could.

It saved my life.

"The next thing I remember is the ground rumbling, like

it did sometimes when there was an avalanche. But this was bigger, louder. It made my legs tremble and my teeth rattle. I turned toward the mountain and saw it . . . shift. Like a giant beast waking from slumber. Snow started cascading down the side and people started screaming. I dropped everything and ran."

Even saying the words make the familiar panic claw at my throat. I tried so hard to reach them that day. My heart felt like it would explode, but I kept pumping my legs and praying my family was safe.

"When I finally made it to my village . . ." I shake my head. "Every last person was frozen solid. I remember seeing a baby first, its tiny face completely covered in ice, its little eyelashes stuck to its cheeks by curls of frost, its lips blue and sprinkled with snow."

I swallow the lump in my throat. I will never forget their faces, frozen in terror. Some caught midrun, others clutching their children tight to their chest. A hard sheen of ice covered their bodies like a blizzard had come and gone in the time it took me to run from the forest to the village. And the silence. Pressing on my ears, as if someone took the chatter of the village and captured it in ice too.

"What about your parents?" Chinua asks, her voice soft.

"Like the others."

A pang runs through me as real and sharp as a blade.

"How did you escape?" Serafima asks.

"I don't know, to be honest. I watched the frost crawl toward me. It lashed out, almost as if it wanted to devour me. At the last moment, the frost changed direction."

I never looked back.

The only sound after my voice dies out comes from the soft crunch of snow beneath the horses' hooves. We ride in silence for hours, no one knowing how to break the tension.

Telling my story had stolen every bit of strength I had. I wanted nothing more than to curl up beneath my furs and sleep until the memory of Ludminka faded once again. It took everything to continue to stare at the stark white snow and the growing shadow of the Biting Mountains instead of succumbing to the tightness still lingering in my chest.

As the sun disappears behind the mountains, Serafima settles us into a small rise in the foothills, the steep sides of the slopes warding off the worst of the winter wind. The group remains silent as we set up camp, Serafima and Ivan putting up the tents, while Chinua, Alik, and I busy ourselves with finding snow to melt, starting a fire, and preparing food.

I handle removing the snow for the fire, using kindling Ivan packed and the driest branches I can find to build it. With a click of a steel flint, I coax the fire to life. Alik takes over as soon as the flames start to melt the snow at its edges. He slings a heavy cooking pot over the fire and warms up a thin gruel with a rabbit Chinua managed to snare.

Serafima drags a log over to the edge of the fire, collapsing on it and placing her hands up to warm them. My legs ache to join her, but I refuse. Something about the girl is off. I can sense it with every fiber of my being.

"Did you know a trader in Ludminka by the name of Iosef?" Serafima asks suddenly, her eyes never moving from the flames.

My brow crinkles at her words as everyone else stills around us. Luiza always said to measure the reaction of a group before responding, and tension blooms between us like a weed. Something lies hidden inside Serafima's question, but I can't divine what.

"No. I didn't get to see any traders who came to Ludminka. I was too young."

She rubs her hands together, her face betraying nothing.

"When you made your escape from your cursed little village, did you happen upon a merchant cart?"

I clench my jaw hard at her tone. "No."

"You see, I always wondered what happened to my father. He was supposed to be on his way home from Ludminka when the ice came. He never got there."

I try to find a smidge of sympathy somewhere in my heart for Serafima. We are connected in a way I wish we weren't. Alik nudges me.

"Oh," I say. "I wish I could help you more."

Serafima looks over her shoulder at me. Her eyes hold nothing but cool indifference. "I never knew what happened to him. I thought maybe he'd suffocated under a mountain of snow, but now I know. Your curse kept him trapped inside that damned village with you."

My mouth drops open.

"Serafima," Ivan shouts, his voice harsh. "This country has spewed enough hate for one lifetime, and I refuse to have you feed into it. If you cannot discern between fact and fiction, you will leave. You heard Valeria's story like the rest of us. The Zladonians had nothing to do with the ice. Do you truly think they would curse themselves just to spite the rest of Strana?"

Serafima glares at Ivan.

"Why was *she* spared when no one else was? It doesn't add up. She's either lying or hiding something."

"What do I have to hide?" I snap. "Why would I lie about my family dying? Do you think I wanted to be an orphan? That I haven't wished every day I had been trapped in the ice with them?"

I swallow at my truth laid bare. The thought has always been with me, tucked in the back of my mind like a hulking beast. I never spoke it aloud, not even to Alik. I know I should feel lucky, blessed by the Brother Gods even.

But I was never grateful for my escape.

I was left in a cold world without a single soul I knew for comfort. I lived, while everyone else froze to death in an event that no one had the answer to. How could I ever feel grateful for that?

Serafima sucks her bottom lip at my words before tucking her head down to study the map in her hand. The empty silence is almost haunting. My gaze slides to Alik. His brows knit and his hand twitches as if he wants to reach out to me but doesn't know how. In the end, he gives me the tiniest of smiles.

I set my bowl down, half-full, no longer interested in eating. Without a word, I slip into the tent and curl in the furs of my bedroll. My chest burns to release the pain building in my heart. I beg my eyes to cry, but they remain dry. My mind seems to ache more than my body does.

The flap of the tent rustles.

"Are you okay?" Alik says softly.

I shake my head. It's the truth, and there's no way I could hide it even if I wanted to. For a long moment Alik doesn't move. I expect him to leave, but instead, he throws his bedroll down and lies beside me. His warmth seeps into my back. I tense, trying to keep myself from touching his body. My muscles quiver and protest with the effort, but my cheeks flame with the idea of curling into him.

Despite my desperate attempts to keep us apart, my body relaxes and my mind goes blank for the first time since I'd told the group about Ludminka. Alik's breathing slows, and I breathe with him until at last I fall into an uneasy sleep.

*I stand at the base of Knnot, looking at the peak. A dome of clouds surrounds it, obscuring it from view, but what I want isn't there. Whispers sound from the darkened mouth of the mine shaft. I tilt my head, trying to catch strains of what is being said. Calm filters through my body. This is what I'm meant to do. This is why I'm here. I move toward the mouth of the mines. The whispers grow louder, surrounding me, pulling me.*

*"Come, child, come," they whisper.*

*"It's safe down here. We can give you the world. Everything you desire can be yours," a second voice says. It curls around me like music, beckoning me forward.*

*"Everything?" I ask.*

*"Everything."*

*"At what price?" I whisper, but take another step forward.*

*"No price. We want to help. We want to cure. We want to heal."*

*I'm nearly inside the mountain now. Vague outlines of over-turned mining carts and heavy wooden beams bracing the walls appear in the dim light. The scents of decaying wood and wet stone filter around me as I take another step. The pebbles at my feet rattle and jump, as if sensing vibrations I can't feel. The voices whisper for me to come closer. To come inside. I put one foot in.*

*Someone grabs my shoulder.*

*I spin and find myself face-to-face with Alik. My heart lurches as he smiles, still bright and beautiful. His white hair falls over his left eye; his deep cobalt eyes are full of all the warmth, happiness, and mischief I remember. He smirks, his full lips twitching and welcoming me. He holds out his hand.*

*"Not yet," he says. "Not yet."*

I gasp as I sit up. Wind whistles through the trees like an angry spirit demanding attention. Embers in the firepit glow orange, allowing just a pinprick of light in the darkness.

The scar at my wrist burns, and I press a hand to it, willing the pain to go away. I force myself back down onto my furs, covering my head with them, and hope I haven't been cursed for my foolishness.

# TEN

A WEEK PASSES WITHOUT AN incident. Serafima makes no mention of our conversation. In fact, she pretends I'm not a part of the group at all. Hours in the saddle leave me sore, and my thighs ache so badly I'm barely able to collapse onto the bedroll at night. Chinua seems to be the only one unaffected by the long hours, bouncing from her horse to gather wood for fires.

Finally, the dawn of the eighth day sees us near a steppe. Serafima leans over her maps, a small smile crawling across her mouth.

"We've made good time," she says. "Thank the Brothers for the mild weather and enough sunshine to melt away any lingering snow."

I eye the steppe in front of us, spread out like a blanket of soft white. I don't trust it. Matta always told us to avoid the one near Ludminka, especially in winter. Out on the steppe, there are no protective foothills, no reprieve from the wind or snow.

"Why do you look so concerned?" Alik says.

"We should go around the steppe," I say. "I don't think—"

"That would take an extra week, at best," Serafima says, not looking up from the map in her hand.

"We have no shelter out there, no wood for a fire, and it'll take two days to cross. We should cling to the hills in case a storm blows up," I say.

"The weather looks fine and the quickest path is straight through. The tents we have will be shelter enough. We continue as I've planned."

"The weather's fine now, but we don't know if it will hold. I know better than anyone how fast it can turn."

Serafima lifts her head, as if asking me to challenge her further.

Anger blossoms in my chest. I can't help but wonder if my concerns would be taken more seriously if I were anything but a *malozla* in her eyes. I'd be willing to bet if Ivan told her to go around, she would.

I swallow down the hatred and shrug, turning away from Serafima.

"Fine. Lead us into danger," I say over my shoulder.

Serafima hisses a sharp intake of breath before Alik's hand closes just above my elbow. I already know what he's going to say. We've had this conversation more times than I care to count.

"Why do you always have to do that?" he whispers low enough that no one but me can hear.

"Do what?"

Alik looks up, eye blazing. "You're letting your temper get the best of you."

"Am I supposed to remain silent while she stupidly risks our lives?" I snap. "You know the steppes can be dangerous."

"Yes, but Sera knows what she's doing. She's been leading traders throughout Strana since she was fifteen."

"That doesn't mean she knows what to do when she's far from a comfortable inn and warm food. Besides, even if she knows I'm right, she'll never admit it. You've seen how she talks to me, looks at me like I personally killed her father. I'm just a dirty *malozla*."

"She's never said that. You can't understand why she's upset about going to Ludminka? She's worried, same as you."

"We are *nothing* alike."

Alik frowns and gives an exasperated sigh. Something about it sets my already tense nerves on edge.

"You side with her," I say bitterly.

"I will never side with anyone over you, but you're being petty. You're letting your anger get in the way, like always. It gets you into situations you can't get out of, pushes you away from people who could be allies. If you truly want this mission to succeed, you'd better start making bridges instead of burning them."

His last sentence stings. I glare at his retreating back, pretending to fiddle with my saddlebag. This was one thing Alik would never understand.

Alik, who never let a nasty word or shove anger him. Alik, who is almost always insufferably in control of his emotions and temper. Alik, who Luiza forced me to learn from because she thought he'd be able to tame whatever dark pit in my stomach makes me say things I regret and blow cover after cover on guild missions. If it weren't for his training, I would've never been able to sneak into the Royal Vestry. My anger at Brother Gavriil's homily would've shown plain on my face. Alik always managed to put his feelings aside and be whoever Luiza needed him to be. He never burned bridges like I did.

Maybe it's because I'm always more than willing to do it for him.

"You two ready?" Ivan calls.

Alik nods, and I take the reins of my horse in my hands. The hill is far too rocky and steep to trust the horses with a rider and all of our packs. We pick our way down slowly until at last the ground levels out. Snow dusts scraggly brambles and long, dead grass. A dark stain on the horizon is the only thing I can make out of the mountains beyond the steppe. That's where we are headed. Two days in this white wilderness.

We all mount without a word and follow Serafima as she starts out across the plain.

"My home was like this," Alik says from beside me.

I glance around at the steppe. It makes sense, enough room for horses to run free, ample amounts of grass to keep their bellies fat and healthy, and plenty of warning if anyone tried to steal them.

"What was it like?" I ask.

Alik rarely spoke about his time before Luiza. She found him after the Czar took his mothers and sister. Just a lost little boy with wobbly legs from hiking for days, wandering around Rurik looking for the carriage that had taken his family.

"In the warmer months, it was wonderful." Alik smiles. "So much green grass, and the wind, gods, I wish you could've smelled it. Clean and pure, like breath from the heavens themselves. Mila would swear she could run to the mountains and back in a day. She tried once but wasn't even gone an hour and was never out of sight of MaMa and Matta. In the summer, there were berries, and MaMa scored the ground to plant things, while Matta took care of our cows. And the horses, oh, the horses. We had two hundred head. We were always brushing them and clipping their hooves. I used to hate it."

He says the last line wistfully, and I wish I could hug him. I used to hate helping my matta in the kitchen, always wanting to be wandering the mines. Now I wish I'd cherished those moments more. They were the only memories I had of my family. And they've faded, melted away like ice on the first day of spring.

"Do you know what happened to them?" Chinua asks.

"I know they were taken by the Storm Hounds." Alik's face is set in stony indifference. "Matta hid me under the hay in our barn. She tried to hide Mila in the cellar, but they found her. I'm not sure what they did with them after that."

My heart aches. Alik only told me once what happened to his family. Tears streamed down his face the entire time, and I could do nothing but sit beside him and hold his hand. We were young then, maybe eleven winters, stuck in the tiny attic bedroom Luiza had us share to keep us from the eyes of the other guildlings. Sometimes I wished I could go back to our cozy attic room, decorated with folded paper stars and draping blankets. It'd been our palace. The one place we felt truly safe.

"I'm sorry," Chinua says.

"It's what happens to everyone from Zladonia," Alik says.

"What about your family?" I ask Chinua.

She shrugs. "There's not much to tell. I came from a large Adamanian family, four older brothers and me. My parents worked in service to the Khan, and he favored our family. Every Adaman must prove their worth before the Khan accepts them into the fold of his kingdom, so I came here. Bringing lovite to him will more than prove I'm worth the investment."

Her eyes don't meet mine, and I get the overwhelming feeling there's something she's not telling me. We fall silent as we continue across the steppe, lost in our own thoughts. It's not until the pink rays of sundown dapple the sparkling snow that Serafima stops.

"We'll camp here." Serafima's eyes cut to me, as if she thinks I'll disagree.

The group's decided against me already. It wouldn't matter if I fought to keep going. We would stay. We set up camp, a smoky fire of wet steppe grass the only thing to keep the chill of the wind off our backs. I eye the horizon as the sun dips beneath the hills in the distance and hope I'm wrong about the unpredictable weather. For all our sakes.

A loud crack jolts me out of my sleep. My eyes spring open. Darkness surrounds me. It takes a long moment to place where the noise is coming from. At last I realize it's the tent. The poles holding the small yurt above us sway in the wind, the hides flapping like a bird desperate to take flight. A sinking feeling falls from my stomach straight to my toes. A storm, it has to be.

"Up," I say in a harsh whisper. "Get up."

I crawl forward, wincing as icy dirt slices into my warm palm. My fingers brush against someone else and I shake them hard. A grumbled moan sounds.

"Hmmm?" It's Chinua, her voice leaden with sleep.

"A storm. There's a storm. We need to get off the steppe as fast as possible."

"What?" She sits up so quickly our heads almost collide.

It's still far too dark to see, any light the moon would've allotted us long since covered by clouds. We're close enough that I feel her shoulders shiver in the sudden cold. The temperature nowhere near the temperate one we'd grown used to over the past week. If we don't move quickly, a blizzard will be upon us. We could lose track of where we're going and walk days out of our way.

"The horses," she whispers, scrambling to her feet.

"We need to wake the others," I say.

"The horses won't last. The temperature's dropped too much. You wake the others, I'll tend to them."

She rustles around before ripping open the tent flap. Wind whips into the small room and tears the flap from her hand. The dim light of dawn illuminates the other forms. I scramble to them, shaking each one until they are awake.

"We've got to leave," I say.

No one fights me. I dart back to my own sleeping roll and dress as quickly as I can, bundle up my furs, and yank the balaclava up over my nose. There's no time to feel vindicated for my argument earlier with Serafima. I'm the first out of the tent, and my heart sinks.

Wind howls down the open plain and crashes against the tent, ripping at the hides. Bulging gray clouds hang low, promising snow. I race to where Chinua furiously tries to untie the horses. Her cheeks are bright red, but her lips are drawn into a tight line.

"We can't keep them," she yells, eyes never leaving her work.

"We can't just let them go," I say.

"They'll never survive. The weather will only turn colder. These aren't winter horses. They were the only ones available in Rurik."

She gestures at the mountains before us. She's right. Zladonia is one of the coldest places in all Strana. We'd had horses when I was a child, but they were covered in thick, shaggy hair, bred to survive even the coldest nights.

As if to insult us, the first snowflakes start to fall heavy and fast.

Ivan strides up behind us. Without a word, he pulls a dagger from his coat and cuts the tangled lines of the horses. He gives one a slap on the rump. They all bolt, taking off for the safety and shelter of the foothills far behind us.

"We carry our things now," he says, voice muffled by his own balaclava.

He tosses Chinua her pack and bedroll as Serafima and Alik pull down the yurt. I rush to help them roll it up as wind whistles across the open plain. Ivan shoulders the bag with the food and we each take our saddlebags, snowshoes dangling off the back. It will be slow going from here, weighed down with so much gear and no animals to help carry it.

There is no other choice.

Snow pounds at us, and we slog through, guided only by

Serafima's compass as she leads us west instead of north, cutting across the steppe to get us out quickly. Blistering wind tears at our faces and snow finds its way into every single exposed crevice. I glance up for a quick check of the others. Ivan now leads, his broad frame digging a path through the snow. Serafima holds out the folds of her coat, attempting to get a good read on her compass. I can just barely make out her blond head, coated in snow. Chinua walks behind her, using Serafima's wide shoulders as a guard against the wind on her chapped face.

Alik and I are the farthest back, and no matter how hard I push, I can't catch up. The wind seems to rip at me, determined I stay in the freezing field until death claims me. Ever so slowly, Ivan leads us into a small patch of trees at the edge of the steppe. The vicious onslaught of wind is all but gone, blocked by the foothills and the thick nest of trees. The ground slopes a little, and my legs fight to keep upright.

Vainly, I try to think of anything other than the cold bite of the wind. The dream I'd had last night slips into my mind unbidden. The yawning mouth of Knnot whispers to me, begging for help.

It's been a long time since I thought of the mountain, my memories always caught up in Ludminka and the family I left trapped there. Knnot was a constant in my life. At a young age, I knew to respect it. My papa bid me to thank the Brother Gods for its seemingly boundless wealth. It's what kept Ludminka warm and comfortable during the long winters. I was always fascinated by it, desperately waiting for the day Papa would take me into the mines with him like he had my two older brothers.

Now, for the first time in ten years, I dreamed of Knnot instead of my village. It should be a relief, but something about it makes my chest squeeze hard and fast. As if the mountain were actually reaching out for me, hungry for the girl who got away.

I try to convince myself it's not an omen. Matta would've said it was, and the thought chills me almost as much as the wind around me. Ivan's fortune-teller said we would reach Knnot.

But she never said we'd all make it out.

# ELEVEN

THE STORM BLOWS US DAYS off course. We spend two long days trekking our way back to our original path, so much slower without the horses. The weather turns bitterly cold, frosting my eyelashes and suffusing its way through my boots to freeze my feet.

Serafima says nothing of our detour. She doesn't even acknowledge that I was right. Instead, her eyes hold nothing but suspicion every time they find me. I heard her whisper to Ivan I had somehow caused it, to prove a point about crossing the steppe. As if I were a champion chosen by the gods and capable of controlling the weather around us. Ivan had told her Zladonians hold no such power, but I can tell she doesn't believe him.

Serafima leads us from the foothills to the slow incline of

the first mountain. The Ral Mountains are the final divide between the southern part of the country and the wild North. Few dare to cross them and those who do definitely don't do so through untested passes in winter. We follow Serafima faithfully, and to her credit, she leads us around treacherous glaciers and through thick forests without veering off course.

The end of the second week sees us halfway up an unnamed mountain, the pass just mere feet above our head. Alik and I, again, bring up the rear. Though he doesn't make a sound, his labored breathing betrays how hard the snowy slope proves for his injured leg.

"Stop," I say through gasps of my own. "Take a rest."

"Are the others stopping?" he asks.

"Damn the others," I reply, and settle to the ground, propping my snowshoes against a hidden rock.

The relief of being off my feet nearly brings tears to my eyes. Begrudgingly, Alik follows suit, leaning back on his elbows.

It's almost a shame we've never looked back until now. The view is stunning. Our path stretches beneath us like a patchwork quilt of land. The steppe lies the farthest away, still a sea of stark white against the far blue hues of the Biting Mountains. The foothills roll like lazy waves up from the plains and give way to the snow-covered branches of the forest we passed through a day ago. My legs ache and my chest burns, but I can't help but feel a rush of pride. We made it such a long way, and Alik did it all without complaint. I glance over and see him massaging his bad leg.

"Let me help."

"No," Alik protests, but I slap his hand away and put mine just above his knee. We traded massages so many times on our missions, it's almost like second nature to help.

My hand stills as I make contact with his leg. The wound is so deep I'm not sure if I'm feeling muscle or bone. What I am certain of is the dull piece of metal beneath the healed skin. I begin to gently rub, but Alik's entire body sits still and tense.

I sigh. "What's wrong?"

"Can't . . . can't you feel it?"

I nod.

"How can you stand to touch it?"

I shrug. "It's just metal, Alik. The final bit of the bolt, I'm guessing?"

It's his turn to nod. "Ivan couldn't get it out. Not without killing me. By the time I'd recuperated enough for him to try again, the wound was already starting to heal, and he didn't want to risk opening it back up."

"It must hurt in this cold."

"You have no idea," Alik says.

I finally look up at him, realizing for the first time how compromising my position is. My face hangs just bare inches away from his own. I flush as I release his leg, no longer feeling as if we're the same pair who were partners a year ago. Some strange shift has occurred between us that I can't quite place.

"Do you remember our first mission to the mountains?" I ask.

Alik gives a humorless laugh. "The time you almost got us killed because you laughed in the baron's face we were supposed to be charming?"

"If that's how you choose to remember it."

"Choose? That's *exactly* what happened."

I laugh. "We're still alive, aren't we?"

Silence falls between us at my words. I don't know what I've been thinking. Alik is lucky to be alive, and we both know that.

"I . . . I'm sorry. I shouldn't have said—"

Alik waves a hand in my direction. "I know, Val. Don't worry."

We stare down at the landscape beneath us for a long moment. I know the others must wonder where we are. They've no doubt reached the top by now. If I had to, I'd fake a turned ankle to save Alik any embarrassment. I just don't want to go up yet. Alik and I had very few moments alone, so even though we are finally together once again, it doesn't really feel as if we are. I want to be able to talk with him without the others hearing, to joke about our horrid guild missions. I want to bask in the fact that he is alive and I have him back. Instead, I was flung into a mission without the chance to really appreciate him.

"Why are you coming with us?" Alik asks quietly.

"For you," I answer automatically.

He turns a calculating gaze my way.

"I don't flatter myself with being the only reason you came with Ivan."

My cheeks go hot at his words. Of course, he is the reason I came with Ivan. He was the scattered piece of my heart I was missing. The idea of getting lovite for the Bright God's champion to save Luiza from the Czar only came after I decided to come to him.

Wasn't it?

"Why did Luiza let you come?" he presses.

"She didn't," I say, and set my jaw, knowing the wheels in his head are likely already turning. "I don't know where she is. I was on a mission. She wanted me to steal from the Vestry, and we were compromised. I have no doubt the Storm Hounds have destroyed the guild by now."

"Why'd she want you to steal from the Vestry in the first place?"

"They had a small stash of lovite. She wanted to give it to the Bright God's champion so he could use it against the Czar. She said the champion is building a rebellion against the Ladislaw, and she knew the country would turn in his favor, so she would go with it."

Alik lets out a snort.

"So you came on this mission to what? Gather lovite for the Bright God's champion yourself?"

I want to lie. I don't want him to think he wasn't worth coming for. The nagging promise we made all those years ago drags at my conscience and I give him a curt nod.

"I hoped he'd take it in exchange for securing Luiza's safety."

"I'm sure Luiza is still very much free. She can slip out of anything." A storm brews on his brow.

"Why are you so angry with her?" I ask.

"Why are you always her pet?"

The ferocity of his words surprises me, and I shoot to my feet, refusing to offer him a hand up.

"Luiza saved us from the streets and from the Czar," I say angrily. "If it weren't for her, we would've been carted to prison just like every other Zladonian. We owe her every-thing." I pause. "I don't know why you suddenly hate her, but I'm not going to sit here and listen to it." I turn and start climbing the steep slope once again.

"You aren't her daughter, you know," he calls after me.

My shoulders tense, but I keep moving and don't look back. I know I am not Luiza's daughter. I had a mother and father of my own. Luiza sees me as a commodity, yes, but she loves me, too. I know she does.

I scale the last bit of the mountain, my legs screaming and my lungs crushing. At long last, the ground levels out. I suck in air and glance around. Serafima studies her maps, which lie strewn across the ground, weighted on the corners with small rocks. Ivan surveys the path before us, and Chinua fidgets with small metal traps. The pass isn't much of a reprieve. It's perhaps four hundred yards in length before it dips down again. Two mountains tower far overhead, their tops obscured by thick white clouds. I'm not quite sure how Serafima managed to find such a tiny place to cross over. I can't look at the way forward without wanting to cry. We've come so far, and yet there is still so much more land to cover.

The sun sits low on the horizon, and I sag against the side of the closest mountain, sighing as my lower back stops aching for the first time all day. It would be madness to attempt the climb down now. It'll be dark long before we finish our descent. Alik crests the top of the rise at last, and I avert my eyes. Instead of going to him as I normally would, I make my way toward Chinua. Her long ebony hair lies in a braid over her shoulder, and her cheeks are pink with wind rash. Still, she looks beautiful, almost vitalized, as if this has been nothing but a quiet walk in the woods.

"Come to help?" she asks at the sound of my boots.

"To be honest, I'm not much use with traps. What are you working on?"

Chinua scoots over and I crouch beside her.

"These are just animal snares," she says, holding up the metal pieces she was studying. "But I haven't had much luck with them. Wrong time of year, I'm guessing."

We'd been subsisting for the past two weeks on the hardtack

and dried meat Ivan had packed. Something fresh would be nice.

"Not much to hunt in the winter. And anything you do catch will be far too skinny to do much good."

"I thought as much," she mumbles. "It's so different from home."

"Is it?" I ask.

"Well, the weather is the same. But so much of the land is wide and open. We have mountains, yes, but they are mostly contained to one corner. Being here is unlike anything I imagined. I shall be glad to see your mountain."

I turn my eyes northward. Knnot is not much more than a smidge on the horizon, but I know its shape. It's haunted my dreams for nearly three weeks.

"It won't be long now," I say. "Then you'll wish you were anywhere else in the world."

"You fear the mountain, yet are willing to travel across the country to see it again?"

"Some things are worth risk and fear."

I keep my eyes locked on my clasped hands, begging them not to stray in Alik's direction.

"How did you learn to make traps?"

She lolls her head to the side to look at me, her eyes flicking briefly over to Alik. I suppose my lie wasn't as well crafted as I hoped.

"My parents," she says simply. "They are great tacticians for our khan. My two eldest brothers took to archery, my younger brother to experiments, and me to traps and explosives."

"Why did you leave home? You said you'd been in Strana a long time—why leave your family?"

The pang of not having a family assaults me. I wish I could still talk to my brothers and my parents.

"There were a lot of reasons." Chinua shrugs. I wait for her to say more. She sighs. "It's . . . far too complicated to get into. But I need the money this mission will provide. Especially now—" Her voices catches. She swallows once. "Now that my mother is dead."

I let the weight of her words roll over me.

"That's hard," I say at last. It isn't the best response, but it seems truer than any other.

I glance over, expecting her to say something. She picks through her bag, counting and recounting the supplies inside.

"We need to get going." Ivan's gruff voice interrupts.

"What?" Serafima's head snaps toward him, her brows tight over her nose.

"Get up. We need to move out," he says.

I glance up at the sky. The sun dips low on the horizon. Before long, it'll be completely dark.

"No, we are supposed to camp here tonight," Serafima says, rising to her feet. "This is the most shelter and level ground we are going to have until we reach Knnot. We need to recuperate."

"It's going to get too dark to see soon. We can't chance a descent," I say.

"I said move out," he growls, turning toward us. The pendant at his neck gleams softly in the growing dusk, the burnished lines of amber bright against the stark white stone. He'd kept it hidden for the past two weeks. Whether because he feared he'd lose it or one of us would steal it and take the lovite for ourselves, I don't know.

"Why?" I ask.

His eyes flash dangerously. "Because I said so. Despite what you may think, I am the leader of this expedition. We've slowed since we lost the horses. We need to make up the ground. Now get up and start moving."

"I think we should wait—" starts Serafima.

Ivan wheels on her. "Move now!"

His roar seems to rattle off the stone peaks above us. No one speaks as we quickly gather our things. My eyes keep straying to Ivan, silhouetted against the dying sun like a shadowed demon. In the entire time we have been with him, Ivan was nothing but good-natured, almost jolly. Why is he all of a sudden pushing when he was content to wait out the storm?

Without so much as another word, Ivan starts trudging down the steep slope off the pass. Ice and snow collect in the treads of my snowshoes and I slip every other step. Alik stumbles behind me, ramming into my shoulder. As we descend, the light fades, and it's hard to see what is hard-packed earth and what is slick, ice-covered stone.

"We've got to stop," I gasp.

My toes ache and my ankles wobble with each step. I need rest. We all do.

"No," Ivan says gruffly. "We go until it's too dark to see."

I bite my lip and clench my hands tight inside my mittens to keep them from lashing out at Ivan. We can make it one more hour.

I hope.

The slick, bald-faced rocks give way to a thick fir forest. It seems too quiet within, the soft crunch of snow the only sound permeating through the trees. No birds sing, no boughs creak. It makes me shiver.

The dark seems to swallow us. Little light filters down through the wide fir branches overhead, and what does is gray and dim. Limbs tug at our clothes as we slip through, dumping snow on our heads. Alik grunts behind me, and Serafima whispers something to him. I glance back to see her slip his arm around her shoulders. I force my gaze to Chinua's back, trying not to think it should be me helping him.

"Ivan, this is far enough," Serafima finally calls. "If we travel any farther, it'll be too dark to see."

"We don't stop until I say we do." Ivan charges forward, not so much as looking over his shoulder at us.

Alik pants as he comes to a stop at Serafima's side. "I can't keep going."

Ivan slows at Alik's words. He turns back toward us, face tight. His eyes drift to Alik's leg.

"Yes, of course," he says.

A long groan suddenly sounds beneath my feet. I slowly look down and my heart stops beating.

I'm standing on ice.

The river current swirls beneath the ice, beckoning to me. The ice can't be more than a few inches thick; it's too early in the season to have frozen solid. I glance up at the others. Chinua charges across the river. The ice creaks under her weight. I back up toward the bank with Ivan and Chinua as spiderweb cracks start to form in the ice. Movement catches my attention on the opposite bank and I look up. Serafima and Alik step into the clearing.

"Stop!" I scream.

Alik looks up at me. Our eyes meet for the briefest moment. Before he drops into the freezing river.

# TWELVE

A CRACK RENDS THE AIR. My heart leaps to my throat as Alik falls in the frigid water to his waist. Serafima fumbles for him, but her weight on the brittle edges proves too much. She falls in headfirst. Alik slips a little as the current tugs at his heavy coat.

Serafima's head bursts through the surface. Again, the water surges around them as if desperate to swallow them whole. Alik loses his footing and the heavy weight of Serafima's limp body drags him down too.

"Alik!" My shriek is loud enough to rival the wind.

I take out a dagger from my utility belt and dart back across the ice. It creaks and groans beneath me but holds. I jump onto the opposite bank and race down to the hole in the river, dropping to my knees. "Alik? Serafima?" I search the gray waters for any sign of them. It can't be that deep, but I know better than anyone how fast your body loses feeling in the cold.

I frantically scan the ice, brushing away the film of snow clinging to it. At last, I see a hand. My heart leaps. I drive my dagger into the ice, breaking a hole, and I grasp the only thing I can see. My fingers curl around sodden wool. I pull with everything in me. My muscles cry out in agony. I ignore them. I won't lose Alik.

*I won't.*

At last, Serafima's blond head breaks the surface. She gasps. Steadying herself with my hand, she tugs hard and Alik bobs to the surface. They both grapple at the edge of the ice. I yank up, and at last their feet find purchase on the bottom of the river and they clamber onto the wet bank.

"Help!" I yell.

Serafima shudders so hard her teeth clack together. Alik doesn't fare much better, his pallid skin turning blue in the cold air. If we don't find shelter soon, we will lose them both to the cold.

"This way," Ivan cries.

I run my gaze along the opposite bank until I spot him and Chinua. He gestures to something before him, but I can't make it out. I'll have to trust him. Serafima coughs, and it sounds as though it's ripped from somewhere deep in her lungs. I slip under her shoulder and glance over. Alik nods, but his lips are nearly purple. I half drag Serafima down the bank, tracking

Chinua and Ivan on the opposite side all the while.

It takes far too long before I reach the path Ivan had gestured at. Wide, flat rocks span the water. Ivan picks his way across to me. He gently removes Serafima, slipping his hands beneath her knees and hoisting her up.

I run back to Alik. "Can you make it?"

"Not alone," he says.

I grab him around the waist, and we make our way to the path. We start our slow walk across. The wind blows so hard I almost fall, my snowshoes skidding across the ice encasing the rocks. Alik trembles with every movement. His feet are the first to go, and he stumbles into me. I manage to catch him before he falls to his knees.

"I can't feel them," he whispers.

The world seems to disappear. I need to get him across. He needs to get out of the wind and wet clothes.

"Chinua!" I scream.

Instantly, she's by my side, looping her arm around Alik's thin body. We drag him to the other side, where Ivan waits with Serafima. He hands me the tent bag, and I glare at him. If he hadn't been so damn determined to make up lost time, Serafima and Alik would be safe and warm in a tent in the pass above us.

"We need to find shelter. Quickly. They are both liable to lose a body part if we don't get them out of this cold," I say.

Ivan gives a brisk nod.

Alik looks so thin and weak in his sopping clothes. I rip off my coat and toss it over him, trying to ignore the bite of the wind. It is near dark now; just enough gray light filters through the bare branches overhead for me to see Alik's lips moving.

"We need to wrap this around him tighter," Chinua says.

I nod, wrapping the coat around his shoulders, tucking it as best I can around his waist. We need fire. We need warmth. Palest hell, we need a village or he and Serafima are as good as dead.

"Valeria," he whispers. I brush away his wet hair, pushing off his eye patch. His scarred eyelid droops over the empty socket, the dark lashes brushing against his cheekbone like neat stitches. I gasp a sob.

"I'm here, Alik," I whisper back. "I'm here."

"Valeria."

I unwrap the scarf from around my neck and put it over his wet hair before looking for Ivan. He bends over Serafima, mimicking my movements. Ivan slings her over his shoulder once more, and Chinua and I stoop to pick up Alik. He's limp between us.

"I'm going to get you to safety," I say. "Don't worry."

He doesn't respond. This time, I take the lead. We tramp through the forest. I shiver in the biting cold, but it's nothing compared to what Serafima and Alik must feel. Anxiety moves my feet. I'm no longer aware of my fatigue or the numbness of my fingers. All I feel is the burning desire to find somewhere safe. Somewhere warm.

Within minutes, we break out of the tree cover and onto a precipice. A small, rocky valley spreads below us. My gut clenches tight as I take it in. Not more than half a mile away is a small encampment. Squat huts line the snow-covered streets, all leading to a barracks. Smoke curls from every chimney, windows aglow with warmth. A wall surrounds the entire compound, four thick battlements placed at the corners. Flags, black and gold, fly from the fortifications.

I gasp. Storm Hounds. But why are they so close to Zladonia?

Alik's teeth chatter. Each second I stand here is another he may lose his life. My stomach twists in knots before I look at Ivan.

"Take her down there." I point to the encampment. "Say what you have to and get her inside. You too, Chinua. I'll take care of Alik."

The relief on their faces is nearly palpable. Anger flushes through my system, and envy. It's not fair they can go to the Storm Hounds and get warm, receive food and medicine, while Alik and I are forced to stay here in the elements. All because of the Czar and his stupid decree.

"Give him to me," I growl.

Chinua's face goes slack, but she slips Alik onto my shoulders. He weighs so much less than I expect. It is still dead weight, and it sags onto my already tight and sore shoulders on top of the tent bag. I don't know how I will make it anywhere, but I must.

"How will we find you again?" Chinua asks.

I feel the briefest flash of affection for her.

"I'll keep close to the mountains on the left. Look for me there. I'll tie my scarf around one of the trees."

She nods, and they turn their backs on Alik and me. Part of me doesn't blame them. If I could, I would be right beside them. But the other part of me hates them down to their very core. The strength of the hate surprises me, but I hold tight to it. It helps me forge a path to the west and the rocky crags at the edge of the valley toward what turns out to be a shallow cave far away from the Storm Hounds.

I breathe a sigh of relief as I lay Alik down as carefully as I can manage. I pull my furs from my pack, piling them atop him. Then I drop the rest of my gear and head back into the wind. I tie my dull gray scarf on the edge of a fir and gather as much dry brush as I can manage. I haul it all back to the cave as night falls.

I get the fire started quickly, piling kindling on as fast as I can. I turn my attention to Alik. He shudders, caught somewhere between unconsciousness and sleep.

He needs to get out of the wet clothes. My cheeks burn as I peel away shirt after shirt until his bare chest gleams in the light. I lay the shirts out on the stone to dry. I tug off his sodden boots and pull off the socks, afraid of what I will see. The skin doesn't look so bad. We might just have avoided frostbite. I massage his feet for a second, willing blood to circulate and warm them back up. Once I'm satisfied the blood is moving again, I avert my eyes as I slip off his pants and throw them over a rock.

I bundle the furs back over him, but he still shivers. He doesn't open his eyes.

"Alik? Can you hear me?" My voice sounds small, even to my own ears. "Please. Answer me."

He doesn't respond.

I know I should snuggle in beside him and offer him my warmth. The thought of pressing my skin against Alik's gives me a shudder of embarrassment as a pang of desire shoots through me.

I refocus and turn to the front of the cave. I put up half the tent, raising the middle pole until it wedges into the ceiling. It keeps most of the wind out. Alik still trembles beneath the furs, but his forehead loosens a bit. I pull out my canteen and press the top to his lips. Water dribbles out and down his chin.

He shivers so hard it feels like he is vibrating. I toss a few more branches onto the fire and stoke the embers until flames lick the wood. But I know there isn't another way to warm him. I have to offer my own body heat.

Pressing my fingernails into my palms to calm my thundering heart, I slide off my clothing until I'm down to the tight band about my chest and the long woolen shorts Ivan had provided. With a deep breath, I slip under the furs beside him, tucking them around us tightly. His skin presses against mine, so cold it could be a fish's underbelly. He shudders again, and I throw my arm around his waist and bring his cold body as close to mine as I can. My entire being burns as ideas of him being awake and circling his arms around me dart into my brain. I hold on.

Keeping him alive is the only thing that matters.

It seems like hours before his body stops trembling and relaxes. The warmth of the cave makes my skin prickle and lulls me toward sleep.

*Whispers roll through the darkness and beckon me forward. I can't make them out, so low and far they sound more like water in a brook than human language. At last, I see a shimmering light. I stumble toward it, desperate for release from the dark void around me.*

*The fire glows brighter until I'm certain it sears my eyes from my head. I hold my hands out before me, desperate to block the light. When my vision clears, I am no longer in the cold shadows. Instead, I stand before a very ordinary-looking door. The latch hangs loose, a green patina staining the metal. A tug in my gut tells me to open it. I place my hand on the handle and warmth tickles up my arm.*

*"Please," a voice begs. "Please."*

*It's desperate. A well of longing and pain so deep and wide I can hardly breathe in its presence. I should open it. I need to. I could save the person inside, free them from their torture. I tug hard at the door. It doesn't so much as budge.*

*I place my hand upon the wood. This time the heat isn't a pleasant tickle. It's a roaring fire that crawls up my arm, wanting to devour me whole.*

I gasp as something bumps my nose. My heart races from my dream, and I try to pull away from the feeling, but a weight at my neck keeps me from moving. My eyes blink open. Dim embers glow before me. Alik's hand touches my nose again. I realize I'm lying on his shoulder, snuggled into the crook of his arm.

The urge to kiss him is almost overwhelming, but instead, I press into his warmth. I remind myself that he thinks of me as a sister, nothing more. I stir to get comfortable, and Alik groans. "Don't move," he grunts. "You're letting in cold air."

My body relaxes, but I scoot away from him, far too conscious of how close our bodies are. "You're alive."

"Last time I checked," he mumbles.

I look him over. His skin is even paler than usual, and deep circles surround his eyes. "You look terrible, just so you know."

He lets out a grumble as he latches onto my arm and pulls me closer to him. "Leave it to you to tease a man after he nearly dies."

My chest tightens as heat blooms on my cheeks. His heart-beat thumps beneath me, steady and sure, and mine quickens at its sound. I inhale and try to imprint every moment of this into my memory. The way he smells of smoke and cold river water, the feeling of his ribs expanding beneath my fingertips.

"You were half dead at most." My voice comes out choked, and I pray Alik doesn't notice.

"Same thing."

"No, you still had nearly a quarter of death to go before you reached near death."

Alik chuckles, and I let a smile crawl across my face.

"What happened? After the river?" he asks.

"We dragged you and Serafima through the forest. We stumbled on a Storm Hound encampment. I told them to go." I try to keep the heat from my voice.

"Storm Hounds? This close to Knnot?"

"I thought the same thing. Why would they be so close to Zladonia? Especially this time of year?"

"Who knows. Maybe the Czar is going to make another attempt at the mountain to retrieve the rest of the lovite," Alik says.

"We better hope not," I say.

We fall silent. My body still lies tense on Alik. This shouldn't make me so nervous. We've shared blankets too many times to count. For some reason, this feels different. I search for a reason to disentangle myself.

"We should probably find something to eat," I say.

"How about instead we stay here. Where it's warm."

"We have no reason to stay here," I say, even though my mind screams at me to agree.

"I'm sure I can come up with a reason," he says, and shifts to face me, our foreheads almost touching. A strange emotion darts across his face, and for a startling moment I think he may kiss me. Instantly, my fingers find my scar and I press them into it, willing it to steady my emotions. Alik's eyes narrow.

"What's wrong, Val?"

"Nothing," I say. I try to put every ounce of Luiza's acting skills into the words.

Alik presses his lips together and shoots me a look that says he clearly doesn't believe me. He unlatches my fingers from my wrist and brings it up before us, turning my hand so my scar is exposed. It stands in stark clarity against my pale skin. Alik brushes his fingertips across it. I suppress a shudder as goose bumps prickle along my arms.

"You only ever touch this when you're upset. I've seen you do it enough times to know."

My secrets bubble at my lips, almost tempting me to speak. I swallow them back.

"I'm just . . . I'm really glad you're alive," I say.

"I think the world will have to try a bit harder than a frozen river." Alik releases my hand. "I've got too much to live for."

A dull silence falls between us. I'm about to get up when Alik speaks again.

"Thank you."

"For what?" I ask.

"Saving me."

I let out a snort. "You just expected me to let you freeze to death? Who would tease me then?"

"It would've been easier to leave me," Alik says seriously. My heart constricts.

"It would've been easier to stay in Rurik, too, but then I wouldn't have you by my side now." My heart thunders as I open my mouth again. "I don't think you understand what you mean to me. I can't lose you. Not again."

He shifts toward me, putting his forehead to mine. I can't bear looking into his eye, so I stare at his chest instead. It rises and falls with his even breathing, and I can't help but take in the long gash, almost angry against his pale skin. I let a finger trace the scar's path and Alik sucks in a deep breath, shuddering beneath my touch.

"Sorry," I whisper.

"Don't be."

We are so close now the air from his mouth brushes against my lips. I want to lean into him. My body aches with the thought of kissing him. He draws closer still, our mouths a whisper apart. The longing courses through me like a bolt of lightning, making me heady. I dare a look up at his face, and my stomach tumbles. Something hungry writes itself across it, his eye burning. He lifts his hand and tucks a strand of hair behind my ear, his fingers trailing along my jaw.

My body hums as I consider that maybe, just maybe, Alik feels the same way about me as I do about him.

Suddenly, snow crunches outside and I whirl away. Heavy footfalls rush toward us, and I snag my dagger from the belt above my head. Cool air wraps around my middle, reminding me I'm shirtless. My cheeks burn as I hurry into my shirt.

Images of black uniforms and cold faces flit through my mind as I put myself between Alik and the front of the cave. I crouch and press a finger to my lips. Alik nods. The canvas wobbles as someone hits it. Whoever it is, they aren't attempting to be quiet. My fingers curl around the cool hilt of my dagger. The flap of the tent flies back and I lunge forward, ready to attack.

# THIRTEEN

I PULL UP SHORT AS I recognize Chinua's dark hair. She carries a bundle in her arms, and her eyes widen as she takes in the sharp point of my dagger. Her gaze drops to the hem of my shirt brushing against my thighs and her cheeks color. She quickly looks away, putting her bundle on the ground.

"Who did you think I was?"

"Storm Hounds," I say. "You saw the scarf?"

"Barely. Snow had swallowed most of it. I never would've seen it if I hadn't known what I was looking for." She opens the bundle, exposing bread, berries in tin cups, and a small bottle of milk with a thick stopper on top

"You don't have the food bag. I couldn't let you starve."

"Thank you," I say. It has been weeks since any of us saw fruit or milk. It almost seems like a gift from the gods. Chinua settles beside the fire, warming her chapped hands.

"Glad to see you awake," she says to Alik.

"Glad to be awake," he responds. "I have Valeria to thank for that."

"We have Valeria to thank for Sera's life, too. She survived the night, but the captain who took care of her said if we hadn't made it to the camp, she would've died before morning. Apparently, it was one of the coldest nights they've had."

"Really?"

She nods, and I hum under my breath. I didn't wake up once. In fact, the cave is downright balmy. The fire isn't much more than a low glow. I suppose the tent blocks most incoming wind, but it still seems like it should've been colder.

"Did they say what they are doing here? I've never heard of Storm Hounds being this far north," Alik says.

"They told Ivan it's some sort of environmental training. They send recruits up north to see how they will survive in this hellish weather. So far, three have died," Chinua says. "I can't believe the Czar would do this."

"He does a lot worse," I say.

"It's odd they just told Ivan what they are doing. Why wouldn't they keep it more of a secret? Or wonder why we are here?" Alik says.

"When they asked, Ivan told them we were sent by a logging company to scan new groves for felling."

"They bought that?" Alik asks.

Chinua shrugs. "Seemed to."

Alik and I make eye contact over the bread I'm cutting. The Storm Hounds have to be lying. There are dozens of other places they could train. Why were they camped nearly a stone's throw from the edge of the Zladonia region? And by the look of their camp, it's been established for quite some time. I wish I'd paid more attention to Luiza's dealings with the Storm Hounds, but she'd always told me to keep hidden.

My throat constricts a bit at the thought of Luiza. I hadn't really thought of her since I found Alik. I can't let the guilt threatening to crash over me take hold. I am doing this for her. The lovite inside Knnot is the only thing I can use to get her back. If there is a her to find.

I hand out a piece of thick bread and a few berries to Alik. I tilt the milk container over the tin cup and see, etched in bold, black lines across the bottom of the glass bottle, two crossed keys with ravens perched on them. My hand rattles, spilling milk over the side of the cup.

"Val?"

Without saying anything, I twist the bottom of the bottle so Alik can see. His lips thin. This is Luiza's guild insignia. She's marked everything the guild owns ever since one member tried to sell guild belongings to make a profit without cutting Luiza in on the deal. Alik and I'd spent far too many nights branding leather saddlebags to be fooled by a fake marking.

"You got this from the Storm Hound encampment?" I ask Chinua.

She nods. "It was all in a back storage room. No one was guarding it, so I figured it was free for the taking."

I turn the edge of the bottle toward her so she can see the emblem. "This is the mark of the Thieves Guild. The only thing I can think is they must've taken all our supplies when they raided it after my failed mission, then transported them where they were most needed."

"What makes you so sure Luiza didn't give it to them?" Alik asks.

"Why would she do that?" I shoot him a look, reminded of our heated conversation on the mountain before the fall into the river. "You have nothing but animosity for Luiza, and I don't understand it." Alik stares down at his hands.

Chinua glances between us and sighs. You both need to stop arguing and eat. You'll need it.

I finally hand the cup of milk over to Alik, who doesn't lift his eyes, then divvy up the rest of the food between Alik and me before eating. The berries burst on my tongue and I could almost kiss Chinua for bringing them. It's been a long time since we had anything other than meat and thin porridge.

"Did Ivan say when he wanted to leave again?" Alik asks.

"As soon as Sera is able. I'll be looking in on you whenever I can."

"We're close now. Only a few days away," I say, hoping I sound casual.

I hadn't wanted to see Knnot before. But the same dream has played through my mind since the first night we left Oleg.

I can't shake the thought of how wonderful it will be to see it again. My home. I dreamed of it so much that it almost feels like that's all it is, a strange vision I can't quite catch.

Chinua's eyes flick quickly over me before she studies the fire. She laces her hands together, and I notice for the first time they are crisscrossed in fine, delicate scars, bright white against her golden-brown skin. She eyes me studying them and splays them out for me to see.

"Almost pretty, don't you think?" she asks.

I can't tell if she is being serious or sarcastic. I nod hesitantly.

She sighs. "That's what I've been telling myself, too. My parents thought them beautiful as well. 'A map of how far you've come' is what my father always said. All I can see is all the times I've failed. Both my parents were generals for the Khan. I wanted to make them proud. And they were. But my skills didn't go unnoticed. The Khan offered my parents more gold than they thought possible for me to become a concubine in his harem. I . . . I felt I had to prove myself first. I needed to show him I was capable of more than raising children."

I tilt my head at her words. The way she stuttered and how she spit out the word *children* makes me think there is another meaning behind what she is saying. I glance over at Alik, but he offers me nothing but a small quirked eyebrow.

My eyes narrow slightly. "Do you think the lovite will be enough to get you out of the proposal?"

It's a guess, but the way Chinua stiffens at my words confirms my suspicion. She has no wish to marry her khan. He must be twice her age.

"No," she spits out bitterly. "I very much think it won't."

Silence, heavy and awkward, filters into the cave, before Chinua gets to her feet. "I'll be back tomorrow."

She smiles, then disappears behind the tent flap and out into the blindingly white landscape. I sip my milk and don't dare look at Alik.

"How are you feeling?" I ask after a few moments.

"Sore," he admits. "But I'll live."

"So, are you going to tell me what your problem is with the guild?" The question bursts from my lips unbidden.

He looks at me with raised brows.

"Like you don't know." His words lash out, full of anger and hurt.

"How could I, since you refuse to tell me?"

"I would've thought Luiza's little daughter would know everything."

I almost jerk back at the venom of his words. "Why do you keep throwing that at me like it's something to be ashamed of?" Alik and I had always vied for Luiza's attention, but he'd never acted like it bothered him. The sudden shift in his mood from when we woke up almost doesn't make sense.

"You're so blind, so devoted to Luiza and the guild that you don't see the evidence in front of your face. Why do you think my letters never reached you, Val? Because *Luiza* didn't want them to."

"How could you even think that?" I snap.

"What do you think happened to them? They just floated away on the wind? I would bet every ounce of lovite left in Knnot that Luiza intercepted and destroyed them. She wouldn't want her prize to run off, would she? Wouldn't want you to run to me, useless and broken."

"You're being ridiculous! Luiza took us in when no one else would. She loved you, Alik. I'm sure of it. She cried with me when I told her that you died. Why would she stop us from being together again? Why wouldn't she want you back at the guild?"

My questions snap out in rapid succession, my voice growing shriller with each one.

"Val, use what she taught you. Look at me. Do you think I am considered an asset anymore? You are. She would've known you'd want to come to me. She couldn't lose her best thief."

"No," I say.

I try not to let the sense of his words seep into me. Luiza did see us as assets. She'd never denied the fact. We made her money, and we all knew that. But she'd never leave one of her own behind. Especially not one she'd practically raised.

"I've had a lot of time to think about it, Val." His voice turns a bit softer. "It's the only thing that makes sense if you truly never received my letters."

"If I *truly* didn't get them? Do you think so little of me that you believe I would leave you alone and hurting if I knew you were alive? You must, if there is even a small part of you that doubts me. Do you think I'm so like Luiza I wouldn't see the use of you? Or did you just like being alone, not having to clean up after my mistakes?"

Alik's jaw goes hard. "What else was I supposed to believe? I've had nothing else to think about for almost a year."

His words slice straight to my heart, and my eyes sting.

"You know me better than anyone in this entire world." My voice shakes. "We grew up together. You were there for my first guild mission, there for every nightmare of Ludminka, there when we stumbled through baking taiga bread, and danced with me at every winter solstice. I would have come to you had I known. I didn't hesitate when Ivan showed me your letter. I agreed immediately."

"You agreed for Luiza. All you wanted was the lovite for the Bright God's champion. You said as much."

"It was an afterthought, Alik. My first thought was you. It's *always* you."

I glare down at him, chest heaving. His face boils with unspoken rage. How did we go from warm comfort to this?

Suddenly, the cave feels far too hot. Sweat breaks out on my brow and behind my knees. The walls press in on me, and I stand. I don't want to stay in here.

"I'm going to go scout around, make sure Chinua covered her tracks and the Storm Hounds can't find us." I tug on my pants and boots. I look back at Alik from the cave. "I spent too many nights with swollen eyes and a broken heart to listen to you call me a liar. You can believe all you want to about Luiza, but don't you *dare* make me into the villain of your story. It isn't fair to me, and the boy I used to know would understand that."

"Val, wait a minute." Alik struggles to his knees, face drawn.

I dart out of the cave before he can get his legs beneath him. Not even the crisp winter air can still my nerves as I race away from the cave.

# FOURTEEN

MY MIND SWIRLS AS I hike away from the cave, wandering aimlessly back the way we came.

The landscape offers nothing but pristine snow and green firs, giving me nothing to focus on besides my churning thoughts. I know Luiza better than anyone in the guild. She wouldn't keep Alik away from me, not if she knew he was alive. She did nothing but care for us since I was a child. How could Alik pretend she'd never done that?

I keep an eye out for swatches of black-and-gold uniforms. The rush of the river surrounds me, and my lungs burn by the time I stop trudging forward. I sigh and press my back to a fir tree, not caring if sap leaks on to my clothes.

The cold air washes over me and calms my mind. I inhale deeply, taking in the clean scent of the forest. The smell reminds me of Ludminka, what it smelled like in the winter, mixed with wood smoke and sweet berry pies. Part of me aches to see it again, but the other parts wish only to go back to Rurik.

I was so young when I left my village. I don't even know if it is my home anymore. I crafted a new family with Luiza, and I do think of her as a surrogate mother. She is the only person I've really loved since the ice devoured Ludminka. I can't just turn my back on her.

I don't understand how Alik can.

I thought we knew each other inside and out. Now it seems like we are strangers piecing back together something that once was. Perhaps the year we spent apart changed him more than I thought. I grab on to the fir branches and scurry up into the tree to give my mind something else to do. I stop halfway, settling against the thick trunk and on top of a *V*-shaped bough. I tuck my hands under my armpits to keep them warm and study the Storm Hound encampment. It's the same as yesterday, flags fluttering in the crisp breeze. It looks like any other Storm Hound garrison I've ever seen. Yet the bottle Chinua brought had the guild marking on it.

It doesn't quite add up. Things have only gotten more confusing since the start of this trip. I long to be back home in my down feather bed in the guild, relaxing under my quilt with a cup of cinnamon tea. That's where things make sense. Where I belong.

I have to remind myself there might not be a guild to return to.

I shift, then freeze as the sound of voices floats to my ears.

"This is getting out of hand," a female's voice says. It almost sounds familiar, but I can't quite place it.

I push myself deeper into the thick fir branches.

"Trust me, I'm well aware. I've not had as much control as I wanted," a male voice says. *Ivan?*

A dark, hooded figure crests the rise, followed by Ivan. My brow creases, and I shift to get a better look. They pull up short a few trees away. I make out Ivan's boots and the hood of his partner through the boughs.

"You think your lack of control is the issue?" hisses the other person. "I've given you as much control as I can. You've lost your horses; you almost lost two members of your party, one of which is crucial to all this. How can I trust you to keep going?"

"We're almost there. I can make it the rest of the way," Ivan says.

"You better, or little Zia will find out what really happened to her *papochka*." The woman's voice takes on an almost child-like sound, mocking Ivan.

A branch cracks somewhere to my right, and I still as the hooded person's head snaps in my direction. My blood runs cold as I finally see her face. A guildling, maybe three or four years my senior. She always went out of her way to garner

Luiza's attention, desperate for a pat on the head. I'd recognize her anywhere. A bolt of horrible realization dawns on me.

Ivan knows someone in the guild, and they are using him to get to Knnot. No doubt the fortune-teller betrayed him for quite a reward. If word got out that someone was able to reach Knnot without coming down with the plague, the guild would want to know the information.

Well, that's what Luiza would've done.

I consider swinging down and demanding to know what is going on. The girl must be trying to maneuver her way into Luiza's position. She might even be the one who sabotaged my mission to the Vestry. There is no way Czar Ladislaw would ignore her contributions if she managed to free Knnot. He'd give whoever managed such a feat anything they wanted, and kill Luiza for failing him.

I watch them say their goodbyes, and the woman heads away from the Storm Hound encampment while Ivan goes toward it. I wait until she is a safe distance away before scrambling down from the tree. I stride toward Ivan. I need to know how the guild is involved in this little expedition of ours.

Ivan's back is in sight, and I open my mouth to call out to him when the ground rattles, sending waves of vibration up my legs. Flashes of Knnot the day my world changed roll through my mind immediately, and my stomach drops. A massive boom shakes the entire valley, and my head snaps toward the noise just in time to see a plume of fire and smoke spit from the Storm Hound encampment.

Forgetting about Ivan, I break into a sprint toward the cave. The Storm Hounds will rip this entire valley apart looking for who caused the explosion. We aren't safe. I need to get Alik out of there as fast as possible. I tear into the cave, terrified someone has found it. Instead, Alik leans over my bag, stuffing the furs inside it, as Chinua breaks down the tent.

"What happened?" I say, trying to catch my breath and dampen the fire at the same time.

"The Storm Hounds found out about you," Chinua says. Her hands shake so hard she almost drops the pole. "I did the only thing I could think of and raced back here to help you."

"How did they find out?"

"I don't know," Chinua says.

Was it Serafima? She's wanted to get rid of me since the start of the mission. Perhaps she thought this was the best way. Or maybe Ivan, using the emergency to hasten our pace to Knnot. I dampen the fire as quickly as I can and cover it with stone dust. It almost looks as if no one was here at all. I move to help Chinua with the tent. My heart thunders. Alik and I can't trust anyone.

"Did they see you leave?" I ask as Alik joins us, still a bit unsteady on his feet.

"They were too concerned with putting out the fires from the explosion," Chinua says with a slight smile. "I knew I needed more time if I wanted to get you two out of here."

"What did you hit?"

"The main barracks. The charge was enough to take out at least the weapon stores and their food vault. It should buy us time to get to Knnot. They won't dare follow us there."

I nod as we finish packing up the rest of the camp in seconds flat. I settle the tent bag onto my aching shoulders. I toss Alik my coat for now, his own still far too wet to wear. I glance around the cave one more time, slinging Alik's still-damp coat across my shoulders. It's as clean as we can make it.

"Are we meeting the others?" I ask.

Part of me secretly hopes we aren't. If we are, I will have to confront Ivan somehow. I want to surprise the truth out of him. Chinua nods, her chin set and determined.

"Follow me and keep your heads down," she says.

A brief moment of paranoia washes over me, and I consider not following her. She could be leading us into a trap. Alik tucks his head down and limps behind her. He seems to trust her, and after what she just did for us, I suppose I should, too. I follow her lead.

Chinua hugs the cliffs of the mountain, keeping far out of sight of the encampment. Every so often she stops and tilts her head, as if listening to something, then starts off again.

We make it behind the Storm Hound encampment without so much as a single Storm Hound sighting. It rubs me the wrong way. They should be crawling over the valley by now. Chinua charges forward, leading us up a foothill, forever pushing for the last set of mountains before Knnot. We march, none of us speaking, not even to clear our throats.

We crest the rise and instantly Chinua falls to her stomach. We mimic her movements as she squirms over the rocky rise and presses her back to the granite outcropping at the top. She checks to make sure Alik is beside me.

"We are almost to the meeting point," she whispers.

We nod, Alik's breath brushing against my cheek. Chinua keeps her body as small as possible. We are too visible up here, even dressed in drab wools. She hides behind every rock, stopping to cover our tracks as best she can before moving out again. She angles our path for a thick grove of trees. I only have time to feel the briefest flash of relief before a low murmur of voices reaches my ears.

"Patrol," Chinua hisses. "They must not know what's happened in the valley yet. Run."

She bolts for the trees. Alik stumbles forward, almost falling face-first into the snow. I help him stand and slip his arm over my shoulder. Alik's weight sags against me as he tries to pick up his pace, pushing me deeper into the snowdrifts. I struggle to lift my legs. My blood runs ice cold as the voices draw nearer, a bark of laughter making my heart jolt. I strain under Alik's weight, pushing myself as hard as I can. It's not enough.

We aren't going to make it.

"Leave me," gasps Alik.

I spare a glance his way. His scarred face is graying and strained. His thin chest heaves with each movement, every step costing him precious strength. Fear flees from my heart, determination filling the void.

"Never," I say.

I push my body as hard as I can, picking my legs up out of the knee-high drifts, snowshoes heavy with wet snow, and plowing forward. Sweat pours down my back, and every single muscle in my body screams. I keep my eyes on the darkened edge of the forest, my mind intent on only one thing. I will get Alik to safety.

Chinua comes into focus in the depths of the shadows beneath the boughs. Her eyes, wide and frightened, keep darting between us and the pass behind. I know the Storm Hounds are close, but they haven't spotted us yet.

I dive forward into the drooping boughs of a fir tree laden with snow. Alik tumbles with me, all limbs and labored breathing. It feels as if we fall forever, but finally my back kisses precious wet snow. I have enough strength to look up and smile. We are beneath the boughs, the snow tinkling down from the disturbed branches, hiding our path.

Alik rolls off me and covers my exposed snowshoes before burying himself next me. Wet snow sinks into Alik's still-damp coat. I shiver, but my body refuses to warm. If the Storm Hounds don't pass us soon, I know I won't last. The cold will claim me.

We wait for what seems like hours before Chinua whispers, "Gone."

I smile. We did it.

Alik rises beside me, brushing away the snow trapping my arms.

"Come on, Valeria," he says.

He studies my face for one moment before slipping the coat he wears onto my shoulders. He lets his hand linger on my arm a beat too long, but I can't make myself look at him.

"Let's find the others," Chinua says.

Alik pulls me up, and we stumble after her, hiking once more toward Knnot.

# FIFTEEN

WE MEET SERAFIMA AND IVAN at the edge of a fir forest and push as far into the night as we can before setting up camp. We don't start a fire, instead huddling close together beneath the tent. We can't risk the Storm Hounds spotting us, and I have no doubt they still follow.

At dawn, we start out again. Our path leads us over pitted limestone to the low slope of the glacier that separates Zladonia from the rest of Strana. It eases upward, but my legs tremble, thinking of finding purchase on the ice. I glance over at Alik, concerned. His face holds nothing but grim determination.

Serafima pulls us to a stop right before the base of the glacier.

"We should be there soon," she says, staring up at it. "Let's keep our strength and start up tomorrow."

We make camp in a flurry, hoisting the yurt and sweeping the ground inside. We're far enough away that Ivan chances a tiny fire. It's far too cold to go without one tonight. The yurt seems to stop most of the smoke, and soon Chinua stirs a thin soup not much more than boiling bones in a broth, and Serafima passes out the last of the bread.

Ivan settles a stack of small branches beside the fire and collapses onto his furs. We all stare at the small dancing orange flame.

"We should've kept going," Ivan says.

Serafima cuts him a glare. "The last time you pushed us, Alik and I almost died. We will stay here."

Ivan grumbles something under his breath. Heat pricks in my chest. The memory of him and the guildling still sits clear at the front of my mind. Something else is going on here. I just can't figure out what.

"Why do you want to get there so quickly, Ivan? We'll be there tomorrow by sunset. Why isn't that fast enough for you?"

"I don't want the Storm Hounds to find us," he says.

"Is that the only reason?" I ask.

Silence blankets the tent, tension sparking between us.

"Of course," Ivan says, his fingers going up to circle his pendant once more. He runs his thumb over it, the bronze filigree shimmering in the firelight.

I clench my jaw so hard a muscle in my cheek ticks. "Where

is your family? I haven't heard you mention them once."

"Val," Alik warns.

"No, I'd really love to know."

"They are as good as dead." Ivan's voice is a harsh rasp.

"As good as dead isn't dead," I say.

"Valeria, stop it," Alik says. "He hasn't seen his family in years. He doesn't know where they are."

I study Ivan's face, the flickering shadows catching in the worn lines, making him seem years older. Alik may have swallowed his lie, but I know better. The guildling Ivan met outside the Storm Hound encampment had as good as admitted the guild is holding his family captive.

I consider pushing Ivan further, but Alik seethes across the fire, so I let the conversation die, fiddling with my scar. I wish it calmed me like it used to, but even it can do nothing to push away the questions swirling through my mind. Or the tight knot of dread coiled deep in my gut.

Knnot lies just up the glacier. Soon, I'll walk into the very village I swore never to return to. Even thinking of seeing the ice-lined streets makes my stomach flip. Nothing about this journey has been what I expected. I thought Alik and I would fall into place like two pieces made whole. I thought this would be like just another guild mission. Instead, it's been nothing but uncertainty.

I glance over at Alik. I don't know where he and I stand anymore, or what happens after we find the lovite. I want to find Luiza and the Bright God's champion to help them over-throw the Czar. But I don't know if I will do that alone, or if Alik will be by my side.

Something deep in my heart says alone. I just wish I knew why.

Silence slithers through us, the crackling fire the only com-pany. I wonder what the others are thinking. Are they afraid of reaching Zladonia and succumbing to the plague? Are they afraid of the ice claiming them as well? I've spent my entire life running from the memory of the ice, constantly afraid it would catch me. Fear grips my heart, and my body sags with the weight. I sink down to my furs and pull them tight over me, wishing the thick blankets could chase away my buzzing thoughts or still the growing tightness around my lungs.

I force myself to take a deep breath, imagining myself back in the attic at the guild. Alik and I laugh on our low pallets, the folded paper stars hanging by twine from the beams over-head. Heat radiates from the chimney behind our heads, and my quilt still smells like my matta. I make myself remember it all, forcing out every thought that isn't of Alik and me until my eyes close with sleep.

*Knnot shimmers before me, bright against the black night. A mighty groan echoes across the starless sky, and the folds of the mountain open, splitting straight up the middle. I step forward. Knnot curls around me in a stony embrace and shadows swallow me once again. I blink against the sudden dark before blue light blooms to life in a river above my head. I follow the soft gleam, dully aware that stone now surrounds me.*

*Before long, the light deposits me in front of a worn door, the bronze handle long since tarnished green. An overwhelming urge to open it comes over me. My hand lifts and curls around the handle. Cool calm rushes up my fingers to nestle around my heart.*

*This is right.*

*"Open me," a hushed voice says.*

*"Why?" My voice sounds leaden.*

*"Freedom. Peace."*

*"Whose?"*

*"Everyone's."*

*"Everyone's, everyone's, everyone's, everyone's."*

*Voices circle me, some high and lilting, others so deep they sound like growls. Suddenly, the surety I felt falls to pieces around me, and I wrench my hand from the door.*

*The voices scream. I clap my hands to my ears to stop it, but they're already inside me, banging against my skull, begging to be released. Their screams grow louder, desperate.*

*Angry.*

*"You will lose everything," one says. It almost sounds like my own voice. "You think you lost something when Ludminka froze? It is nothing compared to what waits for you if you con-tinue to refuse, little girl. That's all you are. A little girl trapped*

*in the body of someone who thinks she's learned something about life."*

*I open my eyes and have to avert them as silver light blasts through the stone surrounding me. A different version of myself stands before me, hair pure white and rippling behind as if caught in an unfelt breeze. My eyes blaze a brighter cobalt than I have ever seen, almost as if they are illuminated from within. Silver light curls around my body, bright and throbbing. The vision of me lifts a finger.*

*"There is always something else to lose."*

I jerk upright. My body shudders and my hands tremble as I study them in the glow of the embers beside me. Normal, except for the scar beneath my left hand. It seems to gleam a liquid silver. I scrub my other hand over it, my heart thundering in my ears. When I finally stop, my wrist is red from rubbing, but there is no sign of the glow I'd seen before.

Maybe it was a trick of the light, a leftover illusion from my dream.

Before the thought has even fully formed, I know it's a lie. Ever since we'd started out on this trip, my scar has turned into something unknown to me. I never gave it more thought beyond using it to calm myself. I don't know why it hurts now. It adds to the mounting panic lacing through my veins.

"Val?"

Alik's sleepy voice makes me jolt, and I knock into the

rocks circling the dying fire. The clatter pulls him up from his furs.

"What's wrong?" He rubs sleep from his face before fixing his gaze on me, his brows tense.

"Nothing. Just a nightmare." I slip my hand beneath the fur so he can't see my scar.

I'm not sure why I don't tell him. I never had dreams that felt so real I was sure they were things I'd somehow forgotten. Alik wouldn't believe me. I almost didn't believe myself.

"Are you sure you're okay? You've been . . . I don't know . . . off since the cave," he says.

"I'm fine," I say far more harshly than I intended.

"You're mad at me." His whisper shoots out like an accusation.

I glance at the other sleeping forms across the fire, but no one stirs. His frustration only adds to the growing anger in my chest. I hate him for getting me into this mess. For calling out every insecurity I have. Every misgiving I've had since we met again forms on my lips and I let the words spill, tired of holding them back.

"Of course I am," I hiss. "How could you believe I'd never want to see you? That I'd lie about your letters? Who do you think I am? Never mind, I know the answer. You think I'm Luiza's miniature. You hate me for defending her, and I don't understand why. You're different, Alik. You aren't the same person you used to be."

"Did you really think I'd be the same?" Alik's voice is flat and cold.

The words hit me like a slap. Yes. That is what I expected. The Alik who could laugh as easily as he could thieve. The one who always knew how to cheer me up and when to talk me down. Not this cold, secretive Alik who wants to prove to the world he is still the same person he used to be.

"I feel like I don't know you anymore," I say. "I want to. But everything I seem to want, you don't. Why do you hate Luiza? Why do you keep pushing me away from her? Why is it so bad that I want to save her?" I hate the way my voice wobbles.

"Because she isn't a good person, Valeria. You don't see it, but all she's done our entire lives is manipulate us into doing exactly what she wants."

"You've always known that. It isn't some revelation that suddenly came to you," I snap. "Are you jealous? She always favored me over you. Is that what you realized as you hid from me?"

Alik's face contorts, his eyes going dark.

"Luiza *found* me. Long before you ever came to Oleg. She knew where I was the entire time." Alik lets out a harsh laugh at the confusion scrawled across my face. "Oh, she didn't tell you? She refused to let me back into the guild, even when I begged. She cast me aside. That's why I was so sure she stopped your letters. Why I was so certain you chose not to come. Why wouldn't Luiza tell you? Like you said, you're her favorite."

The air disappears from my lungs. "You're lying," I whisper.

Luiza would never turn Alik away. She'd practically raised him. She couldn't have seen him suffering and refused to help.

"You know I'm not. I told you, I'm no longer useful. Too broken for Luiza. What use could you have for me if she doesn't?"

White-hot anger lashes through my entire body. "How *dare* you." My voice borders on too loud, and Chinua shifts in her sleep. "You think I'm that heartless?" I hiss. "My heart *shattered* the day you died. I spent months in bed, desperate for anything that reminded me of you. I relived that moment every single night and woke up screaming your name."

I try to suppress the shuddering breaths threatening to break into sobs. If I cry, I know I won't stop. When he doesn't speak, I grit my teeth.

"Are you so desperate to believe I'm like Luiza that you won't listen to the words I'm saying?"

"How do I know you aren't manipulating me like her?" Alik says.

I bite back a frustrated scream.

"Do you want to know what my biggest fear is?" My words are barely more than a whisper. "I'm afraid to watch you die again." My voice trembles as I finally admit it all. "When I left you behind, it was like leaving behind part of myself. It was like someone blew out the candle I used to light my path, and

I had to stumble along without help. Leaving you behind made me realize—"

I choke on the next words, terrified to say them but desperately needing to.

"You're the only thing that matters to me in this world, Alik. You always have been."

Silence follows my words. My anger is gone, replaced only by the dull ache of baring my soul.

"I don't care if you don't believe me," I say. "But I made a promise a long time ago to never lie to you. And I never have. Can you say the same thing?"

He doesn't respond. I wait for what seems like an eternity, but all he does is stare into the red embers. I take a deep breath and lie back on my furs. There is nothing more I can say.

Instead, I turn over what Alik said. Luiza found him and refused to bring him back to the guild. Worse, she never told me he was alive. I don't understand it. Why would she let me suffer when she knew the very thing I wanted more than anything was a few days' ride away? It hurts almost as much as Alik's suspicion.

I have no idea what this means. I'm too tired to even think. I close my eyes and wait for dawn to come.

# SIXTEEN

THE DAY DAWNS BRIGHT AND clear. Ivan and Serafima pore over the map one last time while Chinua banks the fire. I tighten the straps on the tent pack, ignoring everyone around me, and kick snow over the worst of our churning footsteps. We are as ready as we can be. We've seen no evidence of the Storm Hounds following and I can't help but wonder why. Zladonia lies just up the glacier from us. Perhaps they were too afraid to get close to the border? I try to let myself be comforted by the thought, but all it does is remind me of what waits ahead.

"We're ready," Ivan says. "Soon, we will reach Knnot."

My stomach flips at his words, and I shift the pack on my back. The others fall in behind us. I'm glad to walk up front for a little bit. Alik follows, silent and stony, appearing as if I didn't pour my heart out to him. I want to be angry, but instead all I feel is a dull ache in my chest.

The path slopes gently upward, and my heart thunders as the crest of the glacier grows closer. I know what lies at the top. Matta had bid my brothers and me to never go beyond it, too worried about what lay in the wilderness past the soft plains surrounding Ludminka. I charge ahead of Ivan and Serafima as the top comes into view.

My breath hitches as I stare at the scene below. I barely make out the snow-dusted rooftops of Ludminka, still nestled between the fir forest and the slopes of the valley. I trail the overgrown path to the mouth of Knnot and follow the thick lines of the mountain up.

It's all as I remember. I almost feel like if I closed my eyes and tried hard enough, I could smell the cook fires of Ludminka and taste the berries my *babushka* gathered every midwinter. A pressure in my chest releases at the sight of it, as if every moment of my life since the day I left was supposed to lead to this.

At long last, I'm home.

The rest of the group pulls up behind me. They don't speak, in awe as they take in the sight of our quarry for the first time. I wonder what it must be like for them, to see the mountain that faded into legend after the ice claimed Ludminka.

Ivan stands beside me, his pendant resting proudly on his chest. The bronze veins seem to glow and pulse. The fear I'd felt of the ice and plague slowly melt away. Even as we march silently toward my village, it seems to keep whatever curse that circles the town at bay. Stories say no one can step into Zladonia without instantly starting to weaken and pale as the plague takes hold. For all my doubts, Ivan's tale of his magic pendant are true.

It should comfort me. Instead, all I can think about is how he got the pendant in the first place. Was he really given it by an old woman? Or was it the guild all along? Even Luiza? It seems far more likely that whoever he worked with in the guild discovered the artifact and gave it to him.

I turn to Ivan, ready to interrogate him, when something whispers on the wind.

*Valeria.*

I glance behind me to see if the others heard it, but they stare down at Ludminka with wide eyes.

*Come to me.*

It sounds almost . . . loving. Like my matta when she stroked my hair after I hurt myself. Still, no one behind me moves. It's as if they don't hear it at all.

*Valeria.* A breeze picks up and tugs my hair toward the village.

My feet follow the sound on their own. I feel a tug at my core, almost as if a string tightens around my stomach and an unseen puppeteer yanks me forward.

*Come,* the voice commands.

The houses of Ludminka draw steadily closer, and my body begins to tingle, starting at my toes before the feeling works its way up my legs. They go weak and boneless as the wooden slats of the houses draw close enough to touch.

Ludminka looks the same as the day I left it. Wooden houses still stand rot free and freshly painted. The ice encases the thatched roofs and spirals across the windows. Shutters hang half open, frozen hands curled around the edges as if someone were just about to throw them wide. It's all perfectly untouched, as if the world moved forward but Ludminka stood still. I take another step and continue into town.

"I thought there'd be more . . . destruction," Serafima says, pulling me from my thoughts.

"It's as if time stopped," Ivan whispers.

"Should we keep going?" Serafima asks with a tremble in her voice.

"I don't think we have a choice," I say.

I force myself to walk down the familiar streets.

Silence rings through the village. No friendly faces pop out of the brightly shuttered windows, decorated with the familiar red flower designs. It makes me think of the red roses in the window box at my house.

I wonder if they are still there.

I'm not sure where I'm going until my boots hit the cobbled streets of the square. I look up and freeze. Snow stubbornly clings to the crevices between the bricks. The square always bustled with so much activity when I was a child, with people scurrying to buy wares or chasing children. I'd expected it to be empty now, nothing but a ghost of its former self.

Instead, it's teeming with frozen people. Their bodies shine in the late afternoon sun, ice encasing every last one of them. Some are caught midlaugh while others barter wares. Children run, caught in an eternal game of tag.

I never denied the freeze happened. I saw it with my own eyes, watched the ice curl across the floor, intent on devouring me, too. But I didn't expect *this*.

There had been ten summers since I left. Ten years of thaw. Yet every man, woman, and child remains intact, as if they never defrosted. I spin slowly in a circle, the cold around me taking on a new meaning.

Ludminka had been trapped in this endless winter since the day I left. No one ever came back from Zladonia alive. Their weak bodies gave way to the plague long before they reached a way station to report their findings.

I press a hand hard to my mouth, letting the pressure of my woolen mittens against my lips stop the well of tears from forming.

I never should've come back.

I crafted a fairy tale for myself. One where the people of Ludminka died quickly and their bones turned to dust. I never thought they'd still be here, trapped in an icy prison. I have no idea if they will ever thaw, if their souls will ever find peace in the afterlife.

The others gather around, each one looking over the people in the square. My body drains of any sort of hope. Chinua whispers something in her language.

"Cursed," she says. "We have tales of living dead. They slumber during the day in their graves and awaken at night to devour souls."

Serafima examines one of the people from head to toe. She shakes her head.

"Black magic." Her eyes dart to me. "How could you not tell us about this?"

"I told you what I saw that day. I didn't expect this either," I say. My budding panic falls away, replaced by the familiar burn of anger. They all stand there and expect me to have the answers. "I know nothing more than what I already said. I wish I did."

"The Czar was right," Serafima hisses. "The *malozla* cursed this land. You earned your title."

I spring to slap her as she voices my fears to the entire group. "Val, no." Alik catches me around the waist. He stumbles slightly as his body adjusts to the new weight. I turn to face him, ready to claw my way out. He gives an almost imperceptible shake of his head before releasing me and turning on Serafima.

"You truly believe the miners did this, Sera?" Alik says. "You think they damned themselves to an eternity in ice?"

Serafima blinks at Alik's words. "We don't even know if she's telling the truth. For all we know, she isn't even from this village. She could've grown up anywhere in Zladonia, helping whatever dark witch cast this spell."

A cool calm circles me. "You want proof?"

She doesn't respond, but she tilts her chin and clenches her jaw.

If she wants dead bodies, I will give them to her.

My blood burns as I lead us through the silent village. Every window seems to stare at me, every door looks like a trap just begging to be sprung.

At last, roses perched on a windowsill come into view and my entire middle lurches in a sick sob.

My home.

It's so much smaller than I remember. Suddenly, the fervor that carried me all the way to this doorstep is gone. My mouth dries as I take a step toward my door.

I bang the snow off my boots on the small wooden platform nailed a foot above the ground. Even after all this time, it's still habit. It almost feels as if nothing has changed as I reach for the gilded doorknob.

Except everything has.

I push the door open. The hearth is bone cold, the remnants of long-burned logs still clogging the brickwork. I don't want to travel the rest of the way around the single-room cabin, but my eyes catch on my matta's feet. Slowly, my gaze travels up her thin legs until I stare at her stiff body beside the stove, spoon raised halfway to her lips as if about to taste the frozen soup in the pot. Frost clings to the small lines beside her eyes and tiny snowflakes stud her blue lips.

My father sits with his socked feet on the table, his wide mouth stretched into a grin behind his cold pipe. My brothers sit beside him, still caught in their mock argument with smiles plastered across their faces.

My knees wobble and I brace myself against the cold fireplace.

Everything is so familiar. The knot on the floor I helped my father sand down. The burn marks next to the stove where I tried to bake bread and failed. So many memories. So many maybes. My life now isn't what my parents wanted for me. I was supposed to grow up, safe and loved, here. For the last ten years, all I did was search for a place where I felt like I did here. I thought Luiza and the guild was a new home, one I built for myself. But it's just an illusion of a family.

This is my real family.

Tears pour down my face as I place a hand on my mother's cold shoulder.

The others shuffle in behind me. I barely register the sound of their boots. I can't stop staring at my parents. What I wouldn't give for my mother to hug me or my father to ruffle my hair. A hole I've desperately tried to fill gapes open in my chest, aching and raw.

"She looks so much like you," Chinua says.

I glance at my mother's still glossy braid, the graceful curve of her neck, and her merry eyes.

I do look like her.

"Here is your proof, Serafima." My voice comes out thick and harsh. "These are my parents and my brothers. I was here the day the ice devoured everything. I wanted to free them but knew I couldn't. I didn't even try. I gave up. I left them here. Look me in the face now and tell me I'm lying."

Serafima practically trembles as she stares at each face. She doesn't say a word. I shake my head and walk out of the house, unable to stand being there any longer.

Knnot towers over the houses, more obvious than ever now that we are close to the edge of town. My vision blurs as I study the top of the mountain, so steep no one ever managed to summit. I press the heels of my hands into my eyes. I want to stop crying.

I can't.

I spent so many years trying to forget the things I'd never have. My father dancing with me at a summer wedding, my mother watching her only daughter grow. I thought I could replace them with other things, other people, but I was beyond wrong. The dull ache in my chest blooms into something ragged and bleeding. I feel like I'll never be whole again. Boots crunch on the snow behind me, and I know it's Alik without turning around.

"Serafima believes you now," he says.

I don't respond. I hate Serafima for telling me the Czar was right. I hate her for making me see my family again. I hate this stupid, miserable world for taking them away from me.

"I'm sorry you had to see them again." Alik's voice isn't

much more than a whisper. Soft and tender, like he isn't sure he should say it.

Rage chokes my words. I want to scream until there is no voice left in my throat. It's better than this horrible empty feeling. The guilt slithering around me for running from my family.

"Val, I know you're mad at me for last night. I didn't know how to respond. It was stupid of me, and I'm sorry." He takes in a deep breath.

"Are you?" A sour chuckle bursts from my lips before I can stop it.

Alik's hand curves around my shoulder. I let him gently turn me. Tears roll down my face and stain my coat deep brown. He lifts a tentative hand up and brushes them away.

"I am," he says. "You're right, we did grow up together. I was there when Luiza found you; I talked to you when nightmares of the ice woke you. That doesn't just disappear."

I want to ask why he's acting like it does. My voice catches in my throat. I'm too tired to fight anymore. I want to find the Iovite and leave. I never want to think of Ludminka, Knnot, or my parents again.

"Let me help you. Please," he says.

I want to. My mind begs for the comfortable familiarity of his embrace. I want to press my head into his shoulder until I forget Knnot. But how can I when I stand just outside the house where my entire family died, in the village that was taken in a single moment? Any help he can provide would be nothing but false security.

"You can't," I say, and take a step away from him, cold air hitting my cheek, reminding me where his hand had been.

"Val—" he starts to say.

Suddenly, my skin prickles as if something watches me. I search the trees but see nothing besides dying pines. Every single instinct tells me to run, that something evil lurks here.

"We should leave," I say at last.

"Why?" Alik asks.

"There's something wrong about this place," I say.

A mantle of unease settles around us. We both jump as the door of my house creaks open. Chinua strides out and gives my arm a sympathetic squeeze. She is soon followed by Serafima and Ivan.

*Welcome home, Valeria.*

The voice sounds so real and so close that I look over my shoulder to see if anyone is standing there. There's nothing except sparkling snow. My shudder has nothing to do with the cold. Something watches us. I'm sure of it. I open my mouth to ask the others if they feel it, but Serafima slides in front of me before I can. The creeping sensation along my spine vanishes as my anger comes rushing back.

"I . . . am sorry," she says. "I never should've pushed you. I spent most of my life thinking my father was here. Now I hope he isn't. I couldn't . . . I couldn't see him like that, and I should've never forced you to."

I don't know how to respond. Saying it is okay would be

wrong. It will never be okay. Not as long as I stand on the ground before Knnot with the bodies of my family frozen. I turn back toward the mountain, biting the insides of my cheeks so hard the coppery taste of blood fills my mouth.

"Come on," I say. "If we want to make it inside before nightfall, we need to get moving now."

No one speaks as I lead them back through town, careful to avoid the square. Knnot grows ever closer, the height almost dizzying. Something leaden settles into my stomach as I reach the final street at the edge of town.

A single road leads out toward the yawning mouth of the mines not more than a half mile away. In all my dreams of Knnot, the path to the mines was clear. Something dark stains the road halfway between the mines and the village. A thick row of something black and bulky. I push forward. The others pick up the pace without complaint. The closer we get, the more my stomach sinks. It isn't rockfall; that much I can tell.

I'm about one hundred yards away before I stop dead in my tracks. The avalanche fall from ten years ago piles up to my right, making a small mountain of its own. Black dots speckle the top of it, too far away to make out clearly, but I am willing to bet my life it is the exact same thing as what is in front of me.

People.

Not just any people.

Storm Hounds.

# SEVENTEEN

I CONSIDER RUNNING, BUT WE are already too close. They had to have spotted us as we came out of town. If they did, why didn't they shoot?

Ivan comes to stand beside me. "What are you waiting for?"

"Don't you see them?" I nod toward the Storm Hounds.

"Yes, and I also see they aren't moving."

I squint at the group. He's right. They're frozen, just like the people in the village.

We follow the rutted road forward until they're close enough to touch. Unlike everyone in town, their faces aren't frozen in placid, everyday interest. Their eyes are wide with fear, mouths dropped open in screams. Most stand with shields raised and teeth perpetually gritted, facing the entrance of the mine, but others are in the process of tripping, some even sprawled on the ground, clawing their way toward town. Instead of feeling a twinge of sympathy, I feel only vicious satisfaction. They got what they deserved.

"What are they running from?" Chinua asks, voice small.

"The mountain," Ivan responds.

I round the battalion until I stand before them and study their formation, nearly five people long and seven people across. Their terrified faces break through my indifference. I glance over my shoulder at the mountain before studying their faces one more time. They aren't looking at the mouth of the mines, but ten feet above it.

"What are they looking at?" I mumble to myself. I shiver and examine the mountain, searching for what the battalion could've possibly seen. The thick groove running the length is even more pronounced. Some people used to say the mountain cracked when they opened the mine. That the Brother Gods did it to prove how powerful they are, but I never believed it.

The hair on the back of my neck begins to prickle. I'm certain someone watches, their eyes determined to bore into my soul. I glance back at the others, but they still study the Storm Hounds. Wind scrawls between us and Knnot, picking up a dusting of snow. The mouth of the mine lies just two hundred yards away now.

Silence descends on me like a shroud. Not a single bird calls; the wind doesn't whistle through the boughs of the trees to my left. I pick my way forward around deep holes created by wagon wheels and chunks of rock. I'm just about to step into the shadow of the mountain when something catches my eye within Knnot.

A slender form slithers from one shadow to the next.

A jolt runs through my body, and I race back to the others.

"What's wrong?" Ivan asks.

"I thought I . . ." I trail off, feeling like an idiot. They'd never believe me. "Never mind. Are you ready to move? The quicker we get to the vaults, the faster we can leave Ludminka. I don't want to stay a moment longer than I have to."

"You still want to go inside? Now?" Serafima asks.

I shrug. "Why not?"

"Perhaps we should stay in town tonight," Ivan says. "Start again in the morning when the sun is brighter and will be out longer."

"We will be inside a mountain," I say harshly. "We won't see daylight anyway."

"We'll have more time to load the lovite out to the village in the daylight. It's . . . too dangerous now." Ivan's eyes slide to the Storm Hounds before him.

I laugh almost manically.

"*Now* it can wait? We forced our way through blizzards and past Storm Hounds. Two of us almost died from hypothermia, and now you don't want to get what you came for? Don't trust your fortune-teller now? Think that charm around your neck is nothing but a useless piece of rock?"

Ivan's lips thin into small white lines. "Watch your mouth—"

"Or what? You can't get to the vaults without me. You'll wander for days before you find them. You're the one who wanted this. Now you're scared?"

I grind my hand into a fist and relish the feeling of being in control. The group listens to me now. I'm the one with the power.

"You're nothing but a coward," I hiss. "I'll prove to you there isn't anything to fear. You all can go back. I'm staying in the mountain tonight."

"Val, don't do this. You aren't thinking clearly," Alik says.

"I'm not going back into that village," I whisper. "I can't spend the night with all of *them* around me. With my family close but beyond reach. I just can't."

I spin away and let my feet carry me far from the group. I wait for someone to call out, for footsteps to thunder up behind me.

But there's nothing.

My will falters as a small sob escapes my lips. I knew no one would follow, but it didn't stop me from hoping. I really believed Alik would at least try to. I'm left only with the foolish aftermath of my anger. Sweat pours down my back as I finally reach the mouth of the mine. I glance back.

My heart gives a painful thump. I'm alone. Again.

I turn toward the mine. When my father worked here, the

mines had been full of people, light, and the sounds of pick-axes on stone. The days Papa let me come with him were some of the best. I sang with the others and pushed carts full of lovite as fast as I could while my father laughed. I'd never felt happier than when I was tucked deep inside Knnot with him.

Now there is nothing but dilapidated tunnels and deafening silence. It makes my skin prickle.

Spare parts lie scattered about—overturned buckets with rusted bottoms, broken lanterns with the candle buried deep in snow. I glance up at the worn stone above my head. It all looks so familiar, despite the passage of years. As I step into the mine, I get a strange sense of recall. Everything from the patina color of the carts to the dank scent of wet rock and rotting wood is exactly like my dreams. I wrap my arms around myself as I tread deeper.

Two well-worn dirt paths branch out in front of me, one going left, the other going right and down into an oppressive dark tunnel. I don't want to be afraid, but the vast emptiness of Knnot creeps under my skin and settles there.

Tools line the walls in neat piles while metal-plated caps hang on rotting wooden pegs buried deep into the rock. Thick wooden supports hold back stone on the sides and above my head. Papa used to swear they would groan, like the mountain was shifting on top of them.

The eerie calm creeps over my skin, and I'm not so sure I imagined something watching me. Darkness swallows me as

I travel down the right path away from the low light of dusk. What if something *is* in here with me?

My brothers loved the tales about monsters of the mountain, creatures miners only referred to as Those Who Dwell Within. Papa told me Those Who Dwell Within were just monsters in a story, one that mothers told their children to keep them from wandering into the tunnels while the men worked.

My brothers insisted they were real. I heard the miners in the village talk. One man claimed they had leathery white skin, while another said they had silver eyes the size of saucers. Some said they crawled on all fours; others said they moved as if swimming through the air.

I shiver into my coat. It's been so long since fairy-tale monsters were something to be afraid of. I'd been too consumed with the real monsters of Storm Hounds and the Czar. Now, in the midst of this mountain, I'm afraid of fairy tales once again.

A chill runs up my spine and I hunch. I root through my pack until I find a flint and steel among the lanterns Ivan insisted we all carry in case we got separated. I gather them with shaking hands. The flint clicks and sparks against the steel, but the wick of the candle doesn't catch.

A clatter comes from somewhere deeper in the mines, echoing off the rocky walls. I snap my head up and peer into the gloom, my heart jumping at every vague silhouette. I strike the flint again and this time a flame springs to life on the wick and a pool of light slowly blooms around me.

I try to remember the mines as best I can. The handful of times Papa had allowed me inside was so long ago, it's as if another person lived through those memories. I have vague glimpses of the time I got lost, wandering through the caverns until at last I stumbled into my father. I don't remember how I got there or why I'd left him in the first place, no matter how hard I try.

It won't help me now.

I need a place to stay, somewhere safe. My mind latches onto the supervisor's office and a few cabins strung throughout the tunnels. Many workers couldn't return to Ludminka after their shifts, too deep in the mines to make it back out, so they erected tiny caches of goods and pallets to keep them safe. They are as good a place as any to stay.

I make my way farther down the path. My lantern throws odd shapes on the wet walls around me. The rock seems to almost bead, as if it got too hot and began to melt. The ceiling varies in shape, sometimes smooth, other times jagged with deep, dark recesses. I try to avoid looking up. It reminds me of how many miners never made it home. These stone walls would've been the last things they ever saw.

Finally, the path levels out and the walls grow apart until I am standing in a massive hollow. The light trickles up the walls to illuminate the barren ceiling thirty feet above.

The first cache.

My father used to talk about this place often. When lovite was first discovered, this room had been full from floor to ceiling with it. The miners had hacked at the walls, digging deeper until the vein ran dry, leaving nothing but the hollow around me.

I lift the lantern a little higher as I make my way out. The ground slopes dangerously down until it empties into a dark, cavernous hole, the stone around it smooth.

The pits.

Only so much lovite was easily accessible. Some lay far above in the reaches of the mountain, but most lay deeper under the earth. A mine shaft was the only way to reach the rest of it and keep the flow of lovite consistent. Two large pits were dug straight into Knnot's heart. I remember Papa had said the men liked to joke they were the pits to the under-world itself, but he stopped after I crawled into my parents' bed, claiming I'd dreamed of demons there.

The twin shafts are outfitted with a pulley and one wide platform each. Two large cranes sit in the narrow strip of rock between them, the pulleys larger than a wagon wheel dangling overhead. When the mine was worked, two men would turn the crank on the platform to lower it into the shaft. The creak-ing, rattling chain always gave me goose bumps.

The supervisor's cabin lies just to my left, its window facing out toward the cranes and the platforms. It would've been easy to see all the men coming and going from its slightly raised vantage point.

I pick my way forward. One misstep could send me skidding down the sides and straight to the lip of the pit. Too many had died that way. Someone eventually attempted to hammer in large timbers to keep people from tripping into the pits, but it didn't save everyone. I follow the rotting logs to the front of the supervisor's house.

It's a small hut with two windows on either side of the door, one for each pit. A large box full of tiny slots sits on the wall. Men would place their identity cards inside to let the supervisors know who was working that week and who didn't come back. I pull my candle from my lantern and light the two sconces on either side of the door, desperate for more light. The oil surprisingly blazes to life.

I shove the door with my shoulder until the wood gives way. The cabin doesn't hold much. A small bed sits in the left corner, a desk full of papers at its foot. A large hearth with an empty pot graces the back wall. I release the tension in my shoulders as I realize there isn't a frozen corpse in here, too.

I toss my bedroll on top of the bed, then I lock the door and make sure each of the windows is latched tight. Seems silly after I do it, but it makes me feel safer. I snuggle under the furs, the familiar scent washing over me as I bury my nose into them. I keep my hat on and my scarf tied around my neck. Knnot lacks wind, but damp cold seeps from the stone and chills me as surely as a night outdoors would.

I try to adjust to the silence. Not a single sound stirs except my own breathing. Sleep is hard to catch. I drift between waking and dreaming for far too long, my body jolting at every imagined sound. Finally, I drift off.

At first, I think I'm imagining the knocking. My eyelids are too heavy to open, and I'm sure the noise is just part of some strange dream. Then, the knock comes again, louder. My eyes fly open. I lie as still as possible, my heart pounding in my ears.

Visions flash before my eyes of Those Who Dwell Within. A thin, white-skinned monster with large eyes rapping at my door as saliva pours from its mouth. Just waiting for one tasty morsel after ten years without food.

I throw back my furs and grab my blade from the utility belt above my head. I spin to face the door, ready to fight. I creep forward to peek out the window. The light in the sconces has burned low, only illuminating a small area before the door. The path lies empty. Even the dim perimeter holds nothing but shadow.

I suck in a deep breath and unlock the door, slowly trying the handle. It gives easily and the door swings open, the hinges squeaking slightly. My entire body stills. On the path right before the door sits a set of footprints. Large, and strangely human-looking, but with small depressions above the toes like claws. A hard shiver runs up my body. The door bumps against my heels and my legs tingle with the urge to run. Long gouge marks crisscross the front, forming a strange sort of triangle.

Someone or something was here.

The tunnels around me begin to vibrate; the noise rattles between my ears, and I slap my hands over them. It's just like what I felt before Ludminka froze. I scream against the noise and it stops, almost as though I commanded it to.

The hairs on my arms start to rise as a thrum echoes through the caverns, and plumes of dust burst from the pits. The noise rattles through my body as I scream again. It's lost in the cacophony inside the cave. I sprint toward the exit. My heart beats in my ears and bangs against my chest.

The thrum sounds again behind me, and I don't look back.

Something evil lurks in the depths of Knnot.

And I woke it up.

# EIGHTEEN

BY THE TIME I REACH the village streets, I can't feel my legs, and my cheeks burn from wind rash. In my hurry to get out, I'd left everything but my blades behind. The scar at my wrist sears in a blind flash of pain as it touches the rough wool of my tunic. I wince and look down. The edges of it are bright red and raw, as if I'd just burned it. I scoop up fresh snow and press it to my wrist.

It's not hard to see where the others went. They abandoned all thought of covering their tracks as soon as we hit the village.

I turn over the events as I follow the churned snow back toward the village square. How am I supposed to report it to the others? Even if they do believe me, I can guarantee Ivan will still force us all inside.

My hands tremble as I reach the inn doors and nudge them open, afraid to see a common room full of frozen people, but only a single barkeep stands behind the oiled bar, forever drying a silver mug. The others left behind yet another trail. A fire dies in the hearth to my left, a cast-iron skillet of fat beside it. My stomach grumbles and I go to the food bag, digging around until I find dried meat.

"Couldn't stay away?" a voice asks from behind me.

I spin and see Alik. He straightens from where he was slouched against the doorframe.

"What happened?" he asks.

I ignore the question and race toward him, flinging my arms around his neck. I no longer care about our fight or the strange distance between us. I need someone now, and the only person I want is him.

"Val?"

My body still trembles, whether from fear or cold, I'm not sure. He doesn't hesitate in bringing his arms around me, almost as if he'd wanted an excuse to hold me.

I inhale his familiar scent and allow it to wash over me. I'm safe. Here, in his arms, I finally feel safe.

"I'm scared, Alik."

My voice comes out small and quiet.

"Of what?"

"Of . . . everything." My voice breaks. "Ever since we left Oleg, I've had these horrible dreams. I'm always here, in

Knnot, and something pulls me in deeper and deeper. Voices whisper to me. They promise help and safety, and I follow them. I always do. I thought they were just stupid dreams, but just now . . ."

I open my mouth to try and tell my story, but nothing comes out. I shake my head into the hollow of his throat. He seems to understand. He untangles himself and leads me to the fire, flinging his coat over my shoulders as we go. He helps me settle at one of the tables and stokes the embers. As they begin to blaze, I finally find my words. I tell him about the hut beside the pits, the knocks, the vibrations, and dark plumes of dust exploding from below.

"Are your dreams the reason you wake up in the middle of the night?" he asks.

"Yes," I whisper.

"Why did you never tell me?"

Tension hovers in the air between us. The words beg to tumble from my mouth, but part of me fears he'll think I'm irrational. The horrible idea scrawling through my mind sounds wild even to my own ears. How would this new Alik react to it? Before, I'd been able to guess his reaction long before I told him anything, almost able to act out both our parts in the conversation. I don't know anymore.

But I want to.

"It was like Knnot was calling to me. Like it wanted me back here. Now I'm afraid I was the one thing it was missing.

Maybe it's angry I got away that day when no one else did. What if by coming here I've unleashed something worse than the ice or the plague?"

"Then we should leave," he says. "We should run from Strana and never look back. There is an entire world out there, places where people don't know the meaning of the word *malozla*. We could find somewhere warm, maybe next to the ocean. You always said you'd love to swim in it one day."

I bite my lip as Alik's dream flows through me. Us, happy and safe beneath the trees, ocean waves crashing somewhere nearby. Perhaps we'd have a small cottage with a wide garden and chickens clucking happily after insects in the grass. We could start a different life and put everything in Strana far behind us. Just him and me.

The dream fades as reality crashes back on me. If I leave, there will be no one to save Luiza. I wanted enough lovite to ensure her safety, and now it's within my grasp. My body aches to say yes, the word tastes crisp on my lips, but I can't. I can't leave Luiza to the mercy of the Czar. Not after all the years she spent raising me.

My decision must show plainly on my face, because Alik's lips firm.

"You won't go."

"Alik, I can't—"

"Why?" he asks as he shoots to his feet, throwing his arms up. "Why do you want to stay in this miserable place with nothing but bad memories? Why do you keep suffering when you don't have to?"

"I can't leave Luiza," I say.

"You're refusing to save yourself so you can help her? Luiza is more than capable of getting out of any situation she finds herself in. She doesn't need you."

"She does," I grind out, my frustration turning into hot pricks in my eyes.

"She *doesn't*, Val. If you really are so afraid of losing me, then why do you continue to help her? She left me behind. I can't go back. She made that very clear. I will not help her. Not when she cast me aside like a piece of trash."

My chest aches with unshed tears. It hurts that Luiza refused to tell me about Alik, but it's worse that she left him behind. I imagine Alik still in bed, the wound on his chest slowly healing. Luiza standing over him with lips curled in displeasure, telling him to never contact the guild again. He must've felt so alone and lost. Then I never responded to his letters, leaving him even more isolated.

Despite it all, I can't stop myself from loving her. I hate what she did to Alik, more than almost anything, but she did so much for me when I had no one. I don't want to see her die. The Czar destroyed so many lives. I can't let him destroy Luiza's.

"She told me the Bright God's champion had the power to free the Zladonians, overthrow the Czar. I can't ignore that,

Alik. Not if I have the chance to do some real good for once. We spent years helping the Czar keep his power; now we can help cast him down."

"How do you even know that is true? She lied to you about me; what would stop her lying about the Bright God's champion, too?"

"Because—" I snap, but realize I have no retort.

Luiza lied. She lied about the one thing she knew I wanted. She let me suffer through heartbreak, all the while knowing Alik was alive. But it's not like Ivan is any better. I change tactics.

"Ivan is working with the guild."

"No, Val. Stop."

"No. I saw him outside the Storm Hound encampment with one of them. How do I know you aren't the one lying to me?"

Hurt flashes across Alik's face. The same I felt when he accused me of lying.

"I'm not. And he isn't," he says.

"He is. Did you know? Did you help him ruin Luiza's mission and get her caught?"

Alik's eyes go wide. "How could you think I'd do that? How could I have done anything? I couldn't even leave a bed for months! After Luiza saw me, I never spoke to her again. I didn't want to."

"Did you tell Ivan her weaknesses so he could do it? Just because you didn't personally talk to her doesn't mean you didn't have the opportunity to do it," I shoot back.

"You are being ridiculous. You've been nothing but suspicious since you came to Oleg."

"And you've given me reason *not* to be? You lied to me for weeks! And hated me for something you assumed I did. Why shouldn't I be suspicious of you, when you've got a huge motive to hurt Luiza, when you believed I was capable of leaving you to suffer with Ivan in the place you almost died?"

He stares at me, wounded.

"I never hated you, Valeria." His voice is soft. "I could never hate you."

The air in the room stills around us as if it has become too heavy. I blink at Alik as his cheeks redden.

"That wasn't what I felt at all when I thought you refused to come. The only reason I fought so hard to live after Ivan saved me was for you. If I didn't have you, then what was the point? Why had I even tried?"

My breath hitches, and I swallow hard. Being without Alik had brought into stark clarity that he meant more to me than just a partner, than just a friend. I've been too afraid to tell him. I didn't want to break whatever we had if he never felt the same way. But what if he does?

"That . . . that's not what you made it seem like in the cave."

"I was stupid and angry," he says. "I wanted to make you mad, try to trick you into telling me the truth if you had been lying. I never should've done that."

"I never would abandon you like that."

"I know. And even if I didn't, you proved it to me more times than I want to count on our way here." He stills and looks up, his face breaking as he meets my eyes. "I am sorry, Valeria."

The sorrow in his voice is my undoing. I cross the distance between us, no longer wanting to fight. Tears gather on Alik's reddened cheeks. I brush them away with a gentle hand, and he presses his face against my palm.

"I've been afraid since the day I woke up that you wouldn't look at me like you used to," he whispers into the space between us. "I can't stop seeing everything I've lost."

"You got those scars and lost your eye to save me. I will never forget that. When I look at you, I don't see something missing. I see how much you were willing to give up to make sure I survived."

My legs tremble. Something more bubbles into my mind and the world shifts around me. I think I've always known how much I care for Alik, but I can't force the words out.

*I love you. I will always love you.*

It's all I can think. Fear seizes my throat and refuses to release my voice.

He opens his eye and his gaze travels first to my eyes, then down to my lips. Something changes in the space between us. His hand comes up to my waist, the warmth of it pulsing through my tunic.

I take in a shuddering breath as he pulls me closer, his

fingers digging ever so slightly into my hip. He's so close his warm breath scrawls across my mouth. I swallow as my eyes flick down and study his lips. He leans forward a bit more.

This time I know I'm not imagining it. I let my eyes drift closed and allow my body to meld into his. His nose brushes against mine, asking a silent question. One I more than want to answer.

A loud thud rings through the room. We spring apart as the door swings open and Serafima strolls inside. Her eyebrows arch when she sees me, and I hope the inferno blazing across my cheeks isn't as obvious as I think it is.

She pulls off her boots and drops them on the floor before she sits beside the hearth. Serafima cradles her head in her hands and shivers. I'd feel sorry if it were anyone but her.

"You all right?" Alik asks.

She shakes her head. "I was up before dawn to check every single road out of the village for my father's cart. He isn't here."

"I thought he had to be here." The bitter words fall from my lips.

Serafima looks up, but her face lacks the anger and hate I'd grown so accustomed to.

"Apparently, I was wrong. He really must've run away. He must've left before he was supposed to and made it out of the village alive." Her eyes don't leave mine. "I suppose I owe you an apology. I have evidence now that he left our family of his own accord."

I study the wooden floor, not sure of what to say.

"I'm sorry your father isn't here," Alik says, and I'm grateful I don't have to talk.

"I've always hoped he was. At least then he didn't abandon me. But I should've known. I'm never that lucky." Serafima takes a deep breath and raises her head; her eyes are ringed in red. "I've shed my tears for him. It'll be easier to pretend he never existed. After we get the lovite, my mother will never have to work again."

"Your mother?" I ask, surprise curling through me. "You've never mentioned her."

Serafima shrugs. "There's not much to say. After my father died—or, I guess, left—we couldn't afford to stay in Rurik. We moved to the outskirts, and she apprenticed as a seamstress to help us get by. She went blind when I was fifteen summers, and I started navigating for trading caravans after that. I haven't seen her in years."

She swallows hard. Despite myself and all she's said, a pang of empathy laces through me.

"Hopefully, you'll see her soon," I say quietly.

"Hopefully," she says.

It isn't long before Chinua and Ivan wake. Neither of them asks why I'm there; they huddle against the warmth of the hearth with bleary eyes. Chinua quickly makes some porridge and serves everyone. Ivan studies me as he accepts a bowl. He leans against one of the support beams and takes a large bite before speaking.

"Nice to see you again, Valeria."

"I figured you'd want me to guide you to the lovite stores," I say. I will not let him know I got scared on my own and came running back to them. I will not give him the satisfaction. My eyes cut to him, and the smug smile on his lips ignites the quiet anger burning in my gut. "Unless, of course, you have another thief who feels up to it?"

Silence hangs in the air between us for a long moment. I study his posture, trying to decide if he understands the double meaning of my words. I almost spit out the entire story of his meeting with the guild member outside the Storm Hound encampment, but it won't matter after today. My bargain with Ivan ends as soon as I show him the vaults.

"I think you'll do just fine," Ivan says.

I grit my teeth against his cool voice. Once every bowl has been scraped clean and washed, the others gather their scattered things. I follow Alik into the small room where he'd slept last night. The bedclothes lie rumpled against the foot of the bed, and an extra tunic hangs over the small chair in the room. I gather up his things and hand them to him, grabbing his hands before he can move away.

"I will leave with you."

His eye goes wide. "You will?"

I have no reason to stay in Strana. Not when Luiza would use me to get what she needed. She never claimed to not be manipulative, but I never thought she was cruel.

"Let's get all the lovite we can carry and never look back."

# NINETEEN

THE NIGHT'S CHILL STILL CLINGS to the air as we hike, and I shiver as cold air cuts through my thin woolen tunic, cursing my stupidity at leaving my coat behind. Fear dogs my every step and I resist the urge to grab Alik's hand the closer we get to the yawning mouth of Knnot. At last, we step inside the mine. It looks no different from when I left, but it feels wrong.

It takes a few moments of fumbling before someone finally lights a couple of lanterns. The light seems brighter than when I was here last night.

Instead of taking the path toward the pits, I take the left one. It's more gradual, a natural cave as opposed to the other one hewn by human hands.

The cavern twists and turns, stalagmites and stalactites meeting to form long pillars almost like jagged teeth. I slip between them, following the path I remember taking with my father long ago. The path isn't wide and the miners tried hard to cover their tracks to deter thieves, using only the natural bends in the cave as a route.

Small paths lead off into dark holes, some of which I know lead to steep drop-offs or endlessly twist until they dead-end. More than once someone got lost and wandered out days later, half-mad and starving.

Finally, we reach a rounded hall. Skilled laborers had crafted the smooth walls and hung the massive metal doors to hide stores of lovite. Rusted locks still guard the treasure within. I gesture to the room.

"Have your pick. They should all be full."

Papa often spoke of the vaults and how they soon would be too full. Caravans from Rurik came only every other month, even less frequently in the winter when sleighs had to be used. Knnot had enough lovite to last years. It's why the Czar had always been so desperate to claim it.

I let the others crowd in around me. Alik stays by my side as Chinua pulls two gelatinous blobs out of her sack and places them on either side of the door. With a wide grin, she lights them. I stumble back. What is she thinking? An explosion could bring the entire mountain down on us. All Chinua does is turn her head, covering her ears in the process. With a soft bang, the metal of the door crumples, keeping the rest of the wall in place.

"What was that?" I ask, almost afraid of a second explosion.

"*Tersh-ek*. It's an Adamanian explosive that will only deto-nate things within its parameter. Neat, right?"

"More than neat," I say. "I've never seen anything like it."

Serafima grabs the remnants of the door and yanks them off. A gasp rings out and, despite myself, I creep closer. The room is a little smaller than the one we stand in, and just as tall. Lovite chunks stand at the ready, filling the room from floor to ceiling. They gleam in the lantern light, and Serafima picks one up and flicks it. A muted note rings through the caverns, raising the hairs on my neck.

Silence follows before Ivan breaks into a laugh. It echoes off the cavern walls, and he kisses the pendant around his neck.

"We did it," he says between chuckles. "We really did it."

Even I can't deny it's a miracle. No one has been able to stand within Knnot for nearly a decade without succumbing to the plague. Here we are now, standing unchanged before the largest hoard of lovite anyone in Strana has seen in years. We could be kings if we chose to stay in Strana.

But I have no wish to.

I back away from the room and eye the passage we came down. Nothing stirs. Alik goes to Ivan, who holds his arm open for a hug. He slaps Alik's thin back a few times before releasing him to pull lovite from the room, tears of happiness trailing down his weathered face. Alik slowly picks his way toward me.

"We should leave now," he says.

"Don't we need lovite?"

Alik pats a heavy bag hanging at his waist. Years of training tell me it's full enough to get us a couple of steeds and a good distance from Knnot. As the others begin to laugh and toss lovite back and forth between each other, I nod. Now, when they are distracted, is the best time to leave. I'm done with this place for good.

Alik takes my hand, sending soothing heat up my arm, assuring me I'm making the right decision. No one glances at us as we quickly fall into the shadows and hug the side of the wall. The joyful whoops from the others slowly fade as we make our way back up the tunnels. For the briefest moment, I'm upset we left Chinua behind. She is one of the most loyal and trustworthy people on this trip. I know she'll be hurt I didn't say goodbye, but it is for the best. At least, it is for Alik and me.

We skirt the overturned carts, and the bright arch of daylight shooting in from the mouth of the mine finally becomes visible. Excitement courses through my veins.

"We're really going to run away from all of this?" I ask. The relief at being able to choose where I go and who I see hangs on an edge. It seems close enough to grasp.

Alik gives my hand a firm squeeze.

"I promise. We will find somewhere safe," he says with a smile.

I squeeze his hand back. I can picture the rest of our lives now. Golden sunlight filtering down on both of our white heads. We won't wear hats because we finally don't have to. It's beautiful.

We round the slight bend to the outside world. I blink against the bright snow and sun, the blue sky seeming to stretch endlessly above. I can't help but grin as the wind brushes against my cheeks. For the first time since the day Ludminka fell, I truly feel free.

Suddenly, a thwack rings through the brisk air and something buries itself in the snow at my feet. It takes me a moment to realize what it is, and my blood runs cold.

A bolt from a crossbow.

I snap my head up, but Alik pulls me back into the caves.

"What is it?" I ask as another shot echoes off the mountain.

"Storm Hounds," Alik breathes.

I glance over my shoulder, and I count a dozen Storm Hounds dotting the open area between their frozen comrades. We dive for cover behind an overturned cart as they begin to pepper us with crossbow bolts.

"Do you think they tracked us all the way here?" I ask.

Alik nods. "They must have. We rushed to get here, thinking they wouldn't cross into Zladonia. Apparently, we were wrong."

My stomach sinks as I remember all the tracks we made through the village without covering them. The fire we didn't bother hiding the smoke of or sweeping away. We led them to us. Stupid, foolish me, forever believing Alik and I could get away. Strana would never let us escape.

"But how did they reach Ludminka? The plague should've stopped them."

"I have no idea," Alik says.

The Storm Hounds advance. Light gleams off something clutched in their hands, almost as if pieces of the sun were taken from the sky and placed on earth. I squint against the brightness and my stomach turns.

The archers stand behind men with large shields made of pure, glistening lovite. It couldn't be anything else. The bulk of the shield shines pure white, even brighter than the snow. Veins run like small rivers through the surface, but instead of being the cobalt of harvested lovite, they burn a dull copper.

Just like Ivan's pendant.

A rumble sounds from somewhere deep inside Knnot. The rocks overhead grind and groan. Alik pulls me to his chest as a roar of wind echoes from inside the mountain to blast out of its mouth. It numbs me in seconds, so bitingly cold my teeth throb with pain.

My lashes frost over with gleaming crystals, and I watch as the Storm Hounds lift their shields against the wind. It breaks upon them like a wave and their shields sizzle, steam rising from them in thick plumes. The icy breath of wind dies immediately, and Alik and I shudder together.

"What just happened?" he asks.

I shake my head, too focused on the slowly approaching Storm Hounds. Somehow, they'd come prepared to withstand the strange magic that seemed to hold the entire region in its grasp. And they'd done it all with the same material Ivan wears at his neck.

All Ivan's actions come rushing back to me. Him speaking to the fortune-teller, the pendant around his neck he was so certain of, the guild member he consorted with outside the Storm Hound encampment. My breathing starts to speed up as anger chases away the painful cold of the cave.

He must've turned all his information over to the guild. He told them about the pendant the fortune-teller gave him, maybe for his family, maybe for money. It doesn't matter. It gave the guild what they needed to overthrow Luiza. Leverage and money. If Ivan could reach Knnot and open the stores, the guild would operate the lovite mines, not Luiza and the Bright God's champion. The Czar would maintain power, and the Thieves Guild would continue to flourish as it has for a decade.

I break away from the cart and sprint down the passages. Ivan took away our chance at happiness. The Storm Hounds will rush the passages and kill us all without a second thought. Every bit of joy I had crumbles to the dirt and will be ground by the heels of their boots.

I will make Ivan pay for taking away my freedom.

"Val!" Alik calls out behind me, unable to keep up. It

doesn't matter. I won't listen to him defend Ivan.

I almost run straight into Serafima as I break into the large vault. The others have already pulled lovite into the center of the room. Chinua attempts to pick the lock on the second vault as Ivan counts the lovite they've already pulled out. I push Serafima away and head straight for Ivan, who looks over at me just as I pull back my hand and punch him as hard as I can in the nose.

"How could you?" I hiss.

I raise my fist to hit him again, but Serafima catches it.

"Let go of me!"

I try to tug my hand away, but her grip only tightens. She stands a good head taller than me, her broad shoulders and muscled arms far more powerful than my own. More heat floods my system. I tug again, harder. Pain wrenches through my shoulder, but Serafima's grip gives, and I stumble backward. Everyone stares at me. Blood drips down Ivan's face and I'm viciously glad.

"What is wrong with you?" Serafima's voice is a mixture of exasperation and anger.

I whip my finger in Ivan's direction. "He has just doomed us all."

Alik stumbles into the room. He clutches his side and leans against the rock wall, catching his breath. The others look over at him.

"Idiot," Ivan snaps. "I guarantee I have no idea what you're talking about or why you punched me."

"Is that right?" I clutch my fists tighter and relish the feeling of my nails biting into my palms. "What did you tell the Storm Hounds the night you crawled to them for safety? Better yet, what have you told the guild? I saw you talking with one of them just outside the Storm Hound encampment. Have you been working with someone all along? Do they want to overthrow Luiza and take the guild for themselves once they have enough money? Are they the reason you saved Alik? To give you an in to the guild and build your mutiny?"

Ivan's face goes slack with each accusation. "The day I saved Alik I risked everything. I didn't care about lovite. I just cared about saving a life."

"I'll believe that when Strana turns into nothing but sand and dunes," I spit.

"You hateful, stupid girl." Ivan's voice rises. "I said nothing to the Storm Hounds. I told them Sera would die in the cold and gave them all the gold I had left. They asked me for nothing more. As to the guild, they contacted *me*."

"Why would the guild contact you?" I snap.

Ivan's lips thin. "They did want to use me to get into the mines. That's all I know. I was never told more than that."

"And you're telling me that saving Alik despite his connection to the guild was just some sort of coincidence?"

"That's enough," Alik says. "I trust Ivan. He risked his own family to save me that day. No amount of riches would make a man do that. You and I know that better than anyone."

"They have his family. I heard the guildling say it herself," I retort.

"They have them because of Alik," Ivan cuts in, his voice harsh. "I harbored a *malozla*. It's punishable by death. My family would be disgraced, my wife would never be able to marry again. My boy could never hold a job. The guild offered to hide them and alter my papers to say I had died in exchange for me coming here. If I'm dead, they can lead a normal life."

"How did you expect to keep them safe once the entire country learned the name of the man who reopened Knnot?" I ask.

"It wouldn't matter then. I'd have enough money to buy us safety anywhere. All I need is the lovite."

"This is touching. Truly," Serafima cuts in. "But we need to move if we are going to avoid the Storm Hounds. They could come in here any minute."

"Is there any other way out?" Ivan asks.

Everyone's eyes swing to me.

"Not that I know of," I say.

"Who builds something and decides there should only be one way in and out?" Chinua asks.

"Someone trying to protect the most valuable resource in the world," I snap. I press my hands to my face. "I said I never heard of someone talking about it. It doesn't mean there aren't any exits down there. There has to be something, right? In case of a cave-in?"

Alik steps forward. "I refuse to turn myself over to the Storm Hounds without trying."

The others nod their agreement. We watch as everyone clears up and stuffs as much lovite as they can carry into their bags and pockets. If we do manage to get out, they will have more than enough to pay for an entire army to take back the mountain.

Once it seems everyone is ready, I take the lead. I try not to think of the footprints I saw earlier as I wind my way back through the passages toward the front of the mine. It's straight toward the Storm Hounds, but it is the only way to the pits. We have to chance it.

We'll either make it, or die fighting our way past Storm Hounds. Either way, I'm not going without baring my fangs.

# TWENTY

I LEAD US BACK UP the path, going slower and slower until we crawl forward. I don't know what I expect. Maybe for the place to be swarming with Storm Hounds, maybe barricades already erected and archers manning them, ready to pick us off one by one.

Instead, the mouth lies empty. I put my hand up and the others stop behind me. I creep forward until my shoulder bumps the lip of the mine. I chance a glance around it. The Storm Hounds are no closer to the entrance. They mill about the frozen Storm Hounds, studying them, eyeing the entrance, but never coming a step closer.

They've dug their shields into the earth in front of them, like a wall of lovite pushing back the shadows of Knnot. I focus on the veins of amber running through the stark white metal of the shields. Ivan had claimed his pendant was blessed by the hands of the Bright God's champion. It doesn't make sense. How had the Storm Hounds received the same? I frown and head back toward the others.

"They haven't moved," I say.

"At all?" Alik lifts an eyebrow. "They could've cornered us if they rushed in."

"Maybe they figure we don't have enough supplies to last," I say.

"They're right." Chinua shrugs the light food bag slung across her shoulders.

I shake my head. "No. Storm Hounds never wait."

"They're afraid," Ivan says. "No one wants to step inside."

"I don't want to rely on superstition. Eventually, they will get tired of waiting and try to flush us out," I say.

Ivan gestures before him. "Lead the way."

We cling to the shadows, crouching behind overturned carts and fallen beams. We make it into the dark safety of the right-hand passage without being spotted. I let out a long, low breath, which echoes down the corridor as I light a lantern and shuffle through.

The pits lie within view. I gesture for the others to hurry onto the platform while I dart into the supervisor's cabin. My eyes stray to the door, expecting to see the strange etched scratches, but it's clean.

Nothing makes sense.

I shove my coat and sleeping roll back into my canvas bag, then rush out the door and hurry toward the others, who all huddle together on the platform. I toss my bag to Alik and jump on. The wood creaks beneath my feet and sways with my momentum. I take my place beside the pulley.

"Ready?"

"We . . . are going down there?" Chinua asks, her eyes never leaving the mouth of the shaft. It's impossibly black, and even I'm not certain of how far down it goes.

"It's our best chance at safety," I say.

"What's down there?" asks Serafima.

I shrug. "Lovite? More mining equipment, another supply hut. Beyond that, I have no idea."

Memories of my night in the supervisor's cabin curl through my mind. More may lie below besides equipment left behind by miners rushing to get home. Another set of monsters may wait in the darkness, desperate for a bite of mortals. I meet Alik's eyes and raise an eyebrow. He gives me a slow nod. I lick my lips, my hand still resting on the lever.

"When I was here last night I . . . heard something."

"What sort of 'something'?" Serafima says.

"It sounded as though someone was knocking on the door. Then, the mountain shuddered." I know how ridiculous the words sound, but I choke them out anyway. "Dust blew from these pits. I don't know what caused it."

Ivan pulls out his pendant and lets it rest on top of his shirt.

"I don't know what lies within this mountain, but we've got no other choice. Not unless you want to try and face the Storm Hounds head-on. We don't have the weapons or the numbers for that. We're going to have to hope that whatever magic in this pendant let us pass into Ludminka will help us down there too."

"We're just going to wander aimlessly down there and hope we find our way out?" Serafima's voice thins.

"Do you know what the Storm Hounds will do if they catch us?" Alik says. When no one responds, he continues. "Ivan will be hanged for deserting, Valeria and I will go to a *tyur'ma*, or worse, be made to mine the lovite in here until we die. Do you think your fates will be any better? Chinua, you'll go back to the Khan. Serafima, perhaps you won't die, but you'll never find work in Strana again. Not if they catch you with us."

Alik's right. None of us is safe. We won't return to a normal life after this. Not if the Storm Hounds catch us. Chinua is the first to take a shuddering breath.

"Down into the dark we go, then."

The others nod, their faces pale and tight, and I pull the lever. The gears groan to life, moving slowly at first. With a jolt, the platform begins its descent. The illumination from the dying lanterns I lit falls away and we are swallowed whole by darkness.

Serafima rustles beside me. Two sharp clicks echo around

us and light blooms across the platform. I know I should tell her to conserve the last remaining tinder and oil, but I'm too relieved to see light once more.

Other than long scuffs marking the shaft's walls where the platform scraped against the stone, the ride down is dull, full of deep brown rock and the occasional gleam of lovite dust.

The chains start to rattle, and I reach for Alik. Our hands smack together before intertwining. We both squeeze hard as the platform gives a nasty drop. With a final wrench and a high-pitched squeal, the platform breaks into an open cavern. I release Alik and test the ledge. It feels secure enough. I hop off and gesture to the others.

They disembark much faster than they got on, no one wanting to remain on the groaning wooden planks any longer than necessary. We huddle close together, none of us daring to put a toe beyond Serafima's small pool of light.

"Right," Ivan says. "We should probably map out the area, get a feel for the place, and find somewhere to establish a base camp."

Alik nods. "Now that sounds like the colonel I'm used to."

"Colonel?" I ask, Chinua's voice echoing with mine.

Ivan doesn't acknowledge us.

The armies of Strana are few and far between now. Most battalions of the common militia hold no rank higher than captain. A nasty feeling crawls into my stomach. I was willing to believe Ivan when he said he left behind a family and saved

Alik. From the very start he made no play of hiding the fact that he was former military. This entire time I believed him an infantryman who saved the first soul he ever saw close to death. A colonel would've seen hundreds of deaths because there is only one battalion in all of Strana that allows that rank.

And it's the very one we are running from.

I turn to Alik. "He was a colonel? Only the Storm Hounds allow rankings that high."

Alik looks to Ivan, who gives a curt nod. Alik swings his eye back to mine and it begs my forgiveness. "He doesn't work for them anymore."

"He was a Storm Hound," I say quietly. I release him, backing away until I'm in the darkness beyond the light. Even Chinua gives a small gasp of surprise. Serafima does her best to avoid looking at any of us, sealing her guilt in my mind.

"How could you?" I hiss.

"Valeria, just listen to me—" Alik starts.

"Listen? How am I supposed to believe a single thing you say? All this time you've lied to me about him, about how you were saved. And you brought me into this group, let me believe I was safe." I put up my hands as Alik starts toward me and turn to look at Ivan. "The Storm Hounds didn't follow us because they found out about Alik and me. They aren't even following us for the lovite. They came after *you*. You deserted them and walked right into one of their encampments like no one would know who you were? How could someone so stupid manage to make colonel in the Storm Hounds?"

"That encampment was not there the last time I patrolled these roads. There weren't even whispers of it. I had no choice. I had to get Sera to safety."

"You had a choice!" I shout. "You could've stayed with Alik and me. You could've chosen not to endanger this mission and the very boy you claimed to have saved because your moral compass suddenly decided it was pointed in the wrong direction."

"You don't know the things I've seen. I couldn't watch them do it to Alik. I couldn't go through it again."

"How many times did you watch it without lifting a finger, Ivan? One life doesn't erase all the things you've done before," I say with hollow coldness.

Ivan's face drops. He studies his boots before he raises his face back to mine. He looks older than I've ever seen him—his beard a tangle of gray and brown, his weathered face beaten down and broken.

"I know I'm not a good man. I never said I was. The things I watched happen are beyond inexcusable." Silence follows his words as I try to control my breathing. "I'm trying to fix it now."

I chew on the inside of my cheek. There's no way to tell if Ivan is being honest. And I don't care. I can't trust him. Once a Storm Hound, always a Storm Hound. A recruit can't cut ties to something he's been raised to do since he was fifteen years old. He put us in danger and stole any chance of Alik and me making it to safety the moment he stepped into the encampment. He lied about the guild, lied about who he was. And Alik helped him do it.

"You both disgust me," I spit.

I stomp back into the light only long enough to snatch a lantern. Anger gives me the courage I need to push forward. I leave the others to trail behind me. The lantern does little to brighten the massive cavern we stand in. A few lanterns line the walls, and though there's not a lot of oil left, it's enough to keep the cavern lit for at least a couple of weeks, if we burn one at a time. I light the lantern closest to the middle and leave the cavern with the platform behind. After a long moment, the others follow, their steps echoing off the walls.

The fear I feel for the darkened corridors does nothing to touch the white-hot anger burning a hole in my chest. Alik, *my* Alik, hid with a Storm Hound this entire time. The very people who likely killed his mothers and hunted us for years.

Out of it all, the thing that makes me the angriest is the fact that he lied to me about it. He betrayed me on the very principle I thought we both agreed on. I want to know why, but I refuse to turn around and argue with him. I need time to think.

I trudge down the corridors, the stone and wooden beams blurring together so much that I can hardly tell one passage from another.

I know Alik tries to catch up at least twice. His uneven gait is even more noticeable in the silence of Knnot. Both times I push myself into a pace I know he can't match.

I turn, expecting yet another rock corridor, but the air seems to shift as soon as I step inside, as if something titanic moves in front of me. I pull up short, suddenly terrified to go a step farther. The others stop behind me.

"What is it?" Chinua whispers, but in the silence she might as well have shouted.

"The air. Can't you feel it?" I say.

I suck in a deep breath and inch forward. Even the darkness is thicker here, as if my light is nothing more than a small piece of kindling in a moonless night. My knees bang into something solid. With a yelp, I look down. It's nothing more than a low stone wall with a shallow channel running the length of it, leading deeper into the darkness. The crevice of the channel seems wet. I touch my fingers to it, then bring them to my nose.

"Oil," I say.

I remove the candle from the lantern and tip it into the oil, springing back as the wall blazes to life. The fire curls around stone hewn steps. I'm not sure how many times it circles the cavern. Four, maybe five, if my eyes aren't playing tricks on me. The shadows thrown by the flame lap against the far wall, bringing to life a large mural.

A long skeleton painted in blues extends the length of the

wall, its eyeless sockets staring up into a star-daubed sky. Tiny dark figures with weapons prod at the skeleton's feet, a bright ray of sunshine illuminating them, very careful to avoid the toes of the giant skeleton. Alik gasps behind me.

"The Fall of the Pale God," I whisper. "It was my matta's favorite tale. After the Brother Gods grew jealous and spiteful of one another, they started a war that lasted one hundred years. They ripped down mountains and churned plains into valleys in their anger. They fought for so long, they forgot about the world they worked so hard to cultivate. They ruined the very human civilization they helped create. At long last, the Bright God threw down his brother and bade his followers to bury him beneath the earth. His believers didn't know he, too, was injured. The drops of his blood as he hurried from his brother's fallen body are said to still burn today, as hot and red as the day they fell."

"What is it doing all the way down here?" Chinua asks.

I shrug, but the question plagues me.

"Someone probably got bored," Serafima says.

A wind from below flutters the flame, followed by a soft hissing sound, as if the mountain itself disagrees with Serafima's words. It seems to beckon me to take a closer look. Just one more step.

It's an invitation I refuse.

# TWENTY-ONE

"WE CAN LEAVE THE MURAL room for another day," I say, turning and leaving. "We need to find somewhere defensible to sleep, in case the Storm Hounds find the courage to chase us down here. Or, should I say, Ivan down here."

As we enter a new cavern, I drop my lantern. It sputters for a second, then goes out. It doesn't matter.

I don't need it.

I stare at the ceiling, my mouth falling open. A small gasp comes from beside me. Alik stands at my side, his face studded by the bright blue light from above.

Lovite swirls through the rock in the ceiling, emitting a blue glow. The cobalt veins staining the brilliant white of the stone reflect enough light to brighten the entire cavern. The light dims for a moment before a wave starts from the far side and ripples across the ceiling like the surface of a pond disturbed by a stone. I wish I could reach out and touch it.

Lovite loses the ability to glow as soon as it is harvested. I'd only seen the lovite light once, so long ago it almost feels like a dream.

"It's . . . incredible," Alik says at last.

"It almost seems—" I whisper.

"Alive," we say together.

We look at one another. In the rippling blue light, I can make out each achingly familiar feature. His brows draw up and together and his eye shines bright. In that moment, he's so perfect I almost forget how angry I am.

Almost.

"Val. I'm sorry," he says. "I should've told you. I—"

"You promised you'd never lied to me," I say quietly. "Now you've done it twice."

Genuine hurt flickers across his face as the others stumble into the cavern. I look away, unable to take it. I don't know what is true anymore.

"What is this place?" Chinua asks.

"A part of the mine they never finished harvesting," I say. "At one point, this entire cavern would've been full of lovite from the ground to the ceiling. Now there's only these small veins left."

Serafima runs her hand along a vein still left in the wall. It doesn't glow as brightly as the ones above, but it's enough to make her skin gleam blue. Ivan's face cracks into a wide smile as he takes in the ceiling, but I know he isn't appreciating its beauty, he's measuring its worth.

"Do you know how much is left?" Ivan asks.

"More than anyone could mine in a lifetime."

Ivan looks like he will respond, but I don't give him the chance.

"We will set up camp here," I say.

I busy myself with getting everything together. My muscles ache and my head buzzes with exhaustion. I shake out my limbs as I push all the food into the corner farthest from the entrance.

A pang rushes through me. Everything has changed in a single blink.

I watch Alik as he sets out the furs on the pallets left behind by the miners long ago. He doesn't look up as he fixes the corner of the nearest fur, but I know he can feel my eyes.

I swallow the anger clinging in my throat and grab a couple pieces of dried meat. I settle on the fur beside him and hand the food over without looking up.

"Dinner," I say.

"So little."

"I'm trying to ration it. I don't know how long we will be here."

Alik sighs and massages his leg.

We're silent for a few moments, then Alik starts. "I'm sorry

I hid who Ivan was from you. It was wrong of me."

"How many more secrets are you hiding?"

Alik grimaces, but doesn't get a chance to respond as Chinua joins us, shortly followed by Serafima and Ivan. I pass out rations and watch as each of their faces falls, but no one complains. We eat in silence.

"We should get some rest," I say at last. "We don't know how much time we've got or when the Storm Hounds will make their way down here."

The others murmur their agreement, and we all settle down onto our pallets. I listen as, one by one, the people around me slip into an uneasy sleep. Alik rests somewhere above me, his breathing unsteady.

"Why are you still awake?" I whisper.

"I can't sleep when you're angry with me."

"You seemed to just fine two nights ago in the tent."

"I didn't fall asleep then either. I just didn't know what to say to you," Alik responds.

"It seems you never do anymore." I shift so I can look at him. He lies on his stomach, face turned toward me.

"I'm . . . I'm trying, Val. I really am."

"Why didn't you tell me about Ivan?"

"How could I tell you? Our entire lives we've had to run from the Storm Hounds. If Ivan hadn't saved me, I'd still think they crawled straight up from the palest hell."

"So you didn't tell me because you didn't know *how* to tell me?"

"Yeah," Alik says. "I knew you wouldn't want to help Ivan if I told you."

"Well, you're right about that." A question swells inside of me and tumbles out of my mouth before I can stop it. "What actually happened that day on the pier after I ran?"

Alik is silent for a long moment. "After I was sure you were safe, I just stopped fighting. I knew I was dying. I knew how much blood I'd lost. There was no sense in delaying it anymore. And it was . . . freeing. In that moment, nothing mattered. You were safe; I could stop trying. It could all be over. I heard the commander give the order. All I could make out was a silhouette above me with a sword raised. I closed my eyes. I was ready.

"But the blow never came. I heard metal scraping against metal. I opened my eyes, and the man who was supposed to kill me ran his blade through his partner instead. Then he picked me up and ran. That was Ivan—he saved me."

"You really don't think he saved you as a way to get to the lovite?"

"No. I really don't. He didn't talk about it until months after I was better. He said he saved me because he couldn't take one more life. He couldn't have his child growing up thinking it was okay. Apparently, it was something he'd been considering for a long time."

I prop my head on my hands. The lines of his face are so earnest and open, I believe him despite myself. I stick out my hand and raise my pinkie.

"Don't lie to me ever again," I say.

"Never." He links his finger around mine.

We lift our connected hands to our lips and kiss our fists. It's how we've made promises since we were kids. To break it meant to risk death. At least, that's what he said when we were little.

He holds my gaze for a long moment and a flush creeps along my cheeks. I throw myself back down on my pallet.

"Get some sleep," I say.

With a jolt, I startle awake. I'm not sure how long I've been asleep. The world seems to tilt, almost dreamlike. A deep tug pulls at my middle, and I stumble to my feet, following the pull out of the cavern and down the hall toward the mural room.

I know I should be terrified, but the thought is dim.

The room comes into view, and I pick up my pace. The flames still flicker inside the low wall. The shadows throw odd shapes across the mural, making the skull almost seem alive. The large, wide steps curl downward. A lot of effort went into carving them, and I can't fathom why anyone would do it. Why not install another lift? Why paint the mural? They would've had to paint it before making the stairs. It just doesn't make sense. Everything about this room is unnatural.

*"Valeria,"* a soft voice calls from somewhere deep below me.

I freeze. It sounds like the voices from my dreams. My brain screams at me to run, but my body won't obey. It's like

I've fallen into a snowdrift up to my shoulders. Every twitch takes all my effort to perform.

"*Valeria,*" the voice calls again.

This time, though, it's gentle, more familiar.

"Valeria, come, my little *milaya*. You'll be late for dinner."

A knot forms in my stomach. I know that voice. I've wished for it every single night since I left Ludminka. I know it shouldn't be possible, but it's *her* voice.

"Matta?" I whisper.

The word falls from my lips and I need to see her. She'll wrap her arms around me and, at last, I will feel safe. I take one step forward, then another. I make my way down the stairs, ignoring everything besides the sound of my mother's voice. The stairs level out into an unnaturally straight passage. The low wall with the fire runs down the length. I follow it.

The path seems to last forever, but the sound of my mother's voice continues to call me deeper. It sings an old lullaby, the same one she used to hum when I was sick and she was by my bedside, pushing my hair from my face. My heart aches to hear it again.

The scent of baked goods and sweet carnations curls its way down the passage and beckons me closer. It's what my mother always used to smell like from days spent making bread for the village. Tears gather in my eyes.

I want to see her more than anything in the world.

The path narrows and then ends, a heavy wooden door with a rusty bolt my only reward. It looks almost familiar, but

I can't place why. I press my palm to it. The wood is warm to the touch. Almost as if it has been sitting in the summer sun.

"Valeria, my love, are you coming?" my mother calls.

Her voice is just on the other side of the door. I press my ear to it, humming along as she starts another tune. Part of me knows it can't possibly be her. Still, I can't help but wish it is true. Perhaps the magic of the curse caught their souls, and hers is behind this door. Perhaps, if I just open it, they will all be free.

My hand moves down the smooth surface to the patinaed lock. I curl my fingers around the bolt. All I have to do is pull. I can see her smile as she draws me into her. It is all so close. My arm starts to inch back, the bolt scraping against the plate after years of disuse.

"Val!" Suddenly, a strong hand circles my wrist and my eyes pop open.

I spin to face the person behind me, my heart fluttering in my ears, drowning out the sound of my mother, my back pressed hard to the door behind me. I blink a couple of times. The world comes into sharp focus.

"Alik?" I shake my head to clear the fog in my brain. Silence follows my words. I no longer hear the soft humming of my mother, and the door at my back is just as cold as the rest of the cave around it. Alik relaxes his grip and rubs his thumb across my wrist. My scar stands raw and red beneath his touch and I wince. He rips part of his tunic off in a ragged strip and circles it around my wrist, tying it off in a neat knot. I watch his movements as my mind tries to make sense of what happened.

"What are you doing here?"

"I should ask you the same thing," Alik says.

"I . . . I don't remember," I say, and shake my head. "I thought I heard something. It sounded like . . . like my mother."

"Your mother is dead, Val," Alik says softly.

"I know," I say, then sigh. "It just . . . sounded so much like her."

"Maybe you were dreaming," Alik says.

"Maybe," I reply. But I don't think it was a dream. I know I heard my mother's voice. And the smell. It was like walking back into my house after a long day.

"Come back to camp." He tugs my arm until I take a few unwilling steps forward. He wraps his arm around me and lays his forehead against mine. It pushes the icy fear curling around my heart a little farther away.

"Why are you down here?" I mumble into his shirt.

"I woke up and you weren't there. I went out of the cavern just in time to see you slide down the corridor," Alik says.

"Did . . . you hear anything?" I ask.

"No. I didn't hear anything except you humming."

I hug him closer. "I'm scared, Alik."

"Me, too," he says into my hair.

# TWENTY-TWO

*Firelight flickers across the granite, illuminating a grinning skeleton. It struggles to stand, batting away the arc of sunlight overhead before pointing a ragged finger at me.*

*"Why do you continue to run?" Rattling bones clink together as the skeleton seems to take a step forward. "Your life is not your own. Do not struggle."*

*I blink and stand before the long hallway with the door. I don't move, but the door rushes toward me and stops just a hair's breadth from my nose. Without prompting, the door swings open and bright silver light bursts from the edges, washing the entire hall until everything around me sparkles like falling snow.*

*Panic thrums through my body, and I grab the handle before the door can open any farther. I yank hard, willing it to shut, but something on the other side pulls it back. My body lurches forward, but I hold tight. Somehow I know if I let go, something far worse than Storm Hounds or monsters from old tales will escape. I shake with the effort and the metal handle bites into my skin. Blood wells along my palm before dripping to the floor. It disappears as I watch it fall, as if the stone had been waiting to drink something for years beyond counting. I can't let go. My feet slide forward as the thing inside pulls again.*

*I won't let go.*

*Another yank. My boots squeal across the ground.*

*I want to wake up.*

*I force the thought through my mind, willing my muscles to release me from the dream. At first, I'm certain I'm stuck inside, the edges of my mind too firm to escape. I ram myself against it, willing myself to open my eyes. . . .*

I blink and groan as blue light stabs into my vision. My head pounds with every heartbeat, and I press it to the cool stone beneath me and hope the throbbing will go away. Something sticky and warm draws my attention from my head to my right hand. There, slashed across my palm, is a long, thin cut. Blood still trickles from it, as if fresh.

My gut clenches hard at the memory of my dream. Something hides behind that door. I can feel it in my bones. The faster we get out of here, the better.

I push myself up and am greeted by the others already

packing up. Ivan tosses me a hard piece of bread.

"We can't stay here forever," he says gruffly. "We need to map the mine."

I nod. I don't want to spend a moment longer in Knnot than I have to.

"How will we keep track of where we've been?" Serafima asks as she folds her furs.

"We will light the halls," I say. "Everyone should have at least one lantern. It should work long enough for us to find a new route."

"We should explore the mural room first," Ivan says. "Perhaps the painting marks some sort of exit."

"No," Alik and I say together.

The others look at us.

"Val and I decided to look ourselves last night," Alik quickly explains. "There isn't anything but stone down there. There's no way out." The lie is so smooth and nonchalant, I almost believe him.

The others seem to accept this, and we break off into groups of two, with Alik volunteering to stay behind and make sure nothing gets to our food. Chinua and I pair up and take dark hall after dark hall, lighting lanterns where we can. After our second dead end, where Chinua uses a small rock to mark a thick white *X*, she sighs.

"Are we ever going to find a way out of here?" she asks.

"I really don't know. I hope so."

"I keep getting this strange feeling," she says, half to herself. "Like I know I'm going to die here. When I think about my future, I can't see anything beyond the rocks and darkness. It's as if it swallowed me and I can't find my way out."

I put out my hand until I find hers and give it a squeeze. "I won't let that happen to you, Chinua."

"How can you stop it? You're just as lost as everyone else," she says. "You know, back home, it's mostly just open sky. You can see for days, it seems. I always thought that was where I would die, surrounded by family on a warm night with the sound of the wind whispering through the tall blades."

I pull her to a stop. A tear trickles down her cheek and she hurriedly wipes it away.

"You will see the sun again. You will hear the sound of the wind."

Chinua gives me a feeble smile, almost seeming to believe me. A stone settles into my gut as I realize the weight of my promise.

"The mountain makes people think strange things. Humans aren't made to live in darkness. It gives us too much room for imagination. Once we are back in our cozy cavern with the lovite light, you'll feel a little better."

"We might as well go back. We haven't found anything," Chinua says.

I nod, and we retrace our footsteps toward the cavern. We exit the small hall into a slightly larger one, thick timbers as wide as my waist hoisting up the passage. Chinua and I plod on in silence, both our minds on something other than the path ahead of us.

*Clack.*

I straighten, my neck prickling. A loose rock likely fell. No more.

The sound comes again, and I pull closer to Chinua. My breath catches in my throat. Our eyes meet and I know she hears it, too.

I turn slowly, but the path behind us stands shrouded in darkness.

*Click. Clack.*

The sound seems to reverberate around us. I peer into the shadows, willing them to part. The sound comes again. Two rhythmic clacks of rock on rock. I take a step back, the sole of my boot slithering over the stone.

*Click. Clack.*

The clacks are closer this time. Chinua's breathing starts to become erratic.

"We aren't alone," she whispers.

Her words are met by a heavy silence that presses down on my ears.

Then, a single shrill note comes from the shadows closest to us and a dark form takes a step forward.

Chinua screams. The creature mimics it.

A long slender arm snakes into the dim light before I turn

and run. I race after Chinua, who darts around fallen rocks and broken beams. Until now, I thought Those Who Dwell Within were just stories made up by miners.

I never believed they were real.

I glance over my shoulder. A creature sits, hunched, in the center of the path. Its long knees bent; its head tucked between them. All I can make out are the eyes: massive orbs that reflect the small amount of light in the hall. They follow us down the path before it lifts one long, bony finger, and taps it against the rock between its feet.

*Click. Clack.*

Fear courses down my spine, cold and sharp. My legs quicken and I drag Chinua along with me as I race from the creature. Chinua doesn't question my speed. She matches my pace and we run all the way to the safety of the lovite cavern.

"You expect us to believe there are monsters down here with us?" Serafima asks after Chinua and I are done explaining.

"They are real. We were told stories about them all the time when I was little," I say. "They used to say Those Who Dwell Within were miners who got lost and couldn't find their way out. Their skin went white from lack of sun and their eyes wide so they could see in the dark. Everyone believed they were guardians of the mountain, keeping anyone from venturing too far and getting lost like themselves."

"And why would miners who have to harvest lovite want to

stay away from the depths of Knnot?"

I shrug. "I have no idea."

"It likely was a rockfall," Ivan says.

"You just need more rest. There isn't anything in the mines with us. Except maybe the Storm Hounds we are running from," Serafima says.

Ivan clears his throat. Chinua and I had been the only ones to report dead ends. The others turned back when they'd wandered so far their lanterns started to fade. There are other tunnels. More potential exits. But I no longer feel like exploring them.

Our packs full of lovite still sit in a corner. If we can get out, we'll have enough money for a new life, but escape feels impossible, as if Knnot wants nothing more than to hold us here forever.

"We can't stay here," Ivan says. "We have little to no food left. If we don't get out soon, we will starve. And the Storm Hounds won't wait much longer for us to come out. They *will* come for us. I think our best bet is to head to the path I found. It was damp, but I could feel a draft. It's our best option." Ivan points to the path that trails off to the left near the pit entrance. It's close to the area where Chinua and I saw the creature.

"Are we all going?" I ask.

"Yes," Ivan says. "It's our best chance of a way out. We'll pack up and move camp so we don't waste time coming back here if it is one."

"This is defensible," Chinua says. "We shouldn't move positions until we've secured another."

"We are moving camp and we are doing it now," Ivan says firmly, every inch a Storm Hound. "Pack up and move out."

The group sits in stunned silence for a moment before we start packing. I study Ivan. He's been different since we descended into the caves. Thick lines crease beneath his eyes, his skin is ashen, and his shoulders are stooped as if he carries something heavy across them. He saw something deep within the caverns he explored.

I'm sure of it.

In under ten minutes, our camp is disassembled and we head out. I study the ceilings and crevices as we pass, practically jumping at my own shadow. I strain my ears before every turn, hoping to catch the sound of the rocks clicking together.

I never hear a thing.

The walls of Ivan's tunnel glisten in the flickering lantern light. I take in a deep breath. The sharp tang of metallic water prickles the inside of my nose. Maybe Ivan was right to bring us down here. Underground rivers almost always led to a natural exit.

A dull roar begins to build, at first nothing more than a whisper, but it swells until it rings through my ears.

"Water," I say. "We really are near water."

I want to run, but before long, the rocks beneath our feet are dark and slick. It takes all my concentration not to slip.

Alik occasionally has to steady himself on my shoulder. When the roar of the river seems almost too much for my ears, we break into a massive cavern.

Bright cobalt light shimmers throughout a tall wall of solid lovite. The veins glimmer in slow-rolling waves, illuminating the river all the way down as far as the eye can see. Even the water seems to glow slightly, lovite swirling beneath it, embedded in the stone of the riverbed. Before us is a small sandy beach. The water laps lazily at the first couple of inches of sand, but other than that, the beach seems dry. "What now?" Alik asks.

"This is as good a place as any to set up camp. We've gone far enough today."

I stumble onto the beach, thankful for the change in terrain. My ankles roll with each step, and I collapse as close to the wall of the cavern as I can get. I suck in a deep breath, grateful to finally be able to rest. I dig around for my canteen and empty half the contents into my mouth. I sigh and close my eyes.

"You okay?" Alik asks.

"Yeah," I say without opening them. "How are you holding up?"

"My leg feels like someone has been sawing on it, and I can't stop shivering, but I guess it could be worse."

"It always can be, can't it?"

I force my eyes back open, afraid to close them for too long.

I keep close to Alik as Ivan passes around the meager dinner. No one declares they are going to rest. They simply turn to their furs and curl into them, bodies going limp with exhaustion as soon as their heads touch the earth.

"Are you sure you're okay?" Alik asks as he rolls out his own furs.

"I'm too afraid to sleep," I say. "I want to. I'm so tired, but I'm afraid of the dreams. Of creatures lurking somewhere above us."

Alik spreads out the furs and pats the place beside him.

"I'll keep you safe," he says.

I sag at his words and crawl to the spot next to him. He tosses my furs across us and curls one of his arms around my waist. I let the weight and surety of his arm calm me.

"What if there isn't a way out?" I whisper.

"There is," he mumbles.

"How can you be so sure?"

"I just can feel it," Alik says.

"I don't want to lose you, Alik," I say. "Not again."

Alik squeezes me a little tighter. "You won't. I was too stubborn to die last time."

We are silent for a moment. Alik's breathing evens out a little and I think he's asleep before he speaks again.

"I made you a promise. We will get out of Strana. Together," he says. "I know we will."

I snuggle in closer to Alik, willing his hopefulness to

transfer to me. I feel nothing but a cold dread in the pit of my stomach as I drift off into an uneasy sleep.

*"Valeria," the voices whisper to me again. "You need us, Valeria."*

*"I don't need you," I mutter.*

*I open my eyes. A sea of black devours my eyesight, leaving nothing behind. I wave my hands before my face. Cold air whispers between my fingers. I look around for bright lovite but find nothing but empty, cold dark. I can't even hear the roar of the river.*

*"We can show you the way out," they whisper. Long fingers stroke through my hair.*

*I pull away.*

*I spin in a slow circle, willing my eyes to see anything.*

*"What do I have to do in return?"*

*"Tsk, tsk," the voices say. "So suspicious. All you have to do is meet our master."*

*"All right," I say. "Where do I meet your master?"*

*I smell the putridity before they speak, their breath washing over my face.*

*"Open your eyes."*

My eyes snap open, and I instantly put my hands up, prepared for an attack. Nothing happens. Warm fire flickers to my right. I slowly lower my hands. I'm no longer wrapped in

Alik's arm beside the stream. Instead, I stand before the door in the mural room. The fire we lit the last time we were here still flickers in the low trough. A rush of air, like someone inhaling, sounds from the other side of the door. My entire body vibrates and my boots feel as if they've melted to the ground. The cave is no longer cold but boiling hot.

I don't know how I got here. It's hours away from the others.

I shuffle forward and press my ear to the door. Heat rolls from it in waves, and I shiver despite the warm wood. I put my hand on the bolt and my stomach jolts.

This isn't right.

It could be a trap. It could be Those Who Dwell Within playing with my mind. I could be opening a door to madness. The faces of Zladonians struck down by the plague filter to the forefront of my mind, gaunt and wild-eyed.

I step away from the door and run back toward the others as fast as I possibly can.

# TWENTY-THREE

THE NEXT DAY, WE CONTINUE downriver. I haven't told anyone about what happened. No one so much as shifted as I tiptoed back into camp covered in a cold sweat. Two sets of large footprints sat on the bank of the river, only an arm's length from Chinua's resting form. I shuddered, thinking of the creature Chinua and I saw before, now watching us sleep, its clawed toes digging into the sand.

I'd stomped across the evidence until it was nothing more than packed sand. The only thing the revelation would do is scare everyone further. We needed to concentrate on escaping Knnot, not on what hides inside it.

There were always stories of Those Who Dwell Within, told across winter fires or on balmy midsummer nights to scare children. But there were also whispers of something darker.

No one ever told that story. Since Zladonians built Ludminka, there had been whispers that the mountain was alive. My *babushka* spoke of it many times. People who ventured into its caves, before the mines, said it breathed.

I shiver and glance over my shoulder for the hundredth time. I know something is following us. I can feel it as surely as I can feel the rocks beneath my boots or hear the stream splashing beside us.

And I know the others sense it, too. We no longer stretch into a long single line, but bunch together.

I'm not sure how long we've been walking when we come to a drop. The water rushes over the lip and tumbles into darkness far below us. Not a single piece of lovite gleams in the walls surrounding the waterfall, giving us no way to see if there is a way down. Ivan studies the edge before surveying the area. A small tunnel leads into the dark to our left. The opposite bank holds nothing but the tall gleaming wall of lovite and an open cliff falling into the dark pit below. Ivan sighs and sits on the rock.

"Down doesn't make sense," he mumbles to himself. "We need to go out. We need to get out."

I don't know if the others hear him. The desperation of his voice worms its way straight into my core, my fear of being lost inside Knnot threatening to consume me. I grip the lantern in my hand so tightly the metal bites into my palm. It'll die soon anyway; might as well use it for something. I take it to the edge of the waterfall and let it drop, hoping to illuminate a way down. The flickering orange light highlights a stark granite wall before being swallowed by the roar of the waterfall.

There isn't a way down.

The river was our only hope of escape. Now we have nothing.

I collapse beside Ivan. My legs ache more than they ever have, my body weak from days on hardly any food. I wish I could sleep, but I can't force my eyelids to close for fear of hearing the voices again. Even now I'm sure a whisper tugs at the edge of my hearing, begging for attention.

"No!" A cry rips out from the abyss.

My head snaps up. Ivan has gone so pale he almost looks dead.

"Please, don't kill me." A child's voice cries out again. It seems to call from over the edge of the ravine.

"Now." A deeper male voice slithers out from the dark. "You will make a fine bride. You will do exactly what I say. When I say it. Now lift your head and show me that beautiful neck."

The voice makes me shiver. Chinua stiffens, then shrinks in on herself, looking over her shoulder.

"Do you actually think you'll ever be any use?"

My spine straightens. That's Luiza. I would recognize her voice anywhere. I search the group until I find Alik's face, half-hidden behind Serafima.

"You are no use to me now. You should've died when you had the chance." Luiza's voice cracks through the air. Cold and unfeeling, it's unlike anything I ever heard out of her mouth. Alik turns his face away from me.

Another voice overlaps the others, almost impossible to make out as the others keep talking.

"Your father abandoned you," a raspy voice says. One I can tell Serafima recognizes. "He will never come back. He never wanted a daughter. It's your fault he's gone."

"Now undress," the deep male voice says. Chinua slaps her hands over her ears, tears pouring down her cheeks.

"She will never care for you. Not like this. You're nothing but a broken doll." Luiza's voice.

"Have mercy, please," screams the first boy. "Don't kill me. I don't want to die."

The voices rise in a slow crescendo until they practically scream. Ivan's the first to move, bolting up the slippery slope behind us into the darkness, forgetting his bag and lantern.

"Leave me alone," Chinua says as she curls in on herself, putting her hands over her ears. Her mouth moves, but no sound comes out as tears leak down her face. Serafima pushes past her and starts after Ivan.

"Follow me with the supplies when you can," she says to me as she passes.

As soon as she leaves, the cavern falls silent. Not a single sound comes from below, not even the growl of the waterfall.

"Get all the stuff you can carry. We need to move," I say, my voice far too loud in the sudden silence.

Alik nods, and I help Chinua up, half dragging her down the path Ivan took. We stumble through the corridor until we come on to another hall studded with lovite deposits. It twists into darkness at the end. Chinua trembles in my arms. She can't take another bout through the dark.

I find the nearest alcove and let her sit. Alik hands me a thin blanket, and I tuck it around her and offer her the canteen. She takes it but doesn't drink. Her hands shake, the water sloshing around inside.

"It's all right, Chinua," I whisper, and sit beside her. "We are okay. Nothing can get you here."

"How did I hear him?" Chinua mumbles. "He's all the way in Adaman. I thought I'd finally run far enough. I thought I was safe."

Chinua's voice breaks as she turns toward me. Her eyes are wide with fear and tears stain her cheeks. I grasp her freezing hands to steady them.

"I don't know. I think the curse that surrounded Ludminka must've come from in here. Knnot holds something wretched in its core."

"Don't let him find me, Valeria. I can't go back to him. Please. I'd rather die here."

Alik settles in on Chinua's other side. "Who was it?" he asks.

"My khan. He'd taken an interest in me, as my parents were so valuable to his armies. He thought a girl from their stock would make the perfect concubine. My mother had five children, all of them boys aside from me. No doubt he thought I'd give him an heir worthy of his empire. He took me into his palace and . . . evaluated me. He had doctors measure the width of my hips and take pieces of my hair to be assessed by a shaman, certain it would show I was meant to bring greatness to the kingdom. Every concubine he adds to his harem goes through the same thing. But I couldn't do it. I refused, despite my parents' overwhelming pride at me being chosen. It's an honor. One held high above any other."

"Why did you refuse?" I ask.

"I . . ." She lets out a soft, sad sigh. "I don't . . . like men the way other women do."

Alik and I look at each other over Chinua's dark head. She glances up at us.

"My mothers obviously felt the same way," Alik says. Chinua lets out a gasping laugh and continues.

"My mother knew. She said it was obvious from when I was very small. That's why she told me about Ivan's expedition. She told me it was a perfect cover. That I should tell the Khan I wanted to prove myself worthy and bring him lovite as a gift for our union. He lapped it up just as she thought he would. She told me to pack my bags and leave that night before he could change his mind. I didn't get a chance to say goodbye."

"Why return at all, then?" Alik asks.

"He has my entire family at the palace with him. We were all invited to stay for my viewing," she whispers. "If I don't return, I have no doubt he'll kill my brothers for my disobedience. I can't leave my family to that fate. I won't."

I grip her hand and give it a squeeze.

"You're a good person, Chinua. Your mother would be proud," I say.

Her eyes are full of tears as she looks up at me and nods. She finally takes a drink of water. Alik and I sit beside her until her head starts to dip toward her chest. As soon as I am sure she is propped up and soundly asleep, I move away from her warm body heat and into the chill of the cave. Alik's bad leg scrapes against the stone as he stands. I don't turn to face him.

"Was what I heard real?" I ask. "I don't mean was it real now. I know it wasn't. It was madness or magic or demons. But was that what Luiza said to you?"

Alik lets out a soft sigh, and I know the answer before he even opens his mouth.

"Yes."

My heart gives a painful thump. Partly because I'd doubted him, and partly because I'd always truly believed Luiza loved us both. If she was able to say such cruel things to Alik, did she even really care for me? Or was I just another pawn for her to move about her board as she saw fit?

"What else did she say to you?" I ask quietly.

"She said you needed someone whole and capable to take care of you. That you could never love me how I am. I believed it."

Something shatters in my heart. I'd held on to some foolish notion that maybe Alik had taken Luiza's words out of context or that Luiza had been hurt and lashed out when she told him he couldn't come back to the guild. Her voice in the cavern was not one of indecision. She knew exactly what she was doing and exactly what to say to hurt Alik most.

It's too much. Luiza destroying Alik's confidence and shattering his belief in himself. Her knowing he was alive and never letting so much as a hint to me escape that he was. She'd kept me locked in the guild doing mission after mission.

It hurts me all the way to the core. She doesn't deserve my loyalty. She doesn't deserve all the heartache I've gone through simply to get lovite to free her from the Czar and support the champion she was so sure would change the world.

Everything I've done since leaving Ludminka all those years ago was for her. I loved her, despite knowing she worked for the Czar, despite watching her use every single member in the guild to her advantage, believing myself above them because she loved me too. Little did I know she just used my love as a shield, manipulating me like she did everyone else.

"Luiza is a liar. She is a manipulator. And she is wrong. Because . . ." My chest grows tight and I choke around my next words. "Because I do love you, Alik. I always have."

243

Silence stretches between us. My ears roar and I swallow back the saliva rising in my mouth.

Faster than I can blink, Alik closes the distance between us. His hands go under my hair to cradle my face. He brings his lips to mine.

The first brush sends a thrill along my spine. It's soft, almost like a question.

I answer, pulling his body closer and pressing my lips into his.

Hot and cold collide in my chest, swirling through my body. We fit together like we were always supposed to. The warmth of him seeps into me as he moves one hand from my face down my spine to my lower back. I shiver.

Every touch along my skin makes my body sing. Every awful thing we've experienced seems to melt away to a small speck in the back of my mind until it blinks out of existence completely.

It's just Alik and me.

His lips find mine again. This kiss is soft, like a sigh. It sends a tingle up my legs to nestle somewhere deep in my stomach. He pulls away and presses his forehead to mine.

"I love you, too."

A smile tugs at my lips as my heart bursts.

"I always have. Ever since you punched the guild initiate who called us dirty *malozla* and poured water over our heads. And I fell in love with you again nearly every single day since.

You are strong, determined, never afraid to speak your mind or stand up for what is right. I will love you until this world ends and not a day before."

His words are only a whisper, but it fills the cavern like a song.

A year lost because I believed he was dead. Luiza knew for months he wasn't, and never told me.

My temper flares and anger twists through me like a dark cord. What else had Luiza lied about? There were so many stories she'd told me and I'd believed them all, thinking myself the daughter she never had. My body tenses beneath Alik's hands and he studies my face.

"What?" he asks.

"I don't understand why Luiza would do all this. I didn't leave my quarters for almost three months after I thought you died. Why wouldn't she tell me that you were alive? How did she even find you?"

"She must've traced my letters back to Ivan's house. She showed up one day, out of the blue, and climbed through a window to speak to me while he was gone." Alik fidgets with the tips of my fingers before speaking. "Something's been bothering me for a while. I couldn't pinpoint why until now. You said Ivan grabbed you outside of a cache drop, but when he left me, he said he was going to the guild to speak to Luiza. He promised he wouldn't return without you."

A jolt runs through my system at his words. Ivan never

mentioned Luiza. I never even guessed they'd spoken, so sure the guild mutinied against her and he helped. I hadn't even wondered how Ivan found me at the drop site, certain I somehow slipped up and he was able to track me through the city like the Storm Hounds did. But Luiza could've told him exactly where I'd be and roughly what time I'd be there. She must've told him what to do and the exact way to get me to believe him.

It all made some horrible amount of sense. The odd pieces of my journey suddenly were connecting together. Luiza had *wanted* me to come to Knnot. But why? Why not just ask me herself?

"She's playing some sort of game," I say.

"She always is." Alik takes both of my hands in his. "I promise you we *will* find a way out, and then we will never look back."

A high-pitched wail suddenly echoes through the cavern and freezes Alik and me on the spot. That was no human cry.

Something is coming for us.

# TWENTY-FOUR

"WE HAVE TO LEAVE," I say.

I break away from Alik and rush to Chinua. She mumbles as I shake her shoulder, but her head lolls from side to side and she doesn't wake. A cry falls from my lips, and instantly Alik is by my side.

"What's wrong with her?" he asks.

"I have no idea. But we can't wait for her to wake up. Can you help get her onto my shoulders?"

Alik strains for a moment to get her limp form up enough for me to slide my neck under her middle. At last, I square her onto my shoulders and slowly stand, finding my balance. The canteen falls from her loose fingertips, spilling the last of the water across the floor.

"Let's go find the others," I say.

The strange cry echoes again from the river. We charge down the path, and I hope it's the one Ivan and Serafima took. Gone are the rotting timbers and rough-hewn rock, replaced by spotty lovite deposits and hard granite warped by the river itself. The path winds through narrow passages and wide caverns, ever deeper, ever farther from the light of day.

My legs tremble by the time we reach the others. Serafima tends to a bleary-eyed Ivan, offering him small sips of water. She gives us a relieved smile as we stumble into the small chamber.

"Finally found us," Serafima says.

"Chinua is . . . We can't wake her."

"He was the same when I found him. Lay her on the bed-rolls for now. I don't know what's wrong with them, but we will get them through it."

"I heard something in the caverns after you left. I have no idea if it followed us."

"We can't move them, not in this state," Serafima says. "We'll have to set up camp here and keep watch. It's the best we can do."

I sit down beside Serafima and look around, eyeing the small opening at the back of the cavern. It wasn't much more than a gap between two stones, but it was another potential entrance for twisted fingers and bright eyes.

"What just happened?" I ask.

Serafima's mouth firms. "I don't know. It was my mother's

voice I heard, from one of the worst days of my life."

"Mine was from the worst day of my life, too," Alik says, and my heart squeezes at his words.

"The mountain is playing tricks on us. It wants to keep us here," I say.

"Ivan, are you okay? You're shaking," Alik says, putting an arm around the older man.

"I relive that memory almost every night," he says. "I never thought to hear that boy's voice again. It was that day I knew I wanted to desert. I couldn't be a part of something that murdered children. Not when my own wife had just given me a son."

"It took you that long?" I spit before I can stop myself.

Ivan's lips thin, but he doesn't argue. "The Storm Hounds took me in when I was fifteen. My parents sold me off, determined to pay some debt they never even explained. I thought I was doing right by the country. Then the Czar started using us to round up Zladonians. We weren't guardians of a kingdom anymore. We were Ladislaw's personal hunting dogs. I'd never been made to kill a child before. Not until that day. I couldn't disobey the order. I had a wife and a child to think of. I'd be disgraced, barred from any other jobs in the kingdom. And if I deserted, I would be killed and my family would be punished."

"So you offered yourself to the guild," I say, my mind slowly putting the pieces of the puzzle together.

"Luiza promised me my family's safety in return for 'little favors,' as she called them. They were small things at first. Destroying a Storm Hound grain supply with weevils, passing along troop movements and numbers."

"You knew Luiza? Before you saved Alik?" I ask.

"Yes. We'd been in contact for months before I found him."

"She never mentioned he was part of the guild?"

Ivan shakes his head. "I had no idea until I found her trying to sneak from my house after speaking to Alik," Ivan says. "After that, she said if I got you here, she'd release me from her service. I could take all the lovite I could carry from the mountain and run to Adaman with my family."

"Me?" I ask.

Ivan nods.

My mind turns. How long had she been planning this? Had she found Alik and cast him out just so Ivan would have the leverage he needed to get me to come to Knnot? It doesn't make sense.

Nothing seems to anymore.

Now I know I was never a daughter to her. It was a lie to get me to trust her, and I'd been so desperate for a family that I'd fallen right into her trap.

"This was supposed to be my last job. I haven't seen my son in two years. Now I don't know if I ever will."

Ivan buries his face in his hands, and I have to look away. Everyone is broken, tired, scared. Every day we spend underground steals a piece of their hope away. I no longer believe the words I told Chinua. We will never make it out of here. We will die. Or worse, become like those creatures. I press my head into my hands.

"You should sleep." Alik's voice comes from beside me. Ivan now lies on his side, his back to us.

"I can't."

"I've noticed," he says and drapes furs around my neck. "You look like that time you were awake for nearly a week straight on watch for the guild. You need rest or you aren't going to make it to the end."

"If there is an end to reach," I say, half to myself.

"Don't lose hope yet, Val, not when we've come so far. The middle is the hardest part of the journey. You're the one who told me that."

I sigh. I know he is right, but I can't force myself to close my eyes. What if we need to run? What if the creatures come back and steal me away to the door again? What if there isn't another way out? So many what-ifs.

Alik puts one arm around me and pulls me in a little closer.

"Tell you what," he says. "You sleep and I'll watch. Just like we used to. After a few hours, I'll wake you up for your turn."

I nod, and Alik releases me. I settle down next to the feeble flame of the fire. It flickers orange and yellow, and my eyelids grow heavier and heavier, before I'm finally pulled into sleep.

⁓

I'm not sure how long I slept when I finally open my eyes. Our fire is dead, the smoke still curling toward the ceiling. The others sleep in heaps around me. Serafima leans propped against a rock outcropping, eyes closed, with Chinua resting on her legs. Ivan lies curled into the fetal position, his back still toward the rest of us. Only Alik remains upright. He stares at the entrance we came through, eye narrowed.

"Alik?"

He jumps, then puts his finger to his lips. I draw closer to him and look into the passage beyond. Enough lovite shines from farther back in the tunnel to allow dim blue light to filter in. Mist twists around the rocks and creeps toward our party. I shiver in the sudden cold.

"How long has the mist been here?" I whisper.

"An hour. It's been inching closer for about ten minutes."

"Have you heard anything?"

Alik shakes his head.

"I'll wake the others," I say.

A low hiss emanates from the cavern walls. I shake Serafima's foot. Her eyes pop open. I press a finger to my lips and point at the fog. She nods and prods Chinua awake. As if to taunt us, the walls hiss again. I slowly pack up our stuff, careful to be as quiet as possible. Ivan is the last to wake. He takes one look at the fog, then curls back up again. I toss the furs to Serafima and crouch beside Ivan, making sure I can see his face and he can see mine.

"We have to go," I say. "Something stalks us."

"Let it come. We'll never escape anyway," Ivan responds, folding in on himself again.

"You can't just wait here to die."

"Why not? It's what I deserve."

"Ivan," I snap. "If you think you have a sin to atone for, then get up and get us out of here."

He finally looks at me. "What could one ex–Storm Hound do to atone for his crimes?"

"I don't know." I let out an exasperated sigh. "You know where all the prisons are, you know the inner workings of the Storm Hounds. Use that information to free the people you imprisoned. Help the kinsmen of the people you killed."

I grab his forearm and pull with all my might. Slowly, he gets to his feet.

Serafima's hands tremble as she places tin cups one by one into the bag. She fumbles the last one and it falls into the sack with a clang. I tense. It will have heard us.

A loud scrape comes from just beyond the turn in the passage. It's so high-pitched, I wince away from it. The hiss from the walls comes again, followed by the familiar clacking of rocks.

A cry whines through the room and makes the hair on my neck stand on end. It sounds pitiful and too human, almost as if someone were taking their last gasping sobs before death. Shadows move in the passage, the mist swirling around invisible feet. Long nails click against the rock.

It draws closer, and I suck in air as the creature finally makes its way from the shadows. Long gaunt limbs extend from an emaciated body the color of smoke. Wide, bulbous eyes reflect the little light in the room as its head swings toward us.

"They're real," Alik whispers beside me.

The creature takes another step and straightens to full height, its head nearly brushing the cavern ceiling eight feet above. It rolls back its shoulders and straightens its neck and opens its mouth wide. A hoarse scream falls out, putting every inch of my body on edge.

"Run," I hiss.

We force our way into a tight gap at the back of the cavern. My heart beats in my ears as I shove myself through smaller and smaller openings, praying Serafima and Ivan will be able to make it with their broad shoulders. Finally, I pop out into a squat chamber.

The weight of the mountain seems to press down on my shoulders, squeezing and pinching as if it wants to swallow me whole. The only other opening is all the way at the back of the chamber, nothing more than a jagged hole in the floor. I want another way out. We keep going deeper, so far under the earth I fear we will never see sunlight again. My eyes dart to the ceiling, then to the tight walls on either side of me. Nothing.

There is nothing.

Alik tumbles into the chamber, followed by Chinua. Just

the three of us are too big for the small space, our legs tangling and our breath hot enough to make me sweat. We have no other option. We have to keep going down.

I slip into the hole, the rough rock biting my arms and scraping my cheeks. A loose stone gives way, and I skid down the sides, no longer able to support myself. The tight granite gives way, and for a brief moment I fall through open air. I land hard on a stone slab. I start to slip, completely blind in the cavernous dark. My hands scramble to find something, anything, to hold on to as my boots slide farther down the rock. At last, I catch the lip of a boulder and pull myself up with all the strength left inside me. I slam my spine into the mountain at my back and attempt to catch my breath.

My eyes try to focus, straining so hard that pain lances through my head. I squeeze them shut. I can never hope to see anything now. My breathing, harsh and ragged, seems to fill the entire area, and I slowly get it under control, listening hard for something else.

The distant rush of the river sounds to my right. A plop sounds just before me. Then another. Somewhere ahead of me must be water—whether a puddle or a pond, I don't know.

Someone lands beside me and I jump, my heart racing rabbit quick. Boots skid on the rock, and the sound echoes through the cave. I splay out my fingers on the stone before me, looking for whoever followed me inside. It takes a long moment before something warm brushes my fingertips. A hand. I grab it and fingers curl around my wrist.

"Who is it?" I ask.

My voice echoes off the invisible walls.

"Chinua."

I tug her up beside me. She takes in a couple of deep breaths.

"Where are the others?" I ask. It seems too loud.

"Serafima got stuck," Chinua whispers. "Ivan was trying to pull her out. Alik forced me down here."

One by one our party pops out of the tiny opening—Ivan, followed by Serafima. I grasp Chinua's hand, willing myself to hear something other than the quick breaths of the others around me.

"He's coming, right?" I ask no one in particular.

"He was right behind me," Serafima says.

Chinua starts to wheeze. Her other hand flaps against my forearm until she grabs hold, her nails digging deep. Her soft breathing turns into panting, and her lungs whistle as she gasps for air.

"Breathe," I whisper. "It's okay. It will be all right."

"He won't make it," Chinua says, her voice so tight it's almost hard to make out her words. "None of us will. We are going to die down here. All of us. I'm sure of it."

I grip her hand tight. "We won't."

Air squeals between her teeth as she tries to inhale.

"Put your head between your legs," I say. "And then try to count to three before breathing out. Then count to three before breathing in. Once you can do that, try counting to four."

Chinua's entire body shakes, but her legs slowly move up, and she puts her head between her knees. A scrape sounds from above, and my mind conjures images of the creature before I hear the familiar curses of Alik.

His legs swing dangerously near my face. I grab them and pull. A small yelp escapes his mouth as he crashes down on top of me. It's a relief to feel the weight of his body on mine, even if my arms are trapped beneath his chest. He slides off and sits by my side. I grab his hand and, as it tightens around mine, the tension surrounding my heart eases a little.

"We're all here," I say.

"Now what?" Ivan asks.

Chinua takes a long, steadying breath.

"Did anyone manage to keep ahold of their flint and steel?" I ask.

The group mumbles no before Ivan gasps.

"I have them," he says.

I grab the edge of my tunic and rip it off. "The light won't last long, but it will give us enough time to figure out what to do next."

I reach out toward the sound of Ivan's voice. Our knuckles collide. I twist my hand around and stuff the fabric into his fist. Two clicks later, a small flame blazes to life, illuminating our tiny area. We all sit on top of a thin stone ledge. Ivan tosses the fabric over the edge and I catch a scream behind my teeth.

Beneath us, strung out in languid poses across boulders and rock, lie more creatures. Their chests rise and fall, eyes closed as if they couldn't be bothered to wake up as the tattered piece of my tunic burns away. I cover Chinua's mouth and muffle the scream that rushes out of it.

The creature chased us straight into its nest.

# TWENTY-FIVE

OUR ENTRANCE SEEMS TO HAVE gone unnoticed. The first strip of fabric flickers out and, without a word, I rip another piece off my tunic and hand it to Ivan. He lights it once more. The creatures continue to slumber beneath us, so still they could be nothing more than rocks themselves. I force myself to look away from their strange long limbs for an exit. There couldn't be only one way out of here. Not with all the bodies below.

Rocks line the way to my left, large and unwieldy, but we may be able to scramble up them. On the far side of the chamber, the rocks pile so close to the ceiling that I'm not sure we will fit, but it's our only option. I snap my fingers softly, afraid my voice will be too loud. Everyone looks and I point the way forward. I'm met with grim faces, but they know as well as I do it's our best shot of getting out of here.

"We'll need light to make it," Ivan whispers.

"I'll stay behind with the flint and give you as much light as I can, then try and cross it in the dark."

"You can't," Chinua and Alik whisper at the same time.

"It's the only way," I reply, surprised my voice doesn't shake.

The hot spike of fear I'd felt at the creatures melts away, replaced only by the grim desire to get us out. I made a promise to Chinua. I won't give up without a fight. I will not let the others become sacrifices to Knnot.

No one else argues. Ivan slips me the flint and steel, and I rip another shred from my battered tunic and toss the tiny shred of burning cloth into the ground below. I quickly rip off another shred. The acrid scent of burning wool infiltrates the cave as I light another piece. The flame illuminates Alik's face, jaw tight and brows drawn.

"I'll go first," Ivan says.

He scrambles up the first boulder and hobbles from one rock to the next. Before the new strip of fabric is even half burned, he shimmies between the ceiling and the rock and slips into the dark mouth of the crevice. Chinua starts forward, hands trembling as she grasps the ledge of rock. Serafima puts a steadying hand on her shoulder, before kneeling down to give her a boost up. Chinua keeps her eyes trained on the crevice, never faltering. As soon as she reaches the hole, she gives a fleeting glance back and slips through.

Not a single sound echoes from the crevice after they disappear. The strip becomes too hot and I toss it aside, igniting another one, my hands unsteady on the flint and steel. No sound comes from the opposite end of the chamber as Serafima hoists herself up. She slips across the path and into the hole. I hope they are safe in a room full of bright lovite and not being torn apart by another nest of creatures. I shake my head. I can't think like that or I won't make it across at all.

Alik curls an arm around my waist and squeezes me tight. I allow his scent to calm me. He presses his forehead to mine.

"I don't want to leave you," he says.

"You have to. Go, before the strip burns out." I push his chest, sending him toward the safety of the rocks.

My stomach clenches tight as he stands on top of them. I will his leg to hold strong and steady. He made it over mountain ranges and through caves. He can do this. He has to.

He follows the exact same path as the others before him. Just as he reaches the small space on the other side of the chamber, the last remaining light dies out.

Submerged in darkness, I clench my fists tight against the slow squeezing of my chest. Even though I watched everyone cross as carefully as I could, I'm terrified I won't remember the steps. One wrong foot will send me tumbling into a nest of creatures.

I force the images away and start toward the rock. I explore the bald face of the stone, desperately searching for the ledge everyone else used. Finally, my fingers run across the harsh edge of the boulder, and I wrap them around it as tight as I can. I grit my teeth against the bite of the stone as I heft myself up, straining the last couple of inches. My chest slams hard onto the rock before me, knocking the air from my lungs. I try to breath as my boots scrape at the smooth side of the boulder. I shove my hands harder into the ledge, my arms trembling as I manage to get one leg over the top.

I roll onto it, pressing my back hard to the wall. I no longer remember where the ledge is. If I keep close to the rock, I should be safe, but everything seems the same in the dark. It whirls around, and a wave of dizziness takes hold. What if I can't get out? What if I fall?

A flame springs to life feet ahead of me, flooding my vision with light. When my eyes adjust, I realize it's Alik. He lies wedged between ceiling and rock. He holds a burning piece of fabric whose light reflects against the ceiling. I press my hand to the pocket of my pants, but my flint is gone. He must've taken it when he gave me a hug. I try to suppress a smile, feeling stupid I hadn't thought of that before.

I pick my way across the rocks quickly. As soon as I reach Alik, he grabs one of my hands and tosses away the fabric before it can burn his fingers. With Alik's hand guiding me, I slither through the tiny opening.

Alik refuses to let go, using his other arm and legs to move along the passage. We pull ourselves over the rough stone, my muscles screaming as we go. In the never-ending dark, I'm sure we won't make it out. He reaches out with our clasped hands, securing mine on the rough edge of a rock. I move my other hand up and pull with all my strength. I sling one leg over and heft my body onto the lip of the stone.

I am greeted by stars above my head.

For one wonderful moment, I think we somehow made it out. I slowly realize the stars are nothing but distant lovite deposits. They run along a straight line, thick deposits at even intervals curving down to kiss the ground. It almost looks like a grand hall or a courtly ballroom.

"We made it," I say.

"We did. Thanks to you," Alik responds.

I search for the others and find them a little farther up the chamber between two of the thick lovite strips. Chinua runs her hands along the light, seeming to drink it in. I wish I could feel some amount of relief. Instead, all I see is a group of stragglers hopelessly lost and running out of food.

Everyone huddles together as we join them, trying to glean some warmth and a little sleep before forging ahead. I wait as, one by one, they teeter into uneasy slumber brought on by exhaustion. Chinua is the last to go.

Despite the horrible ache in my head telling me to sleep, I can't. We are hopelessly lost. So far from the mines I don't think we'll ever make it back. We have maybe a day of food left and two days of water, despite filling our canteens at the river. We won't leave this mountain alive. Not without help.

My gut twists as I realize I can find exactly that.

The voices that have plagued my dreams only ever said they wanted to help. They've never hurt me. The worst thing they did was lure me to the door at the bottom of the mural room, and if I can find my way there, at least I can get us to daylight, and we can take our chances with the Storm Hounds. They'll be more forgiving than this mountain.

We're out of options. If we wander around in these caves any longer, we will die. Of that, I have no doubt.

I let my body relax against the cool stone floor, allowing my mind to drift. At first, nothing comes. Panic laces through me. Maybe I've ignored the voices for too long. I crush my fingers into my scar and beg for the voices to respond.

"Help me," I whisper into the dark.

*Hello, Valeria*, the voices say.

My body goes limp and warm as the voices crawl into my brain.

*Finally decided to listen?* they ask.

"Take me to him," I say.

The voices don't respond at first. Perhaps I should've begged. My entire body tingles, vibrations running up my legs. A soft flicker sounds to my right.

I know where I am by sound alone.

I open my eyes and am greeted by the door that has haunted my dreams.

The wood seems unchanged, but uneasiness stirs in the pit of my stomach.

I reach for the handle, my stomach in knots. There will be no returning to how things were.

I take a deep breath and yank it open.

The room beyond is completely dark. I hazard one step inside, and the chamber begins to glow a bright blue around my foot before swirling outward until lovite gleams in every corner. I force myself all the way inside, and the door slams shut behind me.

Part of me hopes I'm stuck in a nightmare, but the room lacks the haziness I've grown accustomed to in my dreams.

I tuck my fingers into my arms as the room starts to chill. My breath comes in soft, white plumes from under my nose.

"Welcome," says a deep baritone voice. "I was beginning to think you would never come."

I have to blink several times as a table with two chairs materializes out of the ground. The furniture glows the same bright blue as the room around us. In one chair sits an almost normal-looking man.

His hair seems colorless in the light, tied back at the nape of his neck with a brown ribbon. His clothing looks well made, a pristine white shirt with loose laces at his chest and fine leather breeches. Though a skilled tailor must've made them, as the man is thin enough to be called gaunt. He leans back against the chair.

My heart thunders in my chest. I have seen the man before me in every cabin in Ludminka, seen his picture plastered across numerous chapels. He's thinner than his painted icons, but he is undeniably the same being. I swallow.

"You're . . . you're the Pale God."

He flashes me a smile. "At long last, we meet again."

"Again?"

"I think it's time we finally talk." He gestures to the chair across from him.

# TWENTY-SIX

MY MIND WHIRLS. I AM talking to the Pale God. The one I've pretended for years doesn't exist. This isn't possible. The gods disappeared to the heavens to watch us from above. He can't live inside Knnot. I shudder.

His face slackens as he notices my shiver. "Why, you must be dreadfully uncomfortable. Allow me to change the atmosphere. What do you prefer, hmm?"

He lifts one hand and, with a twirl of his wrist, the air in the room begins to warm. The pungent scent of rose petals floats on a soft breeze. The chamber of blue stone melts away, replaced by a low marble railing of squat posts with a polished wooden banister. Golden sand stretches as far as the eye can see beyond the terrace, rolling in large waves like an ancient ocean.

"Hmm, I think not," he says.

With another flourish, the desert fades away, replaced by a single-room log cabin. A low fire crackles to my right in a brick hearth. A bright yellow-and-pink tablecloth covers a table and hides the Pale God's legs. A small window sits above a counter, looking out on a forest of pine. Even the scent in the air is a familiar mix of burning birchwood and evergreen trees. It's nearly an exact replica of my house. I cross to the table and collapse into the chair, trying to force my mind to accept that I'm in the presence of a *god* performing real magic.

"I apologize for the deplorable state of my chambers when you first arrived. I'm simply not used to having company anymore."

"I . . . understand," I stutter, but I don't. Not really.

When I believed in the Brother Gods, I thought of them as some sort of nebulous entities. Something to believe in because the idea of being alone in this world was too terrifying. Yet, he is real. I almost reach out a hand to touch him.

He leans forward and rests his head on his hands. The action is almost childlike. He studies me. His skin matches his hair in color. Almost paler than I am. The only sign that he actually lives lies in the twinkle of his unnaturally blue eyes, so bright and luminous I have trouble believing they are real.

"You must have so many questions."

I nod. I want to believe this is a dream. That soon I'll wake and laugh about this with Alik.

"You are awake. I can assure you," the Pale God says. "And

please stop calling me the Pale God. It sounds so dry and formal. My name is Kosci."

I allow the name to roll through my mind. He grins at me, showing me a row of perfect teeth, almost too small for his mouth.

"This is where you introduce yourself."

"I'm sorry." I duck my head. "My name is Valeria."

"I know. Don't you remember? We've met before."

I'm taken aback by his response. I file through my memories, searching for a hint of his strange smile or blue eyes. I don't find one.

"I . . . I feel like I would remember that."

"I suppose you probably wouldn't. You were small and human lives don't really begin until they are at least four or five. Such a pitiful waste, those first years." He almost looks remorseful at the fact. "Would you like to remember?"

He taps the inside of my wrist and my scar ignites.

*The image of Kosci and the room swirls away, replaced by a cold, dark cavern. A tiny girl wanders among the stones, patting the round ones with an affectionate laugh. Kosci appears in the far corner of the cavern and watches as the girl spins, staring at the lovite overhead. I startle as the girl tumbles down and I see her face is my own.*

*Little me laughs at the lovite as Kosci detaches himself from the wall.*

269

*"Do you need help, little one?" he asks. He kneels before me and extends a hand.*

*Child me starts at suddenly not being alone, but grins into Kosci's face.*

*"I know you," I say. I touch the tip of his nose and then wrinkle my own. "Your ears are much sillier in your pictures."*

*Kosci gives a dramatic sigh, which makes little me laugh. "They never can get them right, though I'm not sure why. Now let's get you out of here. We don't want to worry your papochka and matta, do we?"*

*I shake my head and take Kosci's hand.*

*I rip my wrist away with a yelp and stare down at the angry welt already forming on it.*

*"I'm sorry, little one," Kosci says and bends down until we are eye level. "I didn't mean to hurt you. Sometimes there are aspects of magic that even I can't control. Come, we will find your family and they will make it all better." Little me takes Kosci's giant hand once again, certain of his trustworthiness.*

The memory swirls again, and I jolt as the log cabin comes into view. Kosci smiles at me over steepled hands.

"I do apologize about your scar. It was never my intention. I hope it hasn't brought you any ill luck."

I rub the raised skin. It's so familiar to me I almost believed I was born with it.

"Why did it happen?" I ask.

"I often save children from the caves. No one deserves to be trapped down here."

"No, why did you burn me? In the memory, it seems like you didn't expect it."

Kosci's brow crinkles a bit. "I didn't know it would brand you. As I said, some things in the magic of the world are beyond my reach. I just knew you needed to get home."

"Does it mean something?"

Kosci studies me for a long moment. "In short, yes. I've touched dozens of humans to lead them from my caves and none of them reacted to my touch as you did. When I went to help you, I expected nothing different."

"I thought the Brother Gods could see all," I say, and Kosci's face tightens.

"My brother"—he says the word through gritted teeth—"and I do see all. Time for us isn't a linear thing. We see things that have happened, or things that will happen. They swirl and mix together, all of them possibilities of what could happen. It's rare we find the thread of reality that is occurring in the moment. Even rarer for the people inside the thread to make the same decisions as they are meant to. The only time we can see our true reality as it unfolds is when we are together, and that hasn't happened in many, many years. So we muddle through with this partial magic and hope for the best."

I try to make sense of his words.

"So without your brother you can see only the maybes of

the future, not what will truly happen?"

Kosci inclines his head. "In your case, after my touch took hold, I could follow your strands more easily. You were always easy to find, and I knew, in that moment, you were more important than either of us could ever imagine."

"If I am so special, why did my entire family freeze to death? Why did the only mother I've known since then betray me for some unknowable reason? I'm nobody."

"You are important *because* of those things. The brand on your wrist marks you as my champion. Doubtless you've heard of my brother's champions. He seems to pick a new one every few years. I can't extend my hand as he can. He saw to that. But you wandered right to me and I have protected you every day since."

"I am your champion? Me?"

"Well, yes. I never would've been able to choose you if you hadn't wandered into my caverns that day, but you have all the qualities I need. The strength of will, the ferocity, that temper. I couldn't ask for better."

"But I have no power. Not like your brother's champion. Or the champions from the tales."

"Of course you don't." Kosci sits back in his chair, a small pout on his lips. "I haven't been able to see you in years and you refused all my invitations here."

"The dreams? I wouldn't call those a welcoming invitation," I say.

Kosci snorts. "I suppose I could've been a bit more direct, but I only supply the message. Your mind conjures the dream. And when those didn't work, I sent my pets and you ran from them, too."

"Those creatures wanted to eat us!"

"No," Kosci says, his face stern for the first time since we started speaking. "They wanted to herd you in the right direction. You would've wandered in those tunnels until you died if I hadn't pushed you the right way."

Kosci twirls his wrist again. A porcelain teapot appears between us, small rosettes circling the lid. Two cups with the same design materialize, and he makes a show of pouring the steaming liquid for the both of us. I wrap my hands around my cup and take a long swig, thankful for any sort of sustenance. I turn over his words as I take another drink.

"You kept me from the frost the day it swallowed Ludminka?" I ask.

He nods. "And I got you from Ludminka to Rurik without dying and made sure Luiza found you so you would be protected. I even warmed the cave when you saved Alik from the river, just to make sure you'd find your way back to me."

"You made Luiza find me? She never cared for me, then. It was just a trick you pulled to keep me safe."

"No." He shakes his head. "I put an idea in her head. I'm not powerful enough for anything else anymore."

"If you care so much about protecting me, why did you

not save Ludminka from the freeze?" I ask. "My village, my family. You watched them die and saved only me when you could've stopped it all and kept me closer to you. Why did you let me suffer, if you cared so much? Why did you trap me inside this wretched mountain with you?"

The questions fall from my mouth like a waterfall, fueled by anger. "If I was a champion like in the old tales, why has my life been nothing but one misery after the next? Weren't they supposed to be blessed? The Bright God's champions had wealth, security, happiness. I've had nothing but suffering my entire life. Why did they get to flourish?"

"There are limits to my abilities. I tried to destroy the humans who followed you here, but they used weapons imbued with my brother's magic. The shields they carry will stop anything I send at them, and I only have so much magic left in my body," he says with a gesture at the lovite above us.

"Lovite is your body?" I ask, my disbelief clear.

"Why do you think it's so strong? It's the bones of a god. Surely you've heard the tale of my brother casting me to the ground and burying me? It's all true. He trapped me here and now I can't get out. It makes choosing a champion of my own to battle my brother a near impossibility. His influence has reigned over this world unchecked for centuries, destroying all the good we created. It's why I needed to reach you. I want to make a deal."

A slow suspicion grows in my core. There are tales of girls

making deals with gods all throughout Strana. It never ends well for the girl, and the deal never is what it seems.

"What is your deal?"

"I will give you all the powers your mortal body can hold. You can use them to free yourself from this place and destroy the Czar. I will consume all the hurt and pain you've felt for years. I will take the burden as my own."

"Why?" I narrow my eyes.

"You were devout, once upon a time. Surely you know it's the role I chose when I fell to this earth. It nourishes me. I will feed on your suffering and regain my strength. Then you will take my heart from this mountain. Once I'm out of this wretched prison, I can form a new body."

He taps the glimmering ember at his throat. A piece of glowing lovite tightly coiled in a spiral around itself sits strung on a thick piece of leather. I inhale, shuddering. The deal seems fair, but it is far too good to come without a larger price I can't see. I sift through all the information Kosci has given. There has to be something I'm missing. My entire body goes cold.

"I want you to answer one question first," I say. He inclines his head and gives me a smile.

"Who caused the ice that covered Ludminka and started the plague that stole lovite from the Zladonians?"

Kosci stays silent for far too long. He drums his fingers across the table. At last, he sighs and splays his hands before him as if asking for my forgiveness.

"It was me."

"All of this suffering was caused by you? You murdered my family and forced all of us from our homes?"

"*Murdered* is a harsh word," he says lightly. "It's more of a sleep."

"You destroyed an entire region. You let the Czar hunt us down like dogs. You ruined my life. You killed the only people to truly love me. Why? To give me enough suffering to feed you for a lifetime?"

The air seems to roar with my fury and my cold fingers curl into my hands.

"I didn't do it to make you hurt," he says softly, but his words seem to fill every inch of space between us. "I did it to protect you. To protect this world. With each piece of lovite mined, I grow weaker, my magic waning as my body is slowly separated piece by piece. If I remain locked here and let my power go, my brother will destroy this world and everyone in it. Prayers make him stronger, fuel his magic. What better way to receive prayers than by ravaging the world? I can siphon away the suffering slowly, but soon it will consume you all. And once it has your soul, it will never release it. Humanity will continue to pray to a deaf god drunk on his own power."

I hold up a hand. "I won't listen to your lies. You're just like everyone else in my life. You want to use me. You'll say anything to get me to agree to freeing you. You deserve to rot beneath the earth for what you did to my parents."

Kosci gives another shrug, his easy manner never dissipating. "This is your choice, Valeria. I will not force you. I *will* leave you with this warning. I will wait two more nights. You must make your decision before the end of the second day. If you decide to refuse my help, you will have to accept whatever terrible life the fates deal you."

"There isn't enough pain in this lifetime that could ever make me agree to your bargain," I spit.

He opens his cupped hand. The pendant from his throat lies there, the glow inside fluttering like the faint beat of a heart. I recoil from it. I know it's his heart before he even opens his mouth.

"I believe you will change your mind, at the end of it all. Once you place my heart around your neck, it will grant you all the power you could ever want. In return, you will free me from this prison. Always remember this price, Valeria. For I will never forget."

I open my mouth to say I will never change my mind, but he forces the pendant into my hand. My fist curls around it almost instinctively. Cold bites at my flesh and worms its way up my arm, reminding me none of this is natural.

"Goodbye, Valeria."

He pushes me out the door before I can speak. I tumble through the air before falling to my knees. I blink a couple of times, my eyes slowly adjusting to the dark of the cavern. My heart falls into the pit of my stomach as I realize where I am.

Back in the belly of Knnot with all the others.

The pendant in my closed fist thrums against my palm. I open my hand and glare down at it, not sure why I even took it. I raise it above my head and almost smash it against the rock beneath my knees. Something stops me. A strange pull in my gut, like a warning. I don't know what would happen to Knnot if I destroyed Kosci's heart. I can't bury us beneath the mountain simply because I am mad at the god locked inside.

I stumble to our bags, suddenly exhausted and more hopeless than ever. I shove the pendant into the depths of my pocket and promise myself I will destroy it and free myself of the person who killed my family.

All I have to do is get out of Knnot.

# TWENTY-SEVEN

SOMEONE SHAKES ME AWAKE AND I groan.

"Come on, Val," Alik says, and he sounds as tired as I feel. "We found something."

My head throbs as I sit up. My encounter with Kosci comes rushing back and the anger leaps into my heart. I will never accept the deal of the god who killed my family. The heat of my rage pushes away the last of my tiredness and I see that the rest of the group gathers a short distance away, huddled around something on the floor.

"What did they find?" I ask.

"It's hard to explain. You have to see it for yourself." Alik holds out his hand and helps me to my feet.

He doesn't let go as we cross to the others. As we get closer, I make out strange runes glowing across the cave floor, like something hot was pressed into the rock to mold it. I blink a couple of times as the runes start to twist into something legible. Instead of strange markings, words ring a small dimple in the stone.

*A gesture of goodwill. This will take you home.*

"I can't make out what it says." Serafima twists her head as she tries to read the words. As I look back down, the words roll into each other, forming the same runes I'd seen as I walked over.

No one besides me can read them. Kosci's made sure of that, too. I bite my tongue. Gods don't help mortals without a price. He's trying to manipulate me, just like Luiza would.

I look around at the wan faces of the party. I can't refuse Kosci's gift, no matter how much I want to. I went to him, hoping for an escape, and he's provided it. We will never make it out of this mountain without his help.

"They are runes," I say, the lie springing easily to my lips. "Miners used them to mark new potential deposits and mining sites. If we follow these, it should lead us out."

The hope on their faces is undeniable, as if I led them to water when they were dying of thirst. Serafima crosses her arms.

"How can you read it?" she asks.

"It's the same sort of rune they always used. It means home," I say.

She raises an eyebrow but says no more.

"Was this here last night?" Ivan asks.

"I think I remember it," Chinua says.

"Spread out, find the next one," Ivan orders.

We scatter. I'm almost as desperate as the rest of them to find the next one. We comb over the rock until Chinua shrieks from the far end of the cave. "I found another one." When I reach her, sure enough, another rune lies at her feet, half-hidden beneath a wall of fallen rock.

"What are we going to do now?" I ask. "There's no way through the rock."

Chinua's smile doesn't fade; in fact, it widens. "Leave it to me."

She rushes back toward our things. When she returns, she opens her hand to display four gelatinous cubes.

"I'll only have a couple left after this, but it can bring down this wall," she says. She looks to Ivan, who gives her a nod. It's the only option we have. Chinua races to the wall and places one cube on the left as high as she can reach, then one as low as she can directly below it. She matches her movement on the right side.

"What about the creatures?" Serafima says. "The noise will bring them straight to us."

"We don't have much of a choice," Alik says.

I can't tell them I know it won't happen. Kosci will keep them away from us now that I've finally met him. He has no reason to release his creatures once again.

We back away as Alik tosses the flint and steel to Chinua, who lights the four cubes in quick succession. She rushes away from the rock wall and hides behind a large boulder. A long moment of silence drags out where the very air seems to shift. Then a boom rocks the cavern; the vibrations rattle along the floor and rocks tumble to crack against stone. I rub my ringing ears and peer through the dust filtering through the air.

A jagged hole mars the entire stone wall. I'm the first to pick my way through the wreckage, the rocks rolling beneath my feet as I cross. On the other side is an empty passage, the lovite deposits still following the strange pattern from the cavern we are in. I study it, the same creeping cold from Kosci's prison clawing at me. These are his bones. Bones of a god. Lovite no longer reminds me of home.

"We better get moving," Ivan says.

He forges ahead into the new path created by Chinua. On his back he carries the few items we have left. The others fall into step behind them. Chinua and I take up the rear. The runes continue to dot the path every twenty or so feet. We follow them cautiously at first. Ivan checks every darkened alcove with a raised knife, Chinua watching our back, turning around and walking backward occasionally to make sure we aren't being followed. After a half hour of nothing but the empty silence of Knnot, even her vigilance starts to wane.

The path winds endlessly upward, but the swelling lovite light never wavers. Sweat pours down my back as the path starts to get steeper. It seems never-ending. We continue to push up and up into the mountain. I don't know where Kosci is leading us or if there was even a path here before he decided to mark the way. My mind is too tired to figure it out.

I don't know how long we hike, but I can hardly breathe by the time Ivan pulls us to a stop. I throw myself to the floor and will the coolness of the stone to soak into my body.

"Can you see anything?" I ask.

Serafima peers down the tunnel, but shakes her head. "Just more lovite."

Silence descends, the space filled with the words we are afraid to say. That we are lost. Again.

I take in a deep breath and something sharp bites the inside of my nose. The dank smell of rock is replaced by something fresher. Cleaner. It almost makes me want to get back up and race down the passage. But I can't force my legs to move.

"We will rest for a few hours, then push forward. We need to put more distance between ourselves and the cavern. The explosion was a necessity, but we don't know what it awoke," Ivan says.

He shrugs off his pack. Sweat clings to his clothing, but he doesn't sit. Instead he peers into the darkness behind us. Alik collapses against the wall and pats the stone beside him. I nestle into the crook of his arm. My body is so exhausted I collapse into a dreamless sleep as soon as I close my eyes. I'm not sure how long I'm out before I jerk awake. I rub my eyes, grit sealing them closed.

Alik stirs a little.

I press a kiss to his forehead.

"Go back to sleep."

"Don't go too far." His voice is muddled with sleep and he rolls over to face the wall. A smile crawls across my face. Even here, in the dark of Knnot, I feel the smallest spark of hope.

I listen to his breathing as he falls back to sleep, eyeing the walls around us. I wonder if Kosci watches me right now. Perhaps that's what woke me. My fingers brush against the pocket where I shoved the pendant.

Kosci's heart bites against my hand, still as cold as the moment he gave it to me. For the briefest second, I wonder what it would be like. I could use Kosci's power to destroy the Storm Hounds outside who are determined to kill us. I'm sure they still wait. How could they pass up the chance to take in a deserter and two *malozla*? They know they have the upper hand. With Kosci's power, I could rain fire down on them with a snap of my fingers and we could all be free.

I could save us all.

But I'd be chained to Kosci, ordered to take his heart from the mountain and out into the world wherever he saw fit. There is no way of knowing what he'd have me do to help him gather strength. If he would use me to destroy his brother. I've seen what happens to the Bright Gods' champions. They get nothing but an early death and a picture painted in the gallery of icons in the royal palace. I can't accept his deal.

Not for me. Not for Strana. Not even for a god.

# TWENTY-EIGHT

IVAN ROUSES US WHAT FEELS like only minutes later, but I know it must've been longer. I stretch my sore muscles as we walk. At long last, the cave terrain levels out. My feet stumble along the suddenly flat path. The lovite veins spread away from each other before us in massive waves of crystalline rock.

"Why didn't they mine this?" Serafima asks.

"They never had a chance," I replied.

We follow the lovite threads along the floor until Chinua perks up. She inhales, long and hard.

"Snow," she says.

She takes off and the rest of us follow, close on her heels. We round a bend and are hit with a blast of freezing air. A jagged opening sits not more than ten paces ahead. Low sunlight spills across the granite floor and a sharp breeze sends scrawls of fresh snow across the stone.

My breath hitches in relief. Kosci delivered. We are free of this mountain and the horror inside of it. We can leave and never look back.

"We made it." Chinua's voice breaks into a sob.

She races toward the entrance, tears already gathering on her eyelashes. I'm right behind her. Wind steals away my breath with its cold, but I don't care. I would gladly freeze in fresh air than rot in the caves a moment longer. Chinua slips out onto the small ledge before the opening.

"There's a path down! It's steep, but we can make it," she calls.

Chinua takes a step forward. A click resounds through the frozen air. A sound I'd recognize anywhere. A pressure plate.

I grab on to Chinua's pack and yank her backward. We tumble back against Knnot just as an explosion rocks the thin ledge before us. I cling to Chinua as the ledge crumbles down the side of Knnot, swallowed by the thick drifts beneath.

"No!" The word rips from Chinua's throat, raw and real.

She scrambles to the edge and stares down at our destroyed path. Tears freeze on her cheeks. She whirls and presses her face into my shoulder. "No."

All that's left of our way out is the tiny ledge Chinua and I now stand on before the entrance, not big enough for more than three people. The soaring hope that filled me when I saw the outside for the first time in days crumbles, lost alongside all my other dreams. My numb fingers wrap around Chinua. I hug her tight, wishing I had another answer.

"We can't stay out here." My voice lacks any sort of emotion. I don't have the strength for it anymore.

"Careful," Alik says from behind us.

He pulls something from the ledge just a half step behind me. After setting it down in the middle of the floor, he takes my arm and gently leads Chinua and me back into the cave. Chinua collapses to the ground and I go down with her. My chest feels like it might break completely.

There is no way out. We are lost.

"What is that?" Serafima says.

Even she weeps, her cheeks bright red and eyes rimmed pink. Ivan stands gray and grim at her side, face caught in ragged despair.

My eyes drift to the metal trap Alik brought inside. The make is far too familiar.

I release Chinua and pull it toward me, deactivating the trigger with a few quick pulls. The metal is so cold it sticks to the moisture on my fingers. I try to steady my trembling hands as I turn the trap over to examine the other side. There, branded clearly, is the Thieves Guild insignia.

"Is that?" breathes Alik from above me.

I nod, brushing my fingers along the symbol, two crossed keys with ravens perched on them. It shouldn't shock me. I'd known what it was as soon as Chinua had stepped on the other one outside. Luiza loved to use these outside the guild, making sure we'd be alerted long before anyone tried to get inside. We were lucky we missed this one or we both would've been dead.

If this is here, there is only one thing it can mean.

The Storm Hounds were never working alone. The guild is helping them, scouting and placing traps everywhere they can, hoping to catch us before we have the chance to escape. Their plan worked. This was the only way out and now the path is nothing but crumbled rock.

The metal bites into my hand and I tighten my grip. This is all Luiza's doing. No one could've planned something this intricate except her.

She wanted me to reach Knnot and show Ivan the way, likely leading the Storm Hounds and half the guild straight to it in doing so. What was a few ingots of lovite when she could give the Bright God's champion an entire mountain of it?

I grit my teeth against the realization of how deep her betrayal ran. She didn't just keep me from Alik, she was manipulating me the entire time I was a part of the guild. Slowly molding me into the willing little being she wanted me to be. Before this, I would've done anything for Luiza. Even died to save her life.

"Are you two going to tell us what that is?" Serafima asks.

I toss the trap toward them with a disgusted scoff and get to my feet.

"This trap was made and used by the Thieves Guild," Alik

says. "They've already been here."

"This is the same Thieves Guild Ivan has been reporting to?" Chinua asks.

"The very same," Alik says. My eyes slice over to Ivan.

"Did you know about this?"

His face is broken and hopeless. I know his answer before he even responds. "No. I swear to you I had no idea what she was planning. I just did as she asked. She said she'd keep my family safe. I had to do it. I *had* to."

Pity replaces the hate I was holding for Ivan. Luiza played Ivan just as well as she did Alik and me. I just don't understand why.

A cold thought snakes its way into my mind. Did she really want the lovite to arm a militia to overthrow the Czar? Or did she want it to get the Czar an even more powerful army? One that could use weapons touched by the Bright God's magic to take back the mountain and restart the lovite trade.

That seems far more likely. Far more profitable for the guild and Luiza than toppling Czar Ladislaw and sending Strana into chaos.

"How did you really come by your pendant?" I ask, my voice not much more than a whisper.

"I told you, a witch gave it to me for saving her life," he says.

"How many days before you found Alik did you save her?" I ask.

"I'm not sure. Maybe a week?" Ivan says. "Why?"

My heart sinks straight to my toes.

"She planned this all," I say to Alik. I turn to the group. "The entire thing was orchestrated by Luiza. She planted the pendant and specifically put the woman in danger, likely with instructions to hand it off to the Storm Hound that saved her. Luiza leaked the report of where Alik and I would be and knew Ivan wouldn't let either of us die. She already had his family and knew he'd do anything to keep them safe. She had to manipulate Alik into staying with Ivan and got me to go searching for him. She would've known I'd never leave Alik's side once I saw him. She would've known it wouldn't matter where Alik was going, that I'd follow and lead you all straight to the hidden vaults."

I thought I couldn't feel emptier than I did when I saw my parents. I was wrong. Luiza's betrayal hurts me down to my very core. I'd clung to her like a silly child, because I was one. I was so desperate for a mother, for a home, that I ignored everything wrong with her. I was stupid enough to believe she felt the same about me.

"But why do it? Why not just use the pendant herself?" Alik asks.

My eyes fall to the scar on my wrist. The very one Luiza planted a kiss on the day I left for the Vestry. A shock runs straight down to my toes.

She knew.

She knew what the scar meant. The Bright God's champion

she so desperately revered must've told her. She didn't save me that day because she had some generous bone in her body or because Kosci planted the idea there. She saved me because she knew I was useful, that one day I'd be able to unlock Knnot for everyone because the Pale God would let me inside.

And if she knew, I was certain Czar Ladislaw did as well.

Luiza hadn't hidden us so well that the Czar never knew we existed. He'd simply turned a blind eye because he knew, just as Luiza did, we were more valuable free than trapped in a prison. From the moment I was caught, he'd likely known Luiza's theory of Knnot and its ability to be reclaimed, which made all the prisons he set up after the fact so much more heinous. He'd known Zladonians were nothing more than people desperate for escape and trapped them all anyway.

I pull out the dagger at my hip and look at the blade. My reflection glares back at me. My ivory skin, the white roots just beginning to peek from Luiza's last dye. She always made sure I looked almost like her twin, down to the very color of my hair, and I'd liked that. I'd wanted to look like her because then maybe I could fill the place as her daughter. I did it all because I loved her. Her betrayal rips me as surely as a real blade would and leaves just as big of a wound.

"For so long I pretended to be one of you," I say to no one in particular. "I dreamed I was like you. To be welcome to walk the streets without worrying about being captured. But you aren't free. You may not be persecuted by the kingdom, but you damn yourselves. You don't care about each other. Other people are just things to manipulate. I'm tired of pretending. I'm tired of running. If my life ends now in the bowels of this mountain, so be it, but I will not go out of this life pretending to be something I am not. I will not let Luiza win. I will fight her as my real self, not as the version she made me."

I twist my hair around itself and slice through it. The dark strands fall and scatter across the pitted floor. My lighter hair tosses in the breeze and I relish the movement. It may not destroy all of Luiza's work, but it does enough.

"What do we do now?" Chinua asks.

Her tears have dried, but her eyes remain vacant, staring out at the pristine mountains beyond the mouth of the cave. I wish we could escape this way. I don't want to spend anymore time trapped in the darkness under a mountain of stone.

But we don't have another choice.

"The only way we are getting out is the way we came in," I say.

Serafima gives a brittle laugh. "What? No. The entire reason we went down into the mine in the first place was because the Storm Hounds had us surrounded. And now we have to double back and return to the starting point? They'll shoot us on sight. And we have wasted days of wandering."

An idea strikes through me hot and fast.

"We need to distract them," I say. "Do something so big they have to leave their posts."

"How can we possibly do that? They've got us cornered," Serafima says.

"It's possible, I suppose. They would've made their way into the mountain by now, hoping to catch us and wanting to be close enough to defend the vaults without choking the hall," says Ivan.

"Where do you think they'd set up their base inside Knnot?" I ask.

"Probably in the hut between the shafts. They would want a choke point, somewhere to catch us where we couldn't easily escape. No better place than coming up on those noisy lifts," Ivan says. "But Storm Hounds won't leave their post for anything short of utter destruction."

I nod. "I'd be willing to bet they are gathering as much lovite as they can from the stores, especially since they are in league with the guild. Luiza wouldn't let all that money go to waste, but she wouldn't use her men to do it. If we were to, say, detonate the vaults, they'd be sure to come running."

"We'd bury the very thing we came for," Serafima protests. "This entire expedition would be for nothing."

"Do you want to get out of here alive?" I ask. She narrows her eyes. "This is our best chance."

"You want to sneak through a Storm Hound base and blow up the lovite? That's insanity. It'll never work. We will be dead before sunset," Serafima says.

"Do you have another idea?" I say.

Serafima clenches her jaw. "No. I don't."

Kosci's pendant pricks cold against my thigh, reminding me of its presence. A whisper of desire runs through me. I could slip the pendant on and get all of us out of here. I could find Luiza and destroy her for what she did to me and Alik. Then I could find the Czar and crush him, too. All it would take is accepting Kosci's deal.

I will not be manipulated again.

"How do you propose we do this, then?" Serafima asks.

"We need something loud and surprising enough to pull them from their posts. Chinua, how much *tersh-ek* do you have left?"

She sorts through her bag before pulling out two final pieces of *tersh-ek*, and I suddenly wish I hadn't destroyed the pressure plate. Not nearly enough for the type of explosion I want, but it will have to do. At the very least, it'll grab their attention.

"Okay, we need someone to place these. The rest of us will wait for the explosion and bolt for the exit as soon as they go to investigate." I level a glance at all of them. "Any volunteers?"

Chinua straightens, her eyes determined. "I can place the *tersh-ek*."

"You're sure?"

She nods. "I want to get out of here. I can do this."

"I know you can," I say. "I want someone to go with her, to watch her back while she places it."

"I'll go," Serafima says, surprising me. She runs her fingers along the hilt of her ax. "I can kill quietly if I need to."

I survey the group. It's not a great plan. It's not even a good one. We've got a single chance, and the sooner we take it, the better.

"How are we going to make it back?" Alik asks. "We can't go back the way we came. It'll take too long and we'll come up the lifts, alerting them all before we reach the vaults."

I turn my gaze to the tight passage behind us. The glimmer of a rune sits a short way down the path, leading back down the mountain in the opposite direction from which we came. We'd made it this far with them. Kosci had delivered a way out. I can't dispute that. I don't want to place my trust in a god who was more than willing to kill to protect himself, but I don't really see another choice.

"We keep following those," I say with a nod toward the rune.

"We don't know where it'll take us," Chinua says.

"I know." A heavy weight shifts onto my shoulders. If this fails, we die. Either at the hands of the Storm Hounds or lost in the mountain.

I have to try. I won't leave this world without a fight.

"I can scout ahead," Alik says. "See where it leads and report back."

"What's the point? It's not like we can go another direction," Serafima says.

Ivan looks out toward the dying sun splashing the mountains on the horizon in oranges and pinks. "Let's rest here for the night. Get as much fresh air as we can. We can start down the path tomorrow."

We drift into an uneasy sleep. My dreams are dogged by Storm Hounds and faceless creatures. I toss and turn until a cold hand slips onto my shoulder. I spring to my feet expecting a guild member, but come face-to-face with Kosci.

"The others can't see you?" I growl and shift farther away from Alik's sleeping form.

"Not unless I want them to, and right now, I don't want to reveal myself."

"My answer is still no," I say.

"You're certain? This plan has almost no chance of actually succeeding, you know. I feel the doubt in your bones."

"Dying is still better than becoming your champion."

"Even if the death isn't your own?" Kosci's eyes stray to the slumbering forms around me.

My heart thuds at his implication, and when I don't respond, he presses a tip of his finger to the place in my pocket where his heart rests. It flares blistering cold at his touch. "I'm here if you need me. You have one more day to make your choice."

The air before me seems to flicker, and he is gone. I suck in a breath, trying to convince myself I'm making the right decision.

# TWENTY-NINE

BRIGHT SUNSHINE POURS INTO THE cave and wakes us for the first time in what seems like years. Shouldering our packs, we follow the runes down a steep slope, traveling deeper into the mountain until the cave makes an abrupt curve.

"We're in the caverns that lead to the Iovite stores," I whisper.

"Already? We haven't been walking for more than a couple of hours," Alik says, his voice hushed.

"Was this path here before?" Chinua asks.

"It must've been. New passes don't just spring up out of the mountain," Serafima says.

Kosci could likely do such things. I glance at Alik. I've wanted to tell him about Kosci since the moment I returned from his room, but every time I opened my mouth, I couldn't. Alik was never one to believe in the gods. Even with the proof hiding inside my pocket, I don't know if he'd believe me.

A darker part of my heart wonders if I haven't told him because I'm still considering Kosci's deal. Alik would never want me to take it. He'd tell me to throw the pendant into the caves and forget about it. I try to convince myself it isn't true, but Kosci's warning the night before still rings in my mind. Am I willing to risk their lives?

I don't know if I am, and the thought scares me.

"It's so small and dark here," I say, at last. "No one probably noticed it."

Boots on stone pound toward us. I shove Ivan back the way we came and scramble in behind him. Just as Chinua slips in, Storm Hounds round the bend with a box full of lovite. I recognize the two Thieves Guild members who bring up the rear, weapons out. All four wear the same sort of stone as Ivan's pendant pinned to their cloaks. The amber lines flicker in the dim light, reminding me just what Luiza has done.

She hadn't been lying about aiding the Bright God's champion. Of course, she hadn't. She's the one who told me the best lies are wrapped in layers of truth. She just lied about what she wanted the lovite for. She must've used what I stole from the Vestry and passed it along to the champion to bless.

I had been so easy to trick. I wonder if she laughed about it after I was gone. If she ever considered how guilty I'd feel, believing I'd compromised the guild and put her in danger. She probably knew how I'd feel and wagered that if my love for Alik wouldn't get me to follow Ivan, my love for her would.

Heat races up my neck as I watch the Storm Hounds march down the path. No one casts a glance in our direction as they round the bend and disappear. I sag against the stone and press my head to the wall. For now, we've avoided detection.

"Of course they're taking the lovite. They're probably betting on us starving," Ivan says.

"We probably will if we don't get out of here soon," Serafima grinds out.

We fall silent. There is only one option before us now. We won't have many chances, if any, where the path is clear. My heart flickers beats of panic. Everything in my being tells me to wait. To gather more information, to do something other than charge in and hope for the best. Our group hasn't eaten in days. We're compromised before we even try.

"Are we ready?" I ask, my voice nothing but a whisper upon the stones.

One by one, they nod.

"Chinua and Serafima will head out first," I say. "We'll count to sixty, then make a move for the entrance. Find a spot to hide after the explosion and run for the exit once all the guards have cleared the halls."

No one protests, and I'm grateful. I don't think I could've handled it. I grasp Chinua's hand and give it a tight squeeze before watching her and Serafima slip into the passage. I slow my breathing as I count, each second landing like a heavy stone on my back. I gesture to Alik and Ivan to follow me.

After the close walls of the interior of the mountain, it almost seems too wide here, too open. I don't waste time in looking around. We dart toward the entrance, and I keep my feet light and my breathing as quiet as possible. Ivan is nearly silent behind me. Years of military training at work, I suppose. We duck behind carts and beams. The closer we get to the mouth of the mine, the harder breathing becomes. Guards litter the area, pacing back and forth, covering every angle. We barely have time to slip behind a fallen ceiling beam before one of them looks our way.

"What now?" Ivan asks.

"We wait."

Too many heartbeats thump by. Each one bringing the nearest guard, a slender boy of no more than twenty, closer to us. Just when he is about to look over the beam, an explosion detonates at the end of the hall.

"What was that?" someone shouts above the tumble of rocks and dirt.

The Storm Hounds scramble toward the noise. They are far faster and stronger than we are. They are prepared for battle, as they always are. It's evident in every movement they make toward the vaults. I pray Serafima and Chinua make it back to safety before the Storm Hounds come.

A flurry of gold-and-black uniforms rush past us. They all shout about losing the lovite and the bad luck of the mines. There seem to be dozens of them. Before long the sound of their charging feet dies down. Ivan, Alik, and I look at each other before pushing away from the walls.

We steal down the last few lengths of corridor, breaking out onto the wide path before the entrance. The open path leading to Ludminka stretches in front of me, a small encampment set off to the left near the avalanche fall. No one stalks about the tents, and tension loosens in my chest. We just have to run. We can be free.

I look back down the left-hand path, searching for Chinua's dark hair or Serafima's frame.

Nothing.

"We've got to go," says Ivan.

"We need Chinua and Serafima," I hiss back.

"We can't wait for them," he says.

I turn my glare toward him, taking in his pallid face and wild eyes. I bite down hard on the inside of my cheek.

"Run, then, you coward," I say. "I'm waiting for them."

I hurry toward the upturned cart beside the wall, Alik behind me. We both duck behind it, sticking our legs into the broken hole in the side to hide them. Ivan hesitates at the entrance before throwing us one last glance and darting outside.

I let a long, harsh sigh out of my nose. Of course he'd run

now that he's gotten what he wanted.

Long moments stretch by, and I don't hear a thing. No Storm Hounds. No hurried footsteps. Nothing. I'm just about to turn to Alik and say we should go when quick gasps sound from our left. I peek over the top to see Chinua and Serafima rushing up the path as fast as they can. I tug Alik out of our hiding space, joining them as we run out the entrance.

Freedom.

Several resounding clicks circle us as Storm Hounds filter from their spots pressed against the side of the mountain, shoving a bloody-nosed Ivan into us. We collide, and they waste no time in surrounding us.

There had never been an escape. The Storm Hounds had been stationed here and told not to move, just in case. Our only hope vanishes like steam on the wind. We will never be free.

The small contingency of Storm Hounds lifts its crossbows, holding them steady at our hearts.

"I knew you'd do something desperate, Ivan Devoski. Destroying the lovite was a fairly good idea. Just not good enough," a cold voice says from behind us.

I spin, and my heart stutters to a halt. Before the entrance stands the commander of the Storm Hounds himself, the same one who chased me through the streets of Rurik the night I robbed the Vestry. He carries his helmet under his arm. When he sees me, he smiles.

Alik reaches for my hand, and I twine my fingers with his. The Storm Hounds lower their crossbows as their commander steps into the ring. He runs an appraising eye over each of us.

Alik tightens his grip on my hand and spins to face me, covering my body with his own as if planning to shield me from the worst of the bolts. I stare into his determined face and wish we had more time.

We should've shared a kiss under open skies and explored the world.

It isn't fair.

The world gave me the thing I wanted most and then ripped it away from me in a heartbeat.

"Seize them," says the commander with a dismissive wave of his hand.

I try to keep ahold of Alik's hand as the Storm Hounds grab our shoulders and rip us apart. His fingers slip through mine, and I turn my gaze toward the sky, praying we'll somehow make it out of this alive.

# THIRTY

THE STORM HOUNDS JUMP TO follow his command. They rip the packs from our backs and check each of us for weapons, stealing away Serafima's ax and my daggers. After making certain we had nothing but the clothes on our backs, they slip heavy manacles around our wrists, all of us leashed together by icy chains as they yank us farther from the entrance of the mines and into the sunlit snow of the road to Ludminka. I squeeze my eyes against the reflection of bright light on snow.

It takes a moment before I can really see. The commander leads us toward the camp I had spotted earlier. I can already imagine the whispers between the other soldiers. He caught the rogue Storm Hound and uncovered *malozlas* too. The commander freed Knnot and now Strana will become a nation of power again. All thanks to him.

Heat simmers beneath my skin. I want to scream, but know it'll do nothing to change things. Alik and I will be shipped off to a prison, Ivan and Serafima will likely be killed for associating with us, and Chinua—poor Chinua—will likely be ransomed back to the Khan, forced to become his concubine.

The commander pushes past the first area of the encampment, primarily wooden pikes for defense and a small weapons station filled with swords and glowing lovite shields. He circles past what is very obviously his tent. The thick black canvas hangs to the ground, firmly pegged in along every edge to keep out the winter chill. Guards stand on either side of the opening. They couldn't be more obvious if they tried. I attempt to memorize everything about it, just on the off chance I do manage to come up with a plan to escape.

It seems odd that Storm Hounds would so blatantly mark out their commanding officer's accommodations. They usually try to maintain equality in an effort to confuse assassins seeking to strike officers down first. The commander must be favored by the Czar to warrant such special attention. Something about it sets me even more on edge.

At last, a small wooden cage comes into view. We are shepherded in, Ivan kicked in the back of the knees so he collapses in the center of the cage. They've placed us here specifically to suffer, likely hoping the exposure to the cold will lower our defenses enough to make us talk. I scan the edge of the encampment, looking for the carriage of metal bars that will take Alik and me away, but I don't see one. Maybe there hasn't been time for one to get here yet.

The commander smirks at us. "Get cozy. You'll be here long enough to loosen your tongues, I promise. I'm sure it'll be a cold night."

"What could he possibly want from us?" Chinua whispers. "We know nothing."

"I have no idea," I say, and move closer to Alik. All I have on is a torn tunic and dirty breeches. Alik wears a heavy woolen sweater and the same pants, our coats lost somewhere in our mad dash to escape. None of us is prepared for the bitter cold of night.

Serafima grips one of the wood bars circling us and tries to rattle it. It doesn't so much as wiggle. She gives a kick and lets out a muffled scream into her arm.

"We spent so much time hoping to get out and *this* is how we'll spend it," she says.

The weight of her words settles on me. This is all my fault. I'd come up with the plan to try and escape Knnot. It failed. There's no one else at fault.

"I won't blame any of you for giving him the information he wants," I say softly.

"I'm not going to tell him anything," Chinua says. "I won't bend to a man who locked me in a cage. Death is preferable to spending my life with the Khan."

Ivan and Serafima don't say anything. I shouldn't feel angry; I gave them permission to give us up. But part of me hoped they'd at least have a little hesitation. We spent weeks together; does that bond mean nothing to them?

Alik's hand curls around mine, already cold. He gives it a squeeze. We don't speak. We always knew the likelihood of ending up in a prison. Nothing will help now. No amount of words or pleading will move the Storm Hounds. They're taught to forget their emotions. The more unfeeling the man, the better the Storm Hound.

Alik stands beside me, as close as he can get. I bring his hand to my mouth, pressing a kiss to his knuckles. All that running, only to be caught now. We should've saved ourselves the starvation and turned ourselves over the first day.

"I promise I will never forget you," I whisper. "Please remember that."

Alik cups my face in his hand and I press into it.

"If you think I won't try to find a way to escape, you're mad. I will find you again, Valeria."

Alik brings my chin toward him. The kiss is soft and tender but desperate. As if he thinks it will be the last time our lips will touch.

Perhaps it will be.

Despite myself, I believe his words, as much as I tell myself I shouldn't. Hope is dangerous in a *tyur'ma*. But I can't help it. Alik will always ignite hope inside me. I pull away, wishing

I could put words to everything swirling in my heart, but I can't. Terror chokes my voice and locks it tight.

I bite the tip of my tongue as Kosci's pendant throbs against my leg. If I slipped on this pendant, if I accepted his deal, we could survive. But I'd be giving in to the power that had no qualms about killing an entire village and letting all Zladonia suffer for his own selfish needs.

I eye the sun hanging low in the sky. I have mere hours to decide.

We sit shivering in the fading light, all of us too nervous to sit on the ground and chill ourselves more. Soon our resolve will fade and we'll have no choice. I tense as a broad Storm Hound approaches. He can't be more than ten years my elder, but lines sit heavy on his brow. He pulls out a key, pointing at me.

"Come."

I bristle but know there isn't any use in resisting. I let him take my upper arm and steer me through the camp toward the commander's tent. As he pushes back the flap, warm air floods over me and I start to shiver.

The tent is elaborate with a low cot near the back wall and a small stove in the center, a pipe directing the smoke out the top. Curtains of lush purples and golds swathe the walls, keeping the heat from leaving. The commander sits with his feet propped up on a small table, a plate of meat resting in one hand. Saliva springs to my lips. How long has it been since I've had a real meal?

"Leave us," the commander says.

The Storm Hound gives a curt nod and disappears through the flap. Unease settles over me. I hope I don't look as nervous and desperate as I feel.

"Valeria, right?" the commander says.

"How do you know my name?"

He gives a broad smile. "Luiza told me all about you, of course."

My blood runs cold. I knew Luiza had betrayed me, but to hear it from this man is something I am not prepared for. I try and let the feeling roll through me, but my temper snares it before I can push it away. How could she turn me over to this man?

The commander takes another bite of meat, juice rolling down his chin. He wipes it away with the back of his hand.

"Why am I here?" I ask at last.

"A favor to Luiza. She asked me to make sure you're safe," he says.

A bark erupts from my lips. "What does she care about my safety?"

"A great deal. She begged me to ensure it."

"You might as well throw me back in the cage," I snarl. "I'll give you nothing."

The commander's eyes snap to mine, hardening for the first time since we started talking. He slowly places his plate on the table.

"Luiza promised you'd be malleable. Said you'd realize it

was better to survive," he says.

"Not for a dog of the Czar and certainly not for the woman who betrayed me."

"We'll see. I have ways of making people talk."

I suppress the shudder trying to climb up my spine. I'd never been tortured. I want to believe I'll withstand it, but part of me is afraid I won't. The commander suddenly pushes to his feet, and I shrink back on instinct. A smirk crosses his lips. He brushes past me and stalks from the tent without another word.

The Storm Hound who'd brought me stands guard just beyond. I catch a glimpse of him as the flap falls back into place. No escaping, then. He'd be on me before I had a chance to so much as lift the tent flap.

I ease myself toward the table, strewn with papers and maps. The commander must truly believe he will break us if he leaves all of his documents unguarded with a thief. I grab the closest page and stare down at it.

The lettering is messy, with large loops and ink droplets, but I can make out a message from the Czar himself, asking the commander to secure Knnot and reestablish the lovite trade. I toss it back on the table. Useless information I'd already guessed.

The next is a map of Strana, small *X*'s dotting it. It takes me a moment before I realize they are prisons. I let my eyes drift to the one nearest Zladonia. It's likely where they plan to take Alik and me. The weather would be harsh and the food meager this far north. My stomach sinks.

At last I find the letter I'd been hoping to. I recognize Luiza's neat hand immediately, more familiar to me than even my own. My heart starts to hammer as I take in who it is addressed to.

*My Lord, the Bright Champion of Strana,*

The commander is not just some highly valued Storm Hound, he is the Bright God's champion.

I scan the rest of the letter. The commander wasn't lying. Luiza did beg him to spare me, saying I would help find new lovite deposits and old trade agreements. Telling him I was more valuable alive than dead, that I would be willing to help to save my own skin.

My blood boils.

Luiza must not know me at all. I would never willingly help a Storm Hound, or the Czar. She paints me as a pathetic creature, desperate to please whichever owner holds the leash. My breath comes hot and heavy in my chest, threatening to break free of my control. Any leftover love I held for Luiza dissipates completely. I crumple the letter and feed it to the stove.

I don't care if the commander realizes it's missing. I don't care if this is my last day alive. I will never again do as Luiza says. I will never bow to the Czar. I would rather fight and die than live a lie.

I jump as a hand clamps on my shoulder. I whirl, expecting the commander, but it's the same Storm Hound who led me to the tent. Without a word, he takes me back outside. Instead of heading toward the cage as I expect, he leads me through camp and toward Knnot.

It looms high above, casting a long shadow. The last of the sunlight still clings to its side, warm fingers against the snowy peak. A circle of black uniforms stands a few paces away with their backs turned toward the center. I stare at their impassive faces as I walk by, hoping my gaze burns each one of them.

The group parts, and I stumble to a stop. In the center of the circle is Ivan, Chinua, Serafima . . . and Alik, all of them on their knees. The commander stands above them, twirling a small dagger as if it were nothing more than a trinket. He grins as I approach, but the smile never reaches his eyes. The Storm Hound behind me forces me forward, shoving me to my knees beside Alik.

He surveys the group, his eyes lingering on Ivan.

"Colonel Devoski." The commander offers a crooked grin. "And here I thought I would never see you again."

"Commander Matvei." Ivan's nod is short.

"The list of your crimes is a long one. Treason, deserting, dealings with *malozla*, stealing, and an unsanctioned expedition into forbidden territory. Just one of those things warrants a trial in the capital." Commander Matvei sighs as if he's simply tired of all Ivan's antics.

"You do not need to lecture me on the laws of the country," Ivan spits.

Commander Matvei tugs off his gloves, baring his waxen skin to the cool air.

"I was originally under orders to bring you back alive, if I could. Seeing as your crimes are too numerous to count and the fact that you put up resistance, I have no choice but to put you down."

Ivan opens his mouth to retort, but it is cut short as Matvei buries a dagger in Ivan's shoulder. He shoves the blade harder and the metal pierces through Ivan's back. He topples, the commander over him, his dark cloak billowing across the snow. He shoves the blade until it's deep in the frozen ground.

Ivan struggles against it for a moment as Commander Matvei stands. Without a word, he unleashes the sword hanging at his hip and drives it through Ivan's throat.

Alik's face goes pale as blood starts to leak from Ivan's mouth, leaving crimson tracks like tears on his chin. Alik's muscles coil as if he plans on springing toward the commander. I wrap my hands around his bicep, shaking my head. The rim of Alik's eye goes red and he grits his teeth hard against the tears. Chinua gasps, placing a hand over her mouth, and Serafima turns away as Ivan's body goes limp.

I watch, letting the image burn into my mind. Yet another life lost to the Czar's justice. Commander Matvei pulls at the thick cord around Ivan's neck and snaps the leather with a single tug. The pendant falls into his hand. He stares down at it before curling his hand around it and turning his eyes to me.

So this is the true glory of the Bright God. The slaughter of humanity. Just as Kosci said.

Matvei takes a step toward Alik and me. Serafima throws herself in front of us.

"They aren't worth your time," she says. "They're nothing."

"Two nothings that managed to break the icy hold of Knnot." He brushes her aside. "I have one of you to thank for finally allowing my Storm Hounds inside the village. If one of you hadn't made this journey, none of this would've been possible. But which one of you is the Pale God's champion? Who did he unlock his mountain for?"

My mind churns as his finger dances between us. How did he know the Pale God had chosen a champion? Before I can think of an answer, his finger lands on Alik.

"You, stand up."

Alik rises from his knees, wincing and grabbing my arm for support as he goes. Matvei's eyes instantly flick over him.

"What's wrong with you, boy?"

"Nothing," I say for Alik. "He's perfectly fine."

"Did I ask you?" Matvei barks.

He crosses to us. His hand snaps out like a viper and clenches Alik's chin. Commander Matvei turns Alik's face from one side to the other, then moves his gaze down his body. Alik tries to shift his weight evenly to both legs, but it's too late. Matvei grabs Alik's thigh. The commander's face goes from momentary shock to calculating in a snap of a finger.

"There's no way you've been chosen by the god." He flings Alik's face away from him with such force, Alik stumbles backward, barely keeping his balance. "You either die here or at a *tyur'ma*. I see no point in wasting rations on someone we won't be paid for. Kill him."

"No." The word rips from my throat.

The commander's eyes snap to mine. "I told you I had ways of making you talk."

Before I can respond, the snap of the crossbow seems to rend the very air. Serafima pushes me out of the way and dives for Alik.

Everything slows to a crawl.

I scream his name and he turns his head toward me. His eyebrows draw together. He knows what comes for him. He's been here before. Serafima's body collides into his, but it's too late.

The bolt hits his chest, and he stumbles, falling with Serafima.

"No," I gasp. "No, no no. Please, no."

I push Serafima out of the way and gather Alik into my arms. Blood pools around the bolt, leaking down his chest. I rip it out and press my hands to the wound, putting as much pressure on it as I can. Warmth seeps through my fingers, staining my hands red.

Alik wheezes in a deep breath. He lifts one hand and lets it stroke my cheek. I press into it. Tears roll down my face, and I free one hand from the wound to press his hand harder to my face, kissing its palm.

"I love you, Valeria."

I sob again, my breath too hard to catch. My entire chest aches like something inside me is breaking apart.

I give up stanching the blood pumping from his chest and gather his shoulders into my arms. He shudders, and I clutch him to me tighter, as if my very presence can keep him alive.

"I love you, too." My breath hitches, but I want him to know. I want it to be the last thing he hears.

He shivers against me. His breath rattles out, and he coughs around the wheeze, blood staining his pale lips.

"Don't let me go alone," he whispers.

"Never." Tears roll off my chin to stain his shoulder. "I will never leave you again."

I allow his hand to fall to his chest and brush his hair out of his face and start to hum a soft lullaby. The same one he used to sing to me when we were young and I was afraid in Luiza's dorm rooms. A small smile spreads across his lips, and his eye slides closed. He lets loose a last breath.

His chest doesn't rise again.

My lungs suddenly don't work. I try to breathe around the squeeze in my ribs, but I can't. He's gone and there was nothing I could do. I tried to save him. I tried to save them all.

Now I've lost Alik twice.

The voices that have plagued me ever since I entered Knnot whisper to me again. They beg me to let them help, let them consume my hurt and my pain, to let them give me the power to take my revenge. I desperately cast my eyes around the circle. Serafima sits with her hands in her lap, staring at Alik's face. Chinua cowers near her. Ivan lies, pinned to the ground, blood still oozing from his wounds.

All of them, broken and lost because of me. I knew the Bright God chose a champion and I still refused Kosci's deal, never once imagining I would find the champion here. It makes a sick amount of sense. If the Bright God could kill me before I came into Kosci's power, he'd never have to worry about a war. Commander Matvei had us trapped. He'd kill us all to serve the Bright God.

My eyes fall to Alik. My poor, beautiful, kind Alik.

Blood still trickles onto my hands, warm and sticky, but he is gone. The fissure in my soul grows wider and deeper until I can't stand it.

The voices whisper to destroy all of Strana like they've destroyed me. A bright ray of light flashes across my face as the sun fades from view. I fumble for my pocket, my hands slick with Alik's blood. At long last, I manage to close my hand around the pendant. I rip it out and stare at the sparkling lovite. I will take all the power Kosci can grant me. I no longer care about the cost. I slip the leather strap over my head.

"I accept your deal," I whisper.

# THIRTY-ONE

I ARCH MY BACK AS something stabs into my chest. I look down, expecting to see a Storm Hound's blade. Instead, my entire chest glows blue where the pendant meets my flesh. It's so bright, I have to look away. I open my mouth to scream as the clawing begins. It rips and tears against my skin, digging its way deeper, into my bones. Everything fades into bright white. My arms begin to fissure, blue light gleaming like veins beneath my skin. A roar sounds in my ears, like a tidal wave before it crashes onto the shore.

"Do not resist me," a deep voice says. Whether in my mind or in the physical world, I can't tell.

I force myself to relax each of my muscles. The pain ebbs away, the roaring stops. Slowly, everything comes back into focus. Every pair of eyes are on me. Some of the Storm Hounds' mouths hang open, their weapons limp at their sides. Chinua's wide eyes reflect only fear; Serafima's mouth is dropped into an O. I smirk.

I'm no longer alone. I'm no longer weak.

I am so much more than I ever was before.

Power courses through my veins. I rise slowly to my feet. Power crackles along my arms and through my torso. I turn my eyes to the Storm Hounds. With a flick of my hand, they fly back. I force the ground to my will, growing sharp rock from the previously smooth snow. The bodies slam into them with dull thuds.

My mouth automatically forms into a whistle. I let out three quick chirps. The creatures that herded us toward Kosci crawl from the mouth of the mine and trickle down the steep sides. They lope across the open field on all fours, long teeth bared. The Storm Hounds scramble to pull up their weapons, but it's too late. They descend onto the Storm Hounds, ripping and biting until the snow churns red with blood.

Commander Matvei manages to cut his way through Kosci's protective monsters. He abandons his brigade without a backward glance and races toward his tent.

I let him. He can wait. First, I will let my creatures take their reward.

I turn my back on the creatures to face the two of us left. "What do you choose? Follow me or die here."

"You aren't Valeria," Serafima whispers.

"I am." I smile. "And so much more. Now choose."

They fear me, yet know I will save them. The power of my magic is obvious now. Better, they respect me as Valeria.

Serafima is the first to fall to her knees. "I serve you."

My eyes slide over to Chinua. Her face firms.

"You promised to lead me from this mountain. You did. I will follow you anywhere."

I smile. "Then let us show them what we are made of."

I lead us forward, head held high. I'm no longer afraid of this haunted land. It is my home.

No, not my home. His power. The God under the Mountain.

*But now it is we,* the deep voice whispers in my head. *Together, we can take Strana. We will win this war, don't you see? You will be able to hear me every time you wear your pendant. Combined, we can stop the Czar and his senseless slaughter. We can stop my brother from ruining this land. We can keep it safe. Make it whole.*

I do see. I can feel the surety of his words flooding through my veins. I have the power to do what I couldn't before. I can free the Zladonians from their prisons. I can allow them to not only survive but flourish.

The Storm Hounds in the encampment move, preparing for my attack and aiming bows at the monsters behind me.

I refuse to let it happen.

I step into the open field. Before they can ready their arrows, I raise my arm. The settled snow before them begins to stir until it rises like a wave. It crashes upon the camp, sending the troops scurrying back. I pull my hand toward my chest and the snow freezes solid.

Matvei calls out orders. Some sort of formation, meaning they will attempt to open fire. They still aren't terrified of me.

That simply won't do.

Instead of waiting for him to give the order to fire, I drop to my knees and shove my fingers into the snow, digging my hand down until I reach the hard earth. I force my power into the earth. My vision goes in and out, alternating between the brilliant white of the churned snow and blackness, before settling on the black. I allow Kosci to take over.

He forces our power into the ground until it connects with a vein of lovite. Instantly, it lights up like a lantern, flaring along the vein back toward the mountain, tracing a path through the tall reaches of Knnot and under the nearby mountains.

The entire ground trembles, rocks tumbling all around us. I don't move. I continue to force my power into the earth, and the lovite drinks it up until it can't take anymore. A crack rings through the air and something sizzles against my skin. Still, I don't look up. Not until the earth rolls beneath me. Chinua and Serafima scream, but I snap at them to hold their places.

A thin line cracks through the earth's surface, darting all the way to the Storm Hounds' encampment. I bare my teeth in a snarl as I shove my fist deeper into the ground. Ice and rock stab into my fingers, but I push past the pain. I open my hand. A pit forms beneath the Storm Hounds' feet and swallows them whole. Their chorus of horrified howls is like music to my ears. I am a giant of frost and snow. They can never hope to compare to the power now sparking at my fingertips.

"That's for Alik," I whisper.

The surviving Storm Hounds flee. No one gives the command, but they've seen too much. I can smell the fear on the air, like the tang of the sweetest flower. Kosci drinks their pain and devours their fear. It only serves to fuel us.

All have fled but a single soul, the heartbeat echoing somewhere to my left. I spin slowly and take in the land. Matvei stands twenty feet away, amber light spilling from his open palms.

"I should've killed you in Rurik when I had the chance," he calls.

I square my shoulders.

"What would've been the fun in that?" I ask, Kosci's voice thrumming below mine in a deeper timbre. "Come out and play, brother. I know you've been waiting for me."

Matvei unsheathes his sword and swings it in a great arc. Fire hurls through the air toward me. I pull up a wall of ice, large enough to protect myself and others behind me.

He is the reason Alik is dead. My anger surges through me, giving more tinder to the flame of my power. I force out a hand and the barrier of ice explodes outward.

I bare my teeth as the shards connect with his shield, burned away before they can slice his flesh.

"Do you really believe you stand a chance against me, little girl? You've had the power of the Pale God for moments. I've prepared for this for years."

He advances, the searing heat rolling off his body melting the snow as he walks.

I will not yield.

I will cut him down and he will pay for Alik's death. The entire kingdom will pay, starting with Luiza and ending with the Czar.

Instead of responding, I lash out, bringing my hand up and crafting long icicles from the melting snow. I shoot them at him in rapid succession, too fast for him to block every one. One manages to catch his arm, and he hisses against the pain. He lunges forward, his blade aimed at my heart. I spin to the side, but he predicts the move. Cold metal bites the flesh of my shoulder. Pure rage burns through my veins and I extend my hands. Long sheaths of ice grow from my fingertips, the edges sharp and deadly.

Matvei's face doesn't so much as twitch at their appearance. He lashes out. I deflect the blow, his metal sword ringing off my frozen weapon with a high-pitched whine. We clash again and again in a flurry of blades. Sweat beads my forehead and rolls down my back. Matvei's trained for years with the Storm Hounds, honing his skill. I'll never best him like this. He bashes his shield into my chest, and I tumble backward, my foot slipping in a patch of half-melted ice.

As I fall, I swipe with my left hand at his exposed wrist. My ice dagger connects, slicing through his skin. He lets out a curse as I hit the ground. Cold mud soaks into my clothes. I try to scramble to my feet, desperate to regain my position before he can strike again. He stabs as I attempt to rise. I cry out as the tip of his sword rips into my side. I roll backward, letting the sword rip from my flesh. I bite the inside of my cheek as pain blooms down my hip and into my leg. I rise to my feet. Blood drips from his wrist and he seethes, emotion finally breaking through his facade.

He charges me. I wait until the last second to move out of the way and he tumbles forward, catching himself at the last moment. He wheels on me, blade raised.

"Enough of this," he growls.

He thrusts the blade high into the air. Calling light from the dusk through will alone. The rays stream down to circle me. I try to move past. My skin sizzles as it touches the bars of light and I back away.

"I haven't spent years waiting for the Pale God's champion to have it be nothing but a girl. The Bright God offered me a glorious battle and instead I trapped a mewling child whose anger is the only thing that keeps her alive."

The bars disappear the instant he's within striking distance. I attempt to jump backward, but I'm too late. His blade connects with my ribs, sawing its way straight to my bone.

I collapse to my knees, hand pressed to the wound at my side. This can't be how it ends. I didn't bargain away my life for all the power of a god to die at the hands of his brother's champion. I want to get to my feet, to keep fighting, but the pain in my ribs keeps me in place.

Matvei places the tip of his blade against the hollow of my throat, and he forces me to look up at him.

"I want to watch you die," he says, a cruel smile twisting his lips.

*Not like this*, whispers Kosci's voice in the back of my mind.

Matvei wrenches back his arm. Without a thought, I press my bloodstained palm to the ground and grin as the temperature instantly plummets. Cooling until steam rises from Matvei's body, and then ever further until frost starts to form on the sweat coating his forearm. Kosci controls me now. He orders my body to stand, the wound on my side zipping closed and scarring over in a blinding flash of pain.

"I will let you rule this world no longer, brother," Kosci says through my mouth.

"Your power is failing. I feel it. You may have stopped me from killing your vessel, but I will escape before you can kill mine. You're weak, Kosci. Far too weak to best me." Matvei's mouth moves, but an entirely different voice speaks. Its low timbre is similar to Kosci's but colder, crueler.

Kosci orders me to cut. My arms move of their own accord, slicing through the frozen arm of the man before me. Matvei's eyes go wide as the limb shatters to pieces around us. The sword clatters to the ground and he clutches his severed arm to his chest.

Before I can do anything more, the air before him shimmers in a ray of golden light. I squeeze my eyes shut against the intensity. By the time I'm able to open them again, Matvei is stumbling into Ludminka and out of sight.

Kosci's hold on my body falters, and I sway. The power I'd felt coursing through my veins moments prior is now just a whisper of its former strength.

*I have power enough for only a few things more. You must decide what they will be. It will return when I'm fed the suffering of this world, but not a moment before. Choose wisely, Valeria.* Kosci's voice rings through my mind like a second consciousness.

Through the power of the pendant, I can tell Matvei's unnatural speed has already carried him to the edge of Ludminka, almost beyond the reach of Kosci's power. There's no point in targeting him. It would be a waste of what is left. Instead, I turn my attention to the other Storm Hounds still trying to escape to the village. I can't allow them to get away.

Not this time.

Not when I have the power to make sure they don't.

I lift my arm, sensing the heartbeats of all the people encapsulated in ice inside the town. For so many years, Kosci kept them alive and safe, knowing he would have use of them. The distant part of me that isn't caught in Kosci's power breaks as I realize my parents are alive. I will get to see them again.

Today I set the cursed villagers of Ludminka free, just like I always dreamed of doing.

The sound of hundreds of icebergs cracking fills the air. The people in the village take in one collective breath, their minds warped and twisted by Kosci's power. *My* power. They are an army of thralls prepared to do my bidding. I want Kosci to free them. They've been trapped long enough.

*Soon*, he says. *We need them to rid us of this plague. They will be too afraid to do it without my power.*

"Kill all but two," I whisper.

The people of Ludminka move as one entity, stumbling on new legs, ready to fight. The first cry pierces the air, the first drops of blood fall to the pristine snow. Then, it's a slaughter. The thralls will kill any who cross their path, except two. Someone must escape to spread word of what is to come. It's no fun if we take them by surprise.

Strana must hear of the anger rising in the north. They must hear rumors of a girl who walks with the soul of a god chained to her neck. With my power, I will be unstoppable.

I turn from the dying Storm Hounds back toward Serafima and Chinua. They are next to Alik, who lies motionless, blood staining his lips and dripping down the side of his mouth. I kneel to the ground beside him and the pendant at my neck gives a wild pulse as if in answer to my question.

I place my hand on his heart and close my eyes.

A cold void of darkness sweeps over me in a wave. A shock ripples down my arm, blue light flaring across my vision. I feel

Alik's wound mending, his heart growing, getting ready for a beat. Another blue shock jolts down my arm.

Alik gasps beneath me.

I open my eyes and stare down. He takes in another deep breath and his eyelid flutters. Before he can open it fully, I collect him into a crushing embrace, even as the last of Kosci's power trickles from my muscles.

"Val?" he croaks. "How? What?"

"Shh," I whisper into his hair, tears pouring down my cheeks. "You're safe. I've got you."

As I hold him, I stare at Ludminka over his head. The village murmurs with activity and confusion, but I now know what I must do. I refuse to let the Czar continue to rule this country, for Luiza to walk free after years of manipulation and control, for Matvei to cause more suffering.

With the pendant still beating at my neck, I know I have the power to end it all. To ruin this world for what it did to me.

Those who once hunted me will now only whisper my name. Those who once sought to control me will bow and praise me before their peers. I will bring them to their knees. They wanted a war. I will give it to them.

Those who feared the gods will now fear me.

I am no longer just Valeria.

I am Vengeance.

# ACKNOWLEDGMENTS

This has been a dream of mine since I was thirteen writing Harry Potter fanfics in my parents' basement. So many people have been by my side on the journey with me and I can confidently say I wouldn't have made it without each and every one of them.

First, I want to thank my parents, Jason and Rebecca. Never once have you questioned my ability to improve. Never once did you tell me getting published was a silly pipe dream. You always supported and encouraged me, finding conferences for me to attend and reading manuscript after manuscript. You always said we could do anything if we tried and those are words I live by. I love you both so much and am so thankful for everything you've given me.

Thank you to my sisters, Katelyn and Diana. You sat in that cold basement with me, helping write fanfics and original stories, and humored me when I wanted to write stories on our Christmas sleepovers. You kept me from at least seven mental breakdowns where I threatened to delete every single book I ever wrote. I wouldn't be here today without your love and unwavering support. You both always believed I could become a published author and never hesitated in building me up when I needed it (or taking me to task when I was being dramatic). I love you both beyond words and am so happy to call you my sisters.

Next I have to thank my partner in crime and lifelong best friend, Mark. I don't know why you decided to marry the neurotic girl you met in band class, but I'm glad you did. You've been with me from the very beginning of this journey. You read every single horrible book that got me to this point and never hesitated in telling me everything I did right (while ignoring all the wrong, which I am also grateful for). You were there for every tear shed and stayed up late into the night listening to every new chapter. Your belief was never-ending. Thank you for wishing for this on every 11:11, shooting star, and backward walk down a hidden druid staircase. I know you did that, even if you never told me. You gave me all the opportunities I needed to make this dream a reality and believed when I couldn't. I love you so much and couldn't ask for anyone better to share my life with.

I will thank my children, Victor and Wesley. First, because they asked me to. Second, because they gave me the final push I needed to make my dreams come true. I wanted to show them that even something as distant as getting a book published was possible. You were mostly good babies, which allowed me to get this work done. I love you both and hope you will read these words someday, even if you don't like the kissing.

Thank you to my in-laws, Kathryn and Conrad. You've been in my life since I was seventeen years old and always took interest in my dreams of becoming an author. Thank you for your quiet support and for watching the boys to give me time to chase my career. I will be forever grateful to you in a way I'm not sure you understand.

I want to thank both sides of my extended family. All the Montgomerys, Morrises, Tupitzas, Hanscoms, and Hurleys. Each and every one of you has buoyed me with your excitement and support.

So many thank-yous to my first critique partner, E. M. Castellan. You have been there through so many different manuscripts, though all my ups and downs, and your support always grounded me and gave me hope. I'm glad WriteOnCon connected us! I am so glad to call you friend and to have you in my life. And thank you to my critique partner Michelle (Tran) Armfield. You helped shape this book and always found the weakest points for me to work through. I am so thankful you were there during one of the hardest parts of my life.

I cannot say thank you enough to my agent, Sarah Landis. You took a chance on this strange book with angry girls and gods and I will be forever grateful. You helped me develop it into a book I could be proud of and championed it with all your heart. Your support and advice mean the world to me. I never, ever could've reached this point without you and I don't think there are enough words to describe my appreciation.

Thank you to my editor, Karen Chaplin, who stayed with me for revision after revision until this book shone like only Karen knew it could. You helped me hone the chaotic nature of my debut into something I can be proud of, and I am so thankful you saw the potential in it. Thank you also to Bria Ragin for answering thousands of questions thoughtfully and quickly. I am so thankful for your help in bringing this book to life!

Thank you to Rachel Simon, who gave me her time and emotional availability for a sensitivity read. You were so helpful and supportive. I will be forever grateful for what you gave me, and I hope to return the favor someday!

To my Sung Room Girls: Sue Hong, Kylie Ann Freeman, Rachel Greenlaw, Dani Moran, Ellie Fitzgerald, and Gabby Taub! I met you when I was uncertain about my place in the writing community. You give me such support and love. I am forever grateful for our Ireland trip. Meeting you all was one of the best things that has happened, and I hope for many more retreats, bar crawls, laughs, and movie screenings. I hope you know I will always be here to love and support you just as you have me. Thank you all for being in my life.

My Lucky 13-ers; Julie Dao, Mara Fitzgerald, Heather Kaczynski, Kati Gardner, Rebecca Caprara. Austin Gilkeson, and Kevin Van Whye, I literally don't know what I would do without you guys. You were there through some of the hardest parts of my writing career and offered advice and a safe haven to come to when things seemed too difficult. Mara and Kevin, thank you so unbelievably much for reading my manuscripts and offering so much helpful advice. You both made my book so much stronger and I know I wouldn't be here without your advice. You both gave me so much of your time and emotional availability and I am beyond grateful.

To my agency siblings: Shelby Mauhrin, Erin Craig, Jennifer Adam, Meredith Tate, Elizabeth Unseth, Jamie Elisabeth, Jennie K. Brown, Julie Abe, Leah Johnson, Amanda Jasper, Lyudmyle Mayorska Hoffman, and all siblings yet to come! I am so glad to have you guys to ask random questions to when I get nervous and to share exciting information with. I am proud to be on Team Landis and watch all your careers grow!

Thank you to all my friends in the nonwriting world: Kayla Hayley, Alayna Wendling, Hilary Behymer, Bethany Williams, Shannon Nicholson, Gifford Bishop, Phil Heppe, Haley Houser, Brittney Henton, and Nikki Eddington for listening to me complain about my books and my journey, for being excited about my successes, and for being interested in my books even if they weren't your cup of tea. You all were more support than you can imagine.

I have to thank every single person at HarperCollins and Quill Tree Books who helped bring my book to life. Thank you to my cover artist, Dadu Shin, who created a more perfect cover than I ever could've dreamed of. Thank you to my production editor, Jon Howard; my copy editor, Martha Schwartz, and my proofreader, Monique Vescia, who did the Lord's work when it came to cleaning up this book and making sure I spelled everything correctly. Thank you to my designer, David DeWitt, for giving me a beautiful book, and to my marketing point person, Sabrina Abballe, for getting it out into the world. Thank you to my publicist, Lauren Levite, for everything you have done. I am so grateful to you all.

And last, I want to thank every reader who took a chance and picked up this book. It is weird to finally be on the shelves after thirteen years of trying, and I will be grateful for each and every one of you. To any of you hoping to get published one day, know that I believe in you. It may seem like an impossible dream, you may want to quit every step of the way, but you can do it. Thank you all.